Labyrinth of Silence

DAVID S. VISCOTT

Labyrinth of Silence

W · W · Norton & Company · Inc · New York

To Judy

Labyrinth of Silence

One

I had no difficulty finding the state mental hospital the first day. I knew the crowded streets well, with their wooden three-family tenements and the narrow alleyways that ran back to yards too shaded for flowers or grass to grow. I knew the smell of cooking chicken and savored the memories it brought back, fragments of a childhood somewhere near this place.

I was a physician and I was also very frightened. Two days earlier I had finished my internship in medicine at one of the most splendid medical meccas in the Midwest, with carpeting on the floor even on the wards. An excellent public relations firm kept the hospital's good name in the regional press, and if you bothered to read the articles you could almost believe that you were enjoying your internship.

It had been a horrible year. I had worked seven days a week and every other night without stop. It had been a sleepless, exhausting blur, an excruciating routine, a humorless walk through a world of physical hurt. For me it had been merely a prerequisite, a boring, aching prerequisite which offered only one reward: it would be over at the end of June and I would be free to return to Boston and begin my residency training in psychiatry.

The fence surrounding the state hospital was made of iron rods attached at intervals to brick posts and was almost a mile long. The morning was hot, the traffic loud; a bus, surer of its way than I, cut me off and I was in the wrong lane and could not turn, so I missed the gate. Somewhere around the corner there was another entrance—a memory from twenty years ago. I followed the fence around the grounds. One part along the road was missing. I remembered when they had torn it down during the Second World War. "They need the iron for bullets," someone had said.

What had I gotten into? I had been so apprehensive and disorganized that morning that I had misplaced my car keys, and by the time my wife finally found them the toast had burned. I had gulped down some orange juice, kissed her, and run out the door. That dreary hospital on a warm July morning, glowing gold through its gray—that was what I had been waiting for. It would mean a chance to put away the bandages and medicines that I had somehow allowed to creep between my medical patients and myself and keep us strangers. It would mean the end of a private dehumanization, the end of a personal era of distance from those I treated. I had hated examining excreta, measuring blood levels of exotic metabolites which had taken on an almost mystical meaning in the minds and hearts of some of my colleagues. Most of all, I had hated knowing that someday some bright-eyed programmer would fix forever all the knowledge

I had tried so desperately to learn onto some distant computer to produce a machine that could diagnose and prescribe more rapidly than I, and without error.

I had fallen prey to the seductive chant of the academicians in my early days in medical school to "be esoteric." I had received a beautiful microscope as a gift from my parents and confess that I enjoyed tinkering with it. It had been fascinating to look through achromatic distortion-free lenses into human cells that had once been alive. Because so much stress was placed on learning the facts, it had sometimes been difficult to remember that what lay stained and mounted, brightly illuminated on the microscope stage below me, had once been human. Although my vision had been clear, my world had grown distorted and one-sided. I had drifted into haematology partly because I enjoyed looking at cells through my microscope and partly because I found the study of diseases of the blood interesting, interesting but removed, and that separation from the patients had bothered me. Haematology turned out to be the most esoteric field in medical school. I had had ambitions before medical school of being a diagnostician, but soon found out that there was no such subspecialty, except in the minds of some patients who wanted to believe that their doctor was better than anyone else's.

It was not surprising that there was so much distance between the doctors in this field and their patients because most of the patients were terribly ill, were dying. My first experience through the wards had been very strange. I was then in my third year of medical school making rounds at night with the resident.

"This thirty-five-year-old man has been admitted to this hospital for the fifth time with a three-year history of chronic myelogenous leukemia. Recent laboratory studies show increased immature forms in the periferal smear and the bone marrow is a chaos of blast forms . . ."

I was pleased—not that the man was ill, but that I understood. Understanding had become a reward in itself. We walked into a totally undistinguished hospital room, a room similar to the ten thousand hospital rooms I would walk into every year for the rest of my life, walk out of, and never remember, to see a patient, a man who looked uncomfortable and pale.

"How are you feeling today? Hmm?" began the resident.

"Okay, but my belly's stiff."

"Hmmm, yes I see that. Take a look at this, Stevens, at the right costal margin. What do you feel?" The resident motioned to me to feel. "Umm. Could you take a deep breath for me, Mr. . . . Mr. . . . Sir?" I didn't know the man's name. No one had mentioned it.

"Jack O'Donnell, Doctor." He looked at me very uncomfortably, sensing, I thought, that I was a student. Perhaps only students cared about names.

"Deep breath, Mr. O'Donnell."

"Ow!"

"Is that tender there?"

"Ow, dammit!"

"I'm sorry. That's fine, deep breath . . . let it out. Fine. Good."

"Well, what do you think?" asked the resident.

I had not wanted to answer in front of the dying man or to alarm him. It would have been out of place to act stupid and make Mr. O'Donnell angry; after all, he was dying. I had wanted to say nothing, but knew that the enormously enlarged liver I had just felt had to be noticed and that the resident, a zealot for everyone palpating every possible abnormality, would make me repeat my examination if I did not reply. So in the finest tradition of obfuscatory camouflage that I had heard and learned to speak, I said, "The hepar is increased in displacement," which meant that the liver was enlarged. The resident nodded and we walked out of the room to continue rounds. We were halfway down the hall when he began again.

"Well, what would *you* do, Doctor?" Residents could call a medical student "doctor" and make it sound like an insult.

"I'd give him blood, packed cells to get his hematocrit up. Do cultures of everything to check out the fever. The medicines haven't worked the last two times so I would omit them and make him comfortable, and follow the laboratory and clinical picture," I said almost automatically.

"Fine . . ." He looked for another chart. "You'll be off this service in one month. Do you think he'll be here?"

"What do you mean?"

"He won't last two weeks."

"Oh . . ."

"Now this is a very interesting case," he said, picking up another chart. "She's a . . ."

"Does he have a family?"

"Who?"

"O'Donnell."

"How would I know? Read the off-service notes and the social-service notes. Hey, where are you going?"

"Back here a minute." I went back into O'Donnell's room. "Hi, Mr. O'Donnell. We're going to be running some tests and giving you some blood. I guess you know the routine. By the way, if there's anything you need, please let us know." I felt hopeless and wanted to do something, anything; but I couldn't bring myself to ask about his family, and went back into the hall.

It was much easier not knowing their names, not knowing their families, not getting attached to them. The residents on that service had seemed to manage their feelings very well. They had kept the patients at a distance. One morning I heard myself call a sixteen-year-old girl "the lymphoma in room 306," and I felt ashamed. I was getting to be like a computer.

My professors had said, "If you want to be a good doctor you have to keep your distance. You have to keep your judgment intact and untainted by personal feelings. It is a necessity." I had watched surgeons drape patients with huge green sheets, more, it seemed, to hide the fact that they were operating on some human creature than to preserve a sterile field. I had not wanted to be like that. I couldn't be like that. Everywhere I looked I had found frightened, hungry patients who wanted five minutes of my time to talk with me. The famous bedside manner I was supposed to cultivate was submerged in four pages of obligatory questions issued by the hospital, questions that I had to ask first, sometimes even before I could look up to see whether the person I was interviewing was a man or a woman, old or young. I was supposed to develop thoroughness, but it only made it more difficult to be at ease. Not all of the important questions were on those sheets. I don't remember ever being asked to find out how a patient felt about being sick.

Somewhere in that sea of numbers, in that endless flood of faces, bellies, lymph nodes, and fevers of unknown origin, I grew despairing. It was not what I had bargained for, it was not a fulfillment of me. As a child I had had a picture of an old country doctor making a visit to a sick child. The sick room was filled with worried people looking to a kindly old man who sat with his chin resting on his hand. I remember wanting to be like that, in control, respected, with the power to help people. It was a childish, even trite, idea, I learned with experience. Though the physician in my childhood picture had had the esteem and love of his patients, I had tried to console myself by thinking that he did not have the knowledge I was ingesting. Somehow the more I learned the more distance I found between the patients and myself, and I could never quite get used to it. When a patient became merely a number and a diagnosis to me, I became a face in a white coat to him. I found that medical training could make you insensitive. The feelings for people that had brought you into the profession in the first place intruded and had to be controlled. We were always too busy to think about our feelings or things like that, and we had to be cool and detached and prepared for any emergency that might present itself in the night.

Just before my internship, when I had only a few months left of medical school, I was scheduled to take a routine clerkship in psychiatry at a small suburban hospital which had the reputation of being the easiest rotation in the entire clinical years. I could come in at nine, read a few records, watch patients get shock treatments, and by two I could leave, my day's work completed. It had been a very strange and uncomfortable place. Most of the patients were being treated by older doctors who seemed unwilling to try to talk to them and who used electroshock therapy for everything. All of the patients were so confused and forgetful from their treatments that interviewing them seemed pointless. The most common comment made by the staff at rounds was, "A few more treatments and she'll be as good as new." I had been horrified by the apparent brutality of what was going on and by the fact that the doctors who were supposed to be interested didn't seem to care. Psychiatry left me cold.

I began to get involved in the assigned reading and discovered the psychoanalytic literature and Freud. While I thought his literary style delightful, I found him difficult to understand and depressingly abstract at first, but his writings grew on me and so did those of his friends and in time even those of some of his enemies.

I grew to dread the morning lineup of patients who were scheduled to get electroshock therapy. They loitered anxiously in the hospital corridor outside the eight-bed dormitory that was converted daily into a shock-treatment ward. Some patients stood mutely, passively, and walked in like robots when the nurse came for them. They were called the "good patients" by the staff. Others pleaded not to go in and insisted that their rights were being violated. They would be reminded that they had signed an operative-permission form and would be coerced, pushed, threatened, and treated like so many mindless children. And no one had seemed to care! The treatment made the patients so confused that later they weren't able to recall what went on anyhow.

Once I was asked to help bring in a depressed old woman who was crying in the hall, refusing to come in. I half-heartedly tried to talk her into the procedure when I really wanted to tell her to turn around and run. She had just calmed down while talking to me when suddenly a large muscular aide came up behind her, picked her up, carried her into the ward, and dropped her unceremoniously on a bed. On the first try the anesthesiologist, inspite of the woman's kicking, found a large vein with his intravenous needle and she went off to sleep to his cooing, senseless babble. I was too shocked to move or speak. I just felt sick.

The anesthesiologist injected an agent which temporarily paralyzes muscles so that the old lady would not move when she got her convulsion. She started trembling all over, and the anesthesiologist said to me, "Those muscle twitchings are called fasciculations. Caused by the drug. Okay, now I'm going to help her breathe and give her some oxygen for about a minute so she doesn't get oxygen-depleted. Okay, Miss Harwood—get those electrodes on!" Miss Harwood, strong, efficient, with a hairy wart on her chin, rubbed some conductive paste on the patient's temples and held the electrodes on tightly. "Okay, doc, hit the button." The psychiatrist, who had been checking his morning appointment book all this time, sprang to life, walked over to the side table, and pressed a red button on a little black box which caused a one-second burst of electricity to flow through the wires to the patient, who grimaced hideously as her muscles tensed. The psychiatrist returned to his appointment book without looking at his convulsing patient and said, "Could we do Mr. Bogen next, Jack? I've got to be at Mount Hebron Hospital at ten." The anesthesiologist nodded as he checked his patient's respirations. All that training compressed into one finger, I thought.

There are proper, well-accepted indications for giving a very small number of psychiatric patients electroshock treatment, but doctors who spend their lives almost exclusively shocking patients manage to find reasons for giving shock to almost everyone. As a personal experiment, partly out of anger at what I had seen, I decided to try psychotherapy with several new patients on the ward who had not yet received shock treatment. I asked the doctor in charge of the ward to withhold shock treatment for these patients during the time I was scheduled to be on the ward. "Oh, you're one of those," he said. "Sure, have a try at it, but don't expect much. Most of these patients have had a good deal of shock before and don't respond very well to anything else." I wanted to see if talking about problems with patients really worked.

I became fascinated by their stories and their troubles and later I was touched and sometimes deeply moved by them. I became aware of a flow of feelings between myself and the patients I talked with, and to my surprise some of them started to get better, better in fact than the patients who were getting electroshock therapy. One woman had never been given the opportunity to say how badly cheated she felt since her forced marriage. She was angry at her mother for making her go through with it because the boy was from a well-to-do family. She doubted whether she really loved her husband. Each time she had brought the question up at home, her husband had run off to her mother and then her entire family had descended on her, telling her how foolish and ungrateful she was. She had received no support from anyone and had not been allowed to leave the house because her family was afraid she would run away. She had become very depressed several times in the past, and each time she had been sent to the hospital to have her treatments and later would return home confused but docile. I asked the social worker to speak with the husband, and I saw them together a few times. As soon as she saw that her husband was willing to listen to her and stop running to her mother with every problem, she brightened up and was able to leave the hospital.

For the first time since I had been in medical school, I felt that it had made a difference that I was there. Not that someone else would have been unable to help, but that what I did, what I said, what I felt was important. I had helped a patient by caring for her, by understanding what was going on in her life and helping her see. I began to get excited about what I was doing. Where before I had contented myself with finding a diagnosis and winning praise for my diagnostic skill from my peers, here I became interested in the patients. When I had been on rotation through other services in medical school and had become curious about the patients' personal lives, I had been told by my teachers that those facts had little bearing on the case. In psychiatry they were the factors that caused the problem itself.

Why were some people timid and retiring when everyone else in their family was aggressive? I wondered why they did the things they did, acting blindly, when even the most superficial glance would reveal trouble ahead. Why did a young woman marry a man exactly like her first husband whom she said she hated? I felt that they must see the world differently than I. Each patient was a world unto himself, undiscovered, secret, and new, and I wanted to be allowed into that world to explore the dark corners and the rubber labyrinths. Each time I would find my way out of someone else's confusion, I saw myself more clearly.

Two afternoons each week Larry Sussmann, the other student who shared the ward with me, and I drove from the hospital to a Veterans' Administration psychiatric clinic in downtown Boston. Larry was very skeptical of psychiatry and we usually discussed problems in metabolism, which was his area of interest. I remember one warm spring day when we were driving in with the top down on my convertible.

"What do you think of the staff at the hospital these past two weeks?" he asked.

"Adequate in medicine, good in surgery," I replied.

"What about psychiatry?"

"They don't do very much, do they? It's too bad. I see a lot of things that I'd like to do, if I had the chance."

"Like with Mrs. Colavito?" Larry asked.

"Oh, of course. She's a fascinating lady, isn't she?"

"You better believe it." He had to shout over the noise of the street. "What a history."

I pulled out into the traffic and listened to Larry give Mrs. Colavito's background.

"Guess what her serum electrophoresis showed? Go ahead, guess. Guess . . . come on. Practically no gamma globulin and a high amount of an unidentified protein. How about that? And her serum lipids, wow! They're *so* screwed up. I've got to get her on some total-balance studies. I bet I could write her up and publish it."

I was suddenly very confused. I had meant her family

background when I said she was interesting. I had meant the fact that she had lost her two oldest sons and in her fantasies had secretly adopted the boy next door without getting his mother's permission and reacted violently when he was late coming home from school or when the boy's real mother didn't show concern for a cut or a cold. But Larry was still talking.

"You know, I wouldn't be surprised if this gal has some kind of storage disease—you know, one of those odd rarities that Dr. Calderone used to tell us about in pathology. I mean, wow, fantastic! All those strange proteins and fats circulating around."

Larry was a good student. He was conscientious, worked hard, and knew what he was talking about. He was sincere and interested. I looked at him sitting next to me, digging out his pipe with a huge metal instrument, the spring wind blowing in his face, almost in a dream over the wonderful abnormalities which appeared in Mrs. Colavito's laboratory tests. I suddenly felt very distant from Larry and his way of looking at patients. I was enormously disenchanted with myself and what my training had come to mean.

The sun was brilliant, and the first flowering bushes and trees scented the air. As we passed the Charles River an eight-man crew disappeared under a bridge. Students were basking in the first warm sun of spring on the Cambridge bank beneath the gilded spires and clock towers of Harvard.

What should I do? Should I spend the rest of my life locked in a world of numbers, of graphs, of things so far removed from what I really felt was important? True, this was a terrible psychiatric rotation and the patients at the hospital were uneducated and unaccustomed to expressing themselves in words, but I had found them fascinating. I had longed to understand their feelings. Of course I knew that Mrs. Colavito had metabolic problems and I understood what that implied, but I found the idea of writing a paper about her as the goal of treatment increasingly upsetting. Medicine had become an extension of the most academic environment imaginable, where we learned to feel that it was more important to prove how smart and inventive we were to our peers and win their approval than it was to relate to patients as people.

I suddenly realized that for the first time I had actually enjoyed working with patients on this rotation even though the hospital was terrible and the staff uninspiring. I had liked what I was doing and for the first time I felt that no computer could have done what I had done, for computers do not feel . . .

Suddenly, I wanted to be a psychiatrist! Suddenly, driving along the willowed banks of the Charles River with the accelerator pushed to the floor, I wanted to be a psychiatrist. Suddenly, with the wind, with the sun, with the sense of spring and new beginnings, I wanted to be a psychiatrist.

"I am going into psychiatry!" I shouted. Larry sat up in his seat, looked at me strangely, and smiled anxiously.

"I am going into psychiatry."

"You are going into the river or a tree. Jesus Christ, you're doing over ninety miles an hour! Slow down, slow down."

I suddenly realized that my hands were squeezing the wheel like a wet towel, and I took my foot off the accelerator. We coasted into a small roadside rest area.

"I . . ."—I turned to Larry and started to smile and then shouted, "I am going to be a psychiatrist."

"Jesus, don't yell."

I had found what I was looking for. I stopped shouting, started the car again, and felt as if I were floating over the other cars, the mossy fens, the granite bridges, the shaded parks of Boston. I was free!

I called on that memory for strength many times during my internship. It once returned like a vision at three in the morning in the emergency room when I felt that all the sick people in the Midwest had been roused together to descend on me. It had appeared again when that year was completed, at the end of the highway driving back East, when the endless flatlands of Indiana and Ohio pulled in their yellow-brown skirts to make room for the lovely, green, enchanting roll of the Berkshires in Massachusetts. The night before I left I had dreamed I was the coxswain of the crew disappearing beneath the spires and the clocks, which had started ringing and were transformed into my alarm, rousing me from sleep.

The hospital was larger than I had remembered. There were huge lawns dotted with patients, and around in back there were three brick houses, apparently for staff members, some children playing in a sand box, the rhythmic whirring of a sprinkler. Some patients wearing pajamas crossed the road. It was like a dream with the characters moving in slow motion or frozen in the icy July air. I was to report to the administration building, and I stopped next to a man standing by the road. "Can you tell me where the administration building is?" He stared at me and at my car and then walked over to me.

"Who are you?" he asked.

"I'm Dr. Stevens," I said in the friendliest way I knew.

"No you're not. That's all." He turned and walked to the curb. I drove on very slowly. A sign read SPEED LIMIT 8 MPH. There was a bench with two women sitting on it.

"Can you tell me where the administration building is?"

"Go away," said one, spitting in my direction.

"Are *you* talking to *me?*" said the other.

I followed the asphalt road around the grounds, passing

hundreds of patients dressed in shabby hospital gray. The buildings were red brick and wood painted gray. Some were almost a century old and because time had not been good to them, they wore their years thanklessly. At the end of the lawn wherever I looked there was the iron fence. The gates were never locked or even closed and although they kept no patients in, they frightened many visitors away. The roads and lawns, the bushes and trees, cottages, infirmary, dormitories, and cafeteria were all strange to me and yet strangely familiar at the same time.

I parked my car and walked toward the front gate. I saw a man wearing a suit walking toward me. I moved along the walk and tried to pretend I did not notice him, but he kept coming closer.

"Robert."

I looked up. How could anyone know my name? I did not know anyone there.

"Robert. Hey, are you deaf?"

"Alan! What are you doing here?"

"Beginning a psychiatry residency."

"Great. So am I."

I grabbed his hand. Alan and I had gone to medical school together. We had shared the same cadaver in anatomy, groaned over examinations together, and had become good friends. He had interned in the East, and neither of us had written. His was a good face to see.

"Alan, I thought you were going into medicine."

"So did I. I'm a convert."

We laughed and found the administration building, where a small crowd of about thirty residents had gathered, waiting for the orientation meeting to begin. They moved slowly up the broad granite stairs into the auditorium and we followed, looking to see if we could recognize anyone, but they were all strangers to us.

We were greeted with the friendly smiles of the hospital staff, nodding and bobbing on the stage, and the outstretched arms of the superintendent, Dr. Larkin, recognizing the old and welcoming the new. He made a few remarks about the history of the place, stressing the fact that Charles Dickens had visited the hospital years before and found it to be enlightened and pleasant. Dr. Larkin was an older man, precise and friendly, who continuously wiped his steel-rimmed glasses while he introduced the staff to us. Some I would never see again. Some I would know too well. Dr. Larkin had a reputation for being a kind, honest, and extremely demanding psychiatrist. When he had interviewed me for my residency appointment the year before he had been cordial and seemed interested and had laughed loudly when I told him how I decided to go into psychiatry. "If you think, don't drive. If you drive, don't think," he said. He actually had a sense of humor, in a dry academic way.

Dr. Larkin coughed through a speech, listing the improvements that had been made over the years. Then he said: "If you think that it is bad here now, you should have seen it ten years ago. A good part of the hospital is closed now. Patient care is better and patients leave sooner. Change takes time and effort. I would like to wish you the best of luck and hope that you will benefit from what you see in your year here with us and that your patients will benefit from what you do. Lunch is being served upstairs, and today only the hospital will pick up the check."

Lunch was brought to us by one of the patients, a sweating, red-faced woman who was enormously overweight. The food was palatable though starchy, and our plates were cleared away the instant they were empty. After lunch Alan and I went to look at the schedule posted on the bulletin board in the basement of the administration building. That day nothing was scheduled for first-year residents except the morning meeting, but it seemed as if every moment of every week was filled for the rest of the year. A ward conference was scheduled every day from eight to nine-thirty. From ten-thirty to twelve-thirty there were teaching conferences of one kind or another. Lunch was from twelve-thirty to one-thirty. Another conference was scheduled from two-thirty to four. In the time remaining, daily ward rounds were to be made with the charge nurse on the day shift and at the change of duty, at four. Each resident was to have a ward meeting with his patients at least once a wwek. Two half hours were to be left open each week to speak with relatives. Three hours a week were to be left open for supervision and two hours were to be spent with the social worker. This left a handful of hours in which to treat patients, assuming that one was all caught up with his paper work. I couldn't believe that schedule.

"Robert?" Alan asked.

"Huh?"

"Are you going to join the bowling league?" He started laughing, and then went on. "Naw, you'd never make the team. Look at this, will you, they have two journal clubs here. Hey, we'll have to join both of these. Don't you love sitting around listening to people reporting on articles? You want to start a breathing club where we sit around and catch our breath?"

"Did you ever see so many conferences?" I asked.

"Well, you may not have time to see any patients while you're here but you'll sure know a shit load of psychiatry when you leave."

Alan and I decided to explore the place and walked across the lawn, a ceramic green of human disarray, to survey what we had inherited. The grounds were immense, and even at a brisk walk—if a patient did not waylay you—it took half an hour to cross them.

We talked about our wards, full of faces nameless to us. We had both been assigned to the chronic service. I had a ward of men, or what was left of men after twenty or thirty years of decay, and Alan had a ward of women. We talked about our fears, of our terrifying new responsibilities and how we would meet them. And we talked about old times and how secure we had been under the wings of our professors. We laughed at our own ignorance and speculated on how we would get along with our new patients.

"Have you ever run a ward meeting?" I asked.

"Once last year when my supervisor went on vacation he asked me to take over the ward for a week, but the patients were nowhere near this sick. Boy, did they put me on the spot—the questions they asked! I don't like working with groups. Anyway, I'll probably never have a group when I'm in private practice. I plan to do a little reading about them, though."

"I guess it all comes with experience and time. I wonder what it will be like sitting alone in front of fifty crazy people."

"Maybe they won't talk to you. That would save a lot of trouble. Or they might attack you."

Suddenly a large woman with stringy black hair that hung to the shoulders of her faded, oversized housedress put her Bible down, started up from her bench across the walk, and motioned to us, calling, "You want to know. You want to know what I think of doctors. Ha! You want to know what I think of psychiatrists?" It was as if she had some power to read our minds and know our fears. Her voice was spellbinding and her words rang like a malediction. "I'll show you!" And she turned around, lifted her skirts, and, laughing with a hideous cackle, urinated on the sidewalk across from us, calling names at us as she walked away.

Actually at the time it was very funny and we laughed

even though we felt that perhaps we shouldn't. But in that moment some of the obstacles we were to face appeared in the open and from then on it was difficult to pretend they were not there.

It was getting late and I decided to go over to my building and inspect my office and see what my ward looked like. The patients were at supper. The ward was deserted, hollow, very still. It had a musty odor with more than a suggestion of urine and it was difficult for me to take a deep breath. Piles of stained linen filled one short hallway. The floor was filthy with cigarette butts and torn newspapers. The nurses' office was locked. I wandered into the main dormitory, which was deathly still in late-afternoon light, diffused and gray in the blighted sun. Diseased beds keeping their wrinkled gray vigil stood waiting in rows for their masters to return.

I walked to the end of the long high-vaulted room and crouched down to look out through an open window at the grounds three floors below. Perhaps I was there for a minute, I do not know, but when I started to get up I saw a dark form standing to one side. My heart began to pound and blood rushed to my head. It was a tall bony man about sixty staring wide-eyed at me; his mouth was open and his arms were bent at the elbows and pulled tightly to his chest. He just stared. He did not move. How long has he been there watching me, I thought. What is he going to do?

He did not move. He did not blink. "I'm Dr. Stevens," I said. He did not respond. He did not move. I walked back to the hallway, turning every few steps to look back. He did not move. I walked through to the day hall and looked again before I went downstairs to my car and home. I saw him, standing, staring. Still he did not move.

Two

The state hospital was in the old neighborhood where I had grown up. When I found the time I walked through the once-familiar streets, looking up my past. I found my old street shabby and cold and the old two-family house where I had lived downstairs from my grandparents needing paint and decaying. Had I been so many years away?

I remembered the day in spring when the city workmen had planted a tree, a maple, in front of my house and how proud I had been that I could make my fingers reach around and touch. Now, dying, strangled from the scars of a wire tied too tight, it gave no shade in summer, only trembling shadows on the dusty street.

In the back yard I remembered the dank, musty smells of my grandfather's porch, the dark, damp, places below where I used to hide, and the mossy beds where I used to crawl on wet green knees. But now children from a different time and race had taken my place and are watching *me* grow old . . .

The more I explored the hospital and my old neighborhood, and the more I remembered of my own life and past, the greater seemed my kinship with the hospital. It was a very strange and dreamlike feeling, a feeling of things not being real, of having been there once before, seeming to know where the buildings were and several times to my surprise almost knowing how the rooms would like inside. It was a sad and lonely feeling.

One helpful thing about the crowded schedule was that I got to see my ward nurse, Miss Barker, three times a day. Miss Barker knew everything that was happening on the wards. There were many bad things about the schedule which were not offset by this. I began my day at eight in the morning by listening to the reports of the aides, the student nurses, and Miss Barker, who always waited to be last. There were always problems with the patients' medications. Bornstein was always too drowsy and needed his medication cut back, Willie was too aggressive and needed more medication to quiet him down. Someone was always asking me to give Willie more medication.

At nine-thirty I went to my office to sit by the phone for an hour. These were my on-call hours, when relatives could get in touch with me if they wanted to. Almost all of the seventy patients on the ward were schizophrenic. Only three had relatives who ever called, and their calls were always the same. They had telephoned each ward doctor the same way for the past twenty-five years. Irving's people wanted to know if he was comfortable; Bill's mother wanted to know if I thought he was doing better; and Kagan's father wanted to debate the etiology of schizophrenia and the rationale of the various treatments which had evolved over the years. He sounded disturbed much of the time and I guessed that talking to his son's doctor on the phone was the only form of treatment he could tolerate. I usually tried to catch up with my paperwork when there were no calls, except on Wednesday when I saw Dr. Glickman for supervision, which I dreaded.

The teaching conferences in the mornings sometimes consisted of going over a patient's record, interviewing a patient, or an impromptu lecture, and at other times there were procedural meetings on how to plan ward excursions or fill out death notices. Once a week there were grand rounds. The only conference worth attending was Dr. Pellegrini's— he was someone very special. He was my other supervisor, but he would see me any time I wanted. In the afternoons there was time to see the social worker twice a week, and to see relatives, though only the three that called on the phone ever visited. I could schedule a ward meeting once a week and see ward patients individually as problems developed if there was enough time remaining. Most of the patients wanted to go home but few of them had homes left to go to.

In the afternoons there were seminars which described the separate units of the hospital—the various workshops where patients could be trained and returned to society, the halfway house, the schools, the psychology department, the statistics department, and the hospital-records department. Once a week Dr. Pellegrini gave a teaching conference. He was the only one who really bothered to prepare his material and whose seminars did not repeat what I had already learned in the assigned reading. Very soon I found that I got more out of the assigned reading than the seminars. Many of the residents still practiced one-upsmanship, which was extremely annoying and time consuming. Others didn't bother to read the material and faked it. The sad part was that few residents even realized it or, worse, they did not seem to care. But the chairs were comfortable and there were rituals of seating, bringing food and coffee, and telling jokes. I loathed the seminars. In the remaining time, I was to meet with one or two patients for individual psychotherapy and with a group of patients once a week for group therapy. It was a full schedule, filled to everyone's satisfaction but my own. The opportunity to get close to patients which I had sought —which was so available if only one had the time for it—was usually consumed by what seemed to me to be trivia. I did not go along with it.

Twice each month I stayed overnight at the hospital as the doctor on call. One of these nights I covered the chronic service and all of the problems that might arise there, and the other I covered the emergency floor, where things were more hectic and unpredictable. I had been a resident only a week when I had my first night assignment. Because of the seminars, the orientation, and the built-in busy-work of the hospital, which isolated the residents from too much exposure to the patients and kept them in the dark about what was really going on, I really did not know my way around the hospital yet and felt completely unprepared. I had been so busy that I knew only a dozen of my seventy patients by name.

That night I stayed on the ward and tried to finish my paperwork, filling out seemingly useless forms. I always seemed to fall behind. It was quiet, and I was able to work uninterrupted for nearly two hours and managed to get caught up. This was remarkable because, being the only doctor for two thousand patients, I had expected no rest, and every time my telephone rang I anticipated suicide and murder.

For the first time since my arrival I found myself with nothing to do and decided to wander through the poorly lit complex of rooms and halls that made up the ward. Just off the cavernous day hall I found a large gymnasium that smelled freshly waxed. It was fully equipped with many games, including, to my delight, a large pool table which, judging by its excellent condition, was rarely used. The heavy door closed behind me. In the light of the fading summer day streaming dustily through the windows I walked around the table following the cue ball for over an hour till I could no longer see, conveniently forgetting where I was and the sickness around me.

When I went to leave, I found that the door was locked and that none of the dozen keys I had been issued could change that fact. I knocked on the door, but no one came. I became restless. Through the heavy metal screen on the window at the side I could see the back porch of my ward and several of my patients sitting and cooling themselves in the evening air. One paced back and forth continuously, Indian style, repeating his pattern over and over again. I went to the window and shouted, "Hello, I'm your doctor. Hello." There was no response. "Hello, I'm locked in the gymnasium. Could you call the aide to let me out?" The man who was pacing suddenly stopped and looked up into the air at nothing and, taking my voice to be another of his hallucinations, smiled knowingly and resumed pacing. I was isolated. I didn't know any of their names. The other patients remained as still as before. Only one man in a rocking chair moved. Surely, I thought, they must know me. They have to know me; after all, I've been their ward doctor for a week. I called again and again. The pacing man stopped for a moment, smiled, and continued to pace.

It was growing quite dark; the shadows were long and the grayness was deep and beginning to take menacing form. I was in darkness and I could not even turn on the lights because the switch was outside. I had rounds to make and the prospect of spending the night in a gymnasium, without even a single light to view the toys of men who had lost their youth, gave me an uneasy, cold feeling. I was as frightened as my patients and I, too, could not make contact or share my loneliness. I called several more times; each time I called a little louder, and each time I got the same response from my patients and the night. Finally a mentally defective patient, one whose name I did know, happened to find himself on the porch during his aimless nightly meanderings, listening to me in the air. After several calls he finally looked my way.

"Who's that?"

"Andy, it's Dr. Stevens."

"What doctor?"

"Your doctor."

"I don't have a doctor. I'm not sick."

"Get the aide, Andy. The aide, get him."

As I waited I thought, I am not even a person to these people. How can I ever reach them? How can I hope to cross this silent space? How can I possibly help them? What could they get from me? Of what use is it for me to try and talk to them? Even if I could for a fleeting moment intrude upon their silence and their isolation, what good would it do? Had Andy found the aide? Did the aide think his story was crazy? Could Andy intrude upon the aide's sanity and reach across the defenses that kept the aide sane? What would I do?

The sun had gone down and the world had become dark. After what seemed like hours on a stage where an actor had forgotten his lines, the aide, Tom, came to the porch and looked across at me. "Well, I'll be damned," he said. "It *is* you. We've been looking for you." A moment later the door opened, letting the yellow light of the corridor into my dark confinement. And Tom was laughing so hard he could not speak. I thanked him, feeling sheepish and a little embarrassed. "You need a special key to get out of there, doc."

"How do you get the patients to listen? What would happen in a real emergency?"

Tom just shrugged, looked at me, and started laughing again. "You're just lucky it's quiet tonight. Hardly anyone listens to Andy. Once we had a patient spend a weekend in there. Wait till I tell them at rounds. By the way, there's a telephone call for you."

I walked to my office on the ward, through the damp halls and dimly lit lounge. How frightened I had been! How hopeless I had felt when no one listened to me. In that world where everyone was insane and I needed help from them, I felt as they must in my world, abandoned, isolated, like a child, and I remembered similar feelings from my past, as in a dream.

King Mycerenus, grave and powerful, an alabaster eternity, is my noble friend. Every time I go to the Museum of Fine Arts I stop by to see him, staring translucently across the centuries. I walk around him and marvel at the size of his giant hands, and when the guard isn't looking, I run my fingers over the cracks and feel where the restorers have filled in with plaster what had once been stone.

I am quite frightened of him, so serious and rigid. Other stone figures might appear to look at you, but no matter where I stand in that cold hollow hall, I can not catch his eye.

I often wonder what it would be like in there at night with all the lights off and only the moon through the skylight showing the way among the carved towers. It gives me chills to think about being locked in with these figures of stone who will not respond.

Whenever I stayed late in the museum, the warning bell at closing always startled me, and I would run to the nearest

exit as if I were being chased by the memory of a roused Mycerenus breathing in the shadows.

The aide opened the ward nurse's office. The telephone
receiver was lying on the desk on a pile of papers.

"Hello, this is Dr. Stevens."

"This is Mrs. Flynn, head nurse in G Building. I have a
lady over here who's very difficult to control. Her name's
Nellie Cohen."

"What's wrong?"

"She's gone into a rage again over her late husband,
died twelve years ago, and is beating her hands against the
walls something terrible, doctor. She says she's destroying his
memory. It's pretty bloody."

"What floor?"

"The second. In G Building."

Crossing the grounds at night for the first time, I felt
strangely alone and apart, like a mariner lost on an unfamil-
iar sea who has heard tales of sea monsters lying in wait to
swallow him up. Although the night was warm, I felt a chill
as I left what was familiar to cross the silent expanse of lawn
dotted with tangled bushes and dark groves of scrub trees. I
started to walk to the other side, which seemed distant and
out of reach, and kept my eye on a light in a patient's room
which served as a beacon.

As I walked through the dark waves of grass blowing in
the damp summer night, I assembled the fragmented forms
of bushes and trees like a child joining the dots by number
to outline a hidden creature in a puzzle. So, too, I filled in
space with faces or forms I thought I saw and made creatures
out of bushes, voices out of murmuring leaves, converted the
movement of a branch into another moving limb. I could
hear the distant sound of a carnival, eerie accompaniment.
From where? Was it my imagination? Did I see lights spin-

ning behind the trees?

One last bush to pass, short and flat against the moonless sky. At last I was sure that what I had seen on my way across the lawn was only trees and bushes. As I got closer, I froze in sudden horror. The bush I had trusted was a man. He lay like a rock that stays submerged when the light is full and appears only on the ebb of day. My legs became detached as I approached and I began to float across the lawn. The other creatures that I saw would disappear in the happy flood of morning light. And the sleeping man, too, would disappear in the sea of faceless people who would be resting on the grass warming in the sun.

G Building, and I was safe! When you are finally safe, it seems foolish to have ever been afraid. Mrs. Flynn was sitting in the treatment room on the second floor with an aide and a breathless woman in a bloody nightgown, Mrs. Cohen.

"Hi, Dr. Stevens. She's pretty calm now. Aren't you, Nellie?" asked Mrs. Flynn. "Tell the doctor."

"Hello. Hello, Mrs. Cohen. Can I take a look at your hand?" She did not answer. I asked again and she held her hand out when the aide prompted her. It looked raw and red. The nurse had cleaned it. "Can you tell me what was going on, Mrs. Cohen?" She looked away. "What was wrong that made you do this?" Mrs. Cohen glared at me and started to tremble. The nurse gave me a look that frightened me, as if I were toying with something I did not understand. I decided to take the nurse's silent warning seriously. After all, Mrs. Cohen seemed to be in control of herself. "I think we should have an X-ray of her hand tomorrow, but it isn't swollen and she can bend it. A simple dressing will do for now." I wrote an order for some sleeping medication and filled out the forms for the lab studies.

"I wouldn't try to talk with her, Doctor," said Mrs. Flynn. "Any time someone discusses things with her, she somehow falls apart, Doctor." The nurse was very serious and was speaking from years of experience with Mrs. Cohen. "Nellie, your hand will be in shape for the carnival tomorrow. Don't worry, the carnival will still be there," she added. I left, relieved that there was little for me to do and that the carnival was real.

What a price to pay. To be silent about the things that hurt the most, to bury all feelings in order to keep one memory from returning, only to have it appear again and again without warning, always with the impact of the first time.

No matter how hard the staff tried to make the patients share an important event in their lives, to feel together, they seldom did. Each patient was a world unto himself and that world was an intensely personal thing with its own logic and its own sense of reality. I could never be sure what something meant to a patient. If he knew, he would seldom tell you about it, and if he did tell you it was difficult to understand. If I questioned Mrs. Cohen I would find only anger and she would lose control and strike out again. There was no purpose to it.

That isolation, which made their world appear mysterious to me, made my world appear terrifying to them. One of us, it seemed, was always locked in a gymnasium, our own separate world, either unable to intrude upon the world of the other or refusing to recognize that it existed.

It had cooled and there was a slight wind blowing. The man on the grass had gone. I walked to the front gate toward the whirring lights of a merry-go-round.

Each summer a touring carnival had the superintendent's permission to set up their equipment on a field in one corner of the hospital grounds, on the condition that the patients would have the run of the place during the day when business was light and pay their own way in the evenings.

There were games of chance, a lindy-loop, a Ferris wheel, re-freshment stalls, and a weather-worn merry-go-round com-plete with prerecorded calliope to which some patients danced. I came and watched.

The patients stand by the hundreds, apprehensive and smiling, restless and fearful of the angry machinery as if it might attack them. Some swear at the contraptions, others touch them cautiously as if they might burn their fingers; finding them safe, they smile, feeling the vibrations. Despite the coaxing and suggestions of nurses and the nudges of aides, some patients are reluctant to go for a ride.

"Don't be silly, Rose. Get on. It won't hurt you."

"No."

"It's only a wooden horse."

"But it moves."

"It's not alive."

"But it moves."

What a bizarre spectacle! On the merry-go-round, fused into one rigid form, wooden horses and wooden riders can-not be separated in their up-and-down travel, a dozen fixed faces spinning in circles, stopping at the place where they first began. The creaking and squeaking Ferris wheel might give a new perspective of the grounds they've lived on for so many long years, had any bothered to look down. Instead, they rock in space and stare at their hands on the bar that keeps them in place in their seats—some bar is always hold-ing them fast.

Cadaverous, they play stiff and unbending while the doting staff see in the patients the delights which they them-selves as children had enjoyed. The nurses and aides retrieve them like children and shower them with praise and, for conspicuous bravery, promise free rides next year.

As the evening grows later, more lights seem to come on, flashing bright colors on shining plastic faces, an unchoreographed masquerade. Some try to buy prizes, some want their money returned when they lose, and some walk away into the night.

A young man in Army fatigues with sergeant's stripes on the sleeve holds out his hand at a booth.

"No, that's not right. This one's a dime. That one's a penny. What are you doing? Hey, you throw those—at the bottles, and try and knock them over. You can't keep those balls. Throw them or get out of here. Come on, now." The townspeople are put off by the patients' strangeness and hurry their children away when the patients speak to them.

"Linda, dear, come over to mommy right away. Leave the nice man alone. . . . Linda, don't bother the nice man."

"But she doesn't bother me."

"Come on, Linda, you're getting tired."

One patient, having his age guessed, finds himself unable to remember.

Parading in gaudy paper leis with stuffed poodles and pandas and plaster clowns, they return with their spoils, taking stuffed toys for children who never visit and empty popcorn boxes as souvenirs.

I went to the residents' on-call room in the administration building. It was a plain room containing only a rocking chair, a bed, a night table with a lamp, telephone, and pads of paper to scribble down emergency calls during the night. Lying in bed I could hear the sounds of the hospital at night coming across the grass. There was a man groaning faintly in the distance and the sound of rattling metal, which sounded as if it came from some place nearby. In the building across the way a door was being pounded into submission without offering any resistance. The carnival and the people were still spinning in my head. The people, all the strange people.

I felt a subtle dread about the hospital, which seemed to

have always been part of my thinking, my attitude. It was an odd feeling, a fear of the forbidding unknown which somehow grew up with me.

When anyone had mentioned the hospital when I was a boy, it was with a nervous smile and an easy hilarity, the way people spoke of things that frightened them. In the summer when school was out I had sometimes walked past and had seen the odd people staring out from behind the iron and stone fence.

I had heard whispered secrets about the place from my friends, and when I went by I always strained to see who was there and who could be so terrible. But no matter how hard I looked, or how close I got to the people in front, they all looked the same to me—very tired, very old, very unhappy.

Later, when I was in my early teens, I heard the hospital mentioned in my own house, but every time I asked about it, the subject would be changed, and I always had the feeling that the place had other whispered secrets to reveal.

Exploring the hospital and its grounds during the day was as adventurous as it was at night. The sun may have made things less frightening on the surface, but the patients and their mysteries managed to find shadows to hide in even if the shadows were mostly in their own minds. Sometimes just by being there I became an unwilling prop in one of their dreams.

No matter what the weather or season she slides around the hospital grounds wearing a heavy purple overcoat. Seeing me a hundred yards away, she stares angrily and then walks toward me.

Twenty steps or less away, she jumps from side to side while I slow down, trying to decide which way to pass, until, an arm's length away, I stop. Then she sways and smiles at me, a funny, toothless, awkward smile, springs open her huge coat and reveals her utter nakedness. In sudden calmness she walks away without a word.

At other times I am an entirely unnoticed audience.

On the ancient tennis court covered with grass veins that flow in the summer wind, he stands waiting for silence from the expectant murmuring crowd to deliver the winning serve in his final match at Wimbledon. He glances down to check his stance in his heavy black leather ankle boots and pulls his toes behind the faded asphalt line. Slowly, in a stuttering arc, he lofts the ball and with a shattering silence smashes it for a fault into a net of air. The crowd breathes as one. He wipes perspiration from his brow onto his blue denim shirt and takes a nervous breath.

He checks his stance again and throws the ball into the air, delivers the service for an ace to win the cup and crown.

In the excitement of the crowd cheering, he forgets and throws his bat away and runs across the court to round the bases and score the winning run. Across the plate, across the lawn, across and gone.

What was perhaps the saddest and most frightening of all was that when the patients were together they seemed the most lonely, the most poignant, and the most suffering.

My building was a maze of corridors that ended blindly, of rooms without windows, of windows that could not be seen through and that admitted no light. Brick, dark, dusty, worn, it was built in older days of a sterner, more confining philosophy of man's impulses toward himself and the world. The doors and locks were ornate and heavy and looked like they had been taken from a medieval castle. It seemed as if no mortal could possibly escape them and you wondered on first seeing them what sort of monsters lurked behind.

Each year the building was painted by patients in vocational therapy who took painful hours to paint a single foot and asked their supervisors' advice about each brush stroke. The walls were always a dark gray with a dark green border on the bottom; if you looked closely, you could see how irregular and shaky the line between the colors was, a public record of the uncertainty of the patient who printed it. The patients' floors were clean—that is, as clean as the patients kept them, a graying brown musty marble, long since impregnated with dirt and the scuff marks of countless shoes pacing back and forth to nowhere. They reflected no light, only time. Each bend in the corridor was a special place to some patient, an area filled with gray light—gray air, it seemed— filled with silence and sometimes a form shuffling along in oversized hospital gray.

I decided to skip some of the daily conferences and try to get to know my patients better. One of the second-year residents, Jerry Bieberman, told me I would be doing well if I even knew my patients' names before I left the chronic service. I had the usual prescribed contact with patients on the ward, which consisted of managing their acute problems when they became upset or filling out prescriptions for an occasional visit home. There were only a few who ever went home and fewer who ever made trouble. By limiting my personal contact to these people I would have ignored the sixty people who were the silent members of a forgotten community. I was not satisfied with the arrangement.

I began to read the long, involved hospital charts and to interview patients. Often when I asked a patient for an interview he would wonder what he had done wrong—it had been that long since some of them had actually talked to a psychiatrist. It was true that each patient had a mental-status examination every year by an elderly state psychiatrist who would stare at the patient for a moment, try to engage him in conversation (which was usually impossible), and make what was essentially a duplicate of the mental-status report from the year before. That report could as easily have been written for the next five years on the same day. Assuming that the patient would be alive then, the report would be as accurate and unchanged, and just as hopeless.

I became fascinated by the patients' early histories, taken when they were first admitted to the hospital. I had three patients with doctoral degrees on my ward, I discovered, and no one seemed to know it! I promptly had their records changed to that effect and insisted that the staff call them "doctor." It was resented by the aides as stupid, but one patient, Dr. MacAuliff, who had been an educator, began to dress more neatly. He had always refused to communicate, but I had him assigned as the general clean-up man in the school for adolescent patients on the grounds. He seemed to enjoy the idea of being in school again and began to make friends with the students. None of us had been able to make friends with him.

The other Ph.D.s on my ward shrugged off their reinstated titles and went back to their hallucinations. I was amazed at what I found when I looked into the records. The patients wouldn't reveal much about themselves, which was to be expected; anyone who spends thirty years in an institution tends to close himself off from the world. But the records told a great deal, if one took the time to look. I found a portrait artist living in the shell of a man and sent him over to art therapy. He resisted going the first few times and he never drew, but eventually he became very fond of the art therapist and spent hours each day helping her with her materials.

Was it possible that there was this much neglect? Why hadn't anyone else bothered to find out who these people were? They were still people, and although they might have changed, time could not wipe out their past or take away credit for their special skills. I asked the ward staff to read the patients' charts, and they found professors as well as peasants. Maybe it was a game that we played to fool ourselves into believing that some of the patients were not hopeless. Sometimes just believing that there is hope is enough to make a patient try. I felt it was worth it, but it was difficult to generate enthusiasm in the staff. One of the aides refused to bother reading the charts and said that there was nothing worthwhile to learn. Tom, the aide who had helped me out of the gymnasium, became very interested in two patients and even called up their relatives to find out why they hadn't visited. Another one of the aides, Stan, betrayed me and my hopes. He told patients about themselves and used what he had earned in reading the records to make fun of them. I was so furious that day when I got home I forced my wife, Anne, to drive clear across the state to Albany with me for a late snack. Anne was very understanding and a good listener with a sense of humor. By the time we got home again we were laughing hysterically about the situations we invented for the people who were oppressing me.

Most of the time I was on my own, reading charts and then making an appointment with a patient to try to find out what had happened to him.

One hot summer day a patient of mine was late for my evaluation appointment with him. I could see the lush green of the trees swaying in diffused silhouette through my office window. The straw-dry uncut grass of an abandoned back field, the proposed site of a new building to replace the one I was in, formed the foreground of the picture I saw through the window. I asked Miss Barker about the patient. She blotted her forehead with a crumpled tissue.

"Look downstairs for him. He always goes to the basement on hot days. It's cooler down there. Crazy or not, he has more sense than we do, sitting up here in this heat. Hey, I've got an idea. Why don't you send in a requisition for funds for a ward picnic?"

Down the green stairs, past the damp, sweating, mossy landings and the sticky handrails of painted metal pipes, I stopped at the foot of the stairs, trying to wipe the grime from my hands. It was dark and, compared to the swelter upstairs, it was cool, musty, and dank. I passed through swinging, squeaking doors into a dark corridor with one naked brown bulb to show the way. A labyrinth of silence. Halls that ended in broom closets or stopped at a brick wall which was supposed to be the entrance to a wing of the building that had been abandoned before it was started.

At the end of the hall I can faintly make out the plaster cast of a human form leaning motionless, as if listening for some forgotten subway. I approach. My own steps, growing louder in my ears, make me feel as if I am being followed by myself. He is an old man, over seventy, staring into the darkness beneath a burnt-out bulb. "Have you seen . . ." I begin, and stop in the middle of my question, realizing the futility of trying to interrupt him—but what if I did interrupt him? But there he is, motionless, leaning against time, little time left for him to push.

I enter a big room filled with large supporting columns and forms, a wax museum. On the floor a huge black man sleeps. A dwarf—a mongoloid—thick-tongued and restless, pats the arm of a blind patient who uses the dwarf as his eyes and buys him candy. Both stand as if in reverence of a god, staring at the dark mysteries of the pipes in the corner.

Cross-legged, gesticulating, creating patterns in the air with bony fingers. First to the ceiling, then to the floor, then to his mouth, over and over, over and over, a cellar spider weaving his web of magic to catch the world and hold it fast, over and over, over and over.

Bloated, in coffee-stained pajamas, red-faced and in deepest sorrow, what was once a living thing holds its head in pain. Grimacing, contorted, a face, a monument to that moment when years ago a love was taken away, leaving the mourner silent to share his emptiness in space with walls and to stretch that moment through time as if it were rubber.

Staring at the window, ashen gray and gray-becoming, a nodding old man muttering "Dorothy, Dorothy, Dorothy" at the summer sun that is not reflected in his dirty window on the world.

The silence is suddenly ended by a loud noise from the hall. A drooling man wearing only underpants appears, walking rapidly—clenched fists, gnashing teeth, head quickly turning, a loud stamp, a growl, a grunt. Seeing me, he glares. You are the intruder, his look says. He goes out as quickly as he came in.

I own the silence once again. I am in a charnel house. I can feel myself sweating. I taste the thick air. I feel the weight of exhaled vinegar breath upon me. I move ahead. Figures grow in the shadows as my eyes begin to see grays among the blackness. Petrified creatures caught and fixed forever in some moment of their life's agony. Scenes from a tunnel ride at an amusement park, but there is no sound of little electric cars running or of switches being tripped or doors snapping open. No squeals of mock terror. The figures in the tableau are silent.

"Yaaaaaa." A piercing hollow yell freezes me, stops my breath, and gives way to silence once again.

There is a door at the end of the room and before I risk going through I turn and ask the silent players, "Has anyone seen . . . ?"

Staring out the window ashen gray and gray-becoming.
Cross-legged, gesticulating.
Red-faced, in deepest sorrow.
Figures moving in the shadows.
Clenched fists, gnashing teeth.

I can hear my voice rebounding in my head as I turn the knob and walk through the door which leads to the laundry. Piles of washable gray pants, baskets of sheets.

No one is there. I feel less alone with the friendly clothing. Somehow it seems that the men's pants and socks have more life, feeling, more purpose than the men who wear them. I find myself holding a piece of white flannel, letting it warm my cold hands in summer.

Three

After a month I had learned to find my way around the grounds and through the buildings in the hospital, but I had yet to learn to find my way through the restricting routine of the days. I was appalled at the hospital conditions. Some-times there were sixty patients sleeping in one dormitory. If a patient became upset and difficult to handle during the night he disturbed everyone in the room and the next day all the patients would be irritable and hard to manage. This led to more difficult nights for others, and the cycle perpetuated itself.

Some of the facilities were good, especially the athletic equipment. But that was not surprising because most on my seventy patients were over fifty years old and had always sat in their corner of the ward and never used the equipment. Little was done for these patients besides providing them with food and shelter. There had been much excitement on the chronic service when tranquilizers had first come out, many patients appeared to get better, but most of them stayed the same or gradually regressed to their old patterns. Perhaps it had only been the new interest the staff took in the patients when they were placed on drugs that caused them to get better in the first place.

Most of all, the ward was understaffed and many members of the staff were either temporary, uninterested, incompetent, or insufficient to the demands placed on them. They were constantly frustrated, short of funds, often short of medicine, and usually short of humor. When I first arrived I felt impotent and helpless with a ward of old and dying schizophrenics. I did not know where to begin and felt I would have to depend upon the ward nurse, Miss Barker, who had been there for years and knew all the problems and how to handle them.

One of the long-cherished routines of the chronic service, part of the standard operating procedure I was expected to follow, was that at least once each week every ward was to have a ward meeting. I was to sit in a large chair at the end of the day hall and preside over my patients, listen to their complaints about the place, and help them find a solution to their problems. What would my first encounter with the patients on the ward be like? What would I say to them? How would I introduce myself? How would I begin? I decided that the best plan was to be friendly and affable, to make no demands at all, and to ask Miss Barker for advice.

"What am I supposed to do? What did the other doctor do?"

"Doctor Rosatti always asked questions. Nobody ever answered them, but he asked a lot of questions like how were they, or did they want to go on a picnic or have a party."

"Picnic or party? But they're all so old."

"Don't kid yourself. They love picnics. Getting outside and sitting in the sun and eating. It's a very big deal to them. Look, you can start the meeting any time you want. I have a few things to do in here and I'll be out to join you in a minute. I know all their names so I can help you out with that, at least. Dr. Rosatti's meetings lasted about ten minutes. He said that even was more than he could stand."

The day hall was filled with patients. I looked out on a sea of gray—gray pants, gray shirts, gray faces; a sea of eyes staring blankly, of hands rubbing themselves in anguish, a sea of postures fixed in time. I looked down each sorry row for one face to direct my comments to, for one person to try and contact, for one person to meet, but all I saw was a flat sea of gray. The only motion in the room was a patient rocking in the back and the aides shifting their weight.

"I am your new doctor, Dr. Stevens. I am replacing Dr. Rosatti, who has left for another hospital in New York. I know a few of you by sight but I'm afraid I don't know many of you by name yet. I hope to get to talk to each of you soon and to discuss your problems and see what I can do to help or to make you more comfortable. If there are any problems or questions that any of you would like to discuss now, please feel free to bring them up."

I sat back in the iron-ribbed chair and sank down into the sticky plastic cushions that were falling apart at the seams, the moldy stuffing falling out. I looked around at the pictures on the walls. There was one of a ship someone had painted in occupational therapy, a large red ship with yellow and blue sails and the name *Santa Maria* on it.

On the other walls there were seed pictures. The patients took seeds of various shapes and colors and pasted them in patterns on a board; usually they were still-lifes. Every ward had at least one representation of the masks of comedy and tragedy portrayed in seeds hanging on its walls. I supposed that it was a very popular motif because the occupational therapists thought it offered a convenient way for the patients to express their feelings. There was an orange hooked rug with a design I could not make out directly opposite my chair.

I had exhausted the pictures in the day hall and found it very difficult to look at the patients. They were professionals at staring and I was only a novice. It would have been no contest. I looked at the television set for a moment and at the empty chair next to me, which was reserved for Miss Barker.

Where was she? Time seemed immeasurable. Finally, after many minutes, she came in.

"How are things going?" she whispered as she sat down.

I did not reply, but she looked at my face and then at the patients and nodded with a serious look. We got along quite well at the start and tried to help each other out as much as possible. She was very concerned. We both took a deep breath and waited.

Silence. Perhaps ten minutes.

"I, I . . . I've got a question."

Someone spoke. I was as happy as I could ever remember being. Someone spoke!

"That's John," the nurse whispered.

"Can I go home for the weekend? Can I go home for the weekend?"

"Have you been home in the past?"

"I went last month. I went last month."

"Well, then, you and I and the nurse will sit down after the meeting and discuss it."

I had taken the safe way out. I did not know this man

and, as grateful as I was to him for breaking the silence, I did not want to promise anything I could not deliver.

Suddenly a robust-looking man who had been sitting in the back stood up, waved his arms in all directions, and began to speak, loudly and as if he had some sort of authority.

"Glad to see you here, doc, I'm Larry. It's good to have a good doc here. You're a good doc to have here, doc. Lots of docs come through here. I've seen lots of docs, but you're a good doc, doc. We've heard all about you, doc. We're glad to have you here, doc. I hope that you are better than that other stupid doc."

Where did he come from, I wondered. At least he was talking. Everyone else remained quiet and didn't seem aware that this man had been talking. Miss Barker was busy helping a patient with a button and was unable to offer me any help. There was the silence again. You could have sung all four stanzas of the national anthem in that silence. It was an oppressive and demanding silence. I had the feeling that I should say something, but what should I say? I looked around at the seed pictures again and could feel my skin crawl.

A patient in front of me said, "Bread and water, bread and water," but he was talking to himself.

"Hey, doc," the talkative man began, "I think that they are all afraid of you." He started walking around the day hall like a monitor in an examination. "Yeh, it always takes them a while to get used to the new doc. And you got to admit, doc, that you're a new doc, doc. No matter how you look at it. How old are you, doc? You married, doc?" I noticed the nurse look at me when he asked that question. "Where'd you go to school, doc? Are you really a doc, doc?" He started laughing very hard, and as if trying to make me feel better he added, "I'm only kidding, doc."

I asked, "Is there anything that any of you would like to

talk about? Anything about the ward, or suggestions you might have to make things here go a little better?" In my fright about the patients not having anything to say I did not understand what the man had told me—that the patients would really like to know who I was and what I wanted of them. But I was afraid of revealing myself to them. I missed that opportunity and went off in another direction.

"I'm going to have a suggestion box made and will lock it and place it in the lounge. Those of you who wish to can put comments into it. I'll open the box at our ward meetings and read the suggestions aloud."

"Hey, that's a good idea, doc. That's an idea. That's a real good idea, doc."

I was frankly very pleased with myself then, but gradually over the next month I came to see that incident as a failure of communication with the patients, as a convenient way of keeping distant and uninvolved.

"Can I go home for the weekend? I would like that. I would like that."

"I'll speak to the nurse."

"I would like that. I would really like that."

Again the silence took over the ward.

"Where do you want to put the suggestion box, doc? A lot of good places, doc. Right on top of the TV. That's a good place to put it."

"How do the rest of you feel about it?"

"I would like to go home for the weekend. I would like that."

I smiled and nodded at him. Tom and Stan, the aides in the back, were smiling and trying to quiet hallucinating patients and keep them from disturbing the others. I would have welcomed a new disturbance at that point. A few stragglers, who I found would always be late for meetings, filtered in.

"Put it on the TV. That'll be perfect. A good place to

put it. Right on the TV set, square in the middle. Right in front of the antenna. Made of wood, a good thing."

A man dressed in a bathrobe and pajamas started to cough. He couldn't stop and I felt myself developing a tickle in my throat and was forced to clear it several times. Another man who had been silent and motionless during the entire meeting stood up and said, "I've got to go," and walked out of the meeting. I longed to follow him.

"Can I go home for the weekend?"

"You guys got to learn to keep this place clean," the talkative man began, with his back to me. He had walked across the hall and stood directly in front of me, totally upstaging me and pushing a broom in earnest. "If you don't learn how to keep this place clean, it'll be a rotten place to live. Tell 'em, doc, huh, doc? You don't live here, doc, so you don't know. You live out in the suburbs with the little woman and the kids, big house, lots of money, doc? Well, this place is filthy, doc, and you ought to know something about it."

He brushed some dirt into a pile and pushed some patients out of the path of his broom. He had done this many times before, I guessed, because some of the men lifted their legs automatically when he went by to let him through. When he reached the side of the room he leaned angrily against the wall and his face grew red. Then he stormed out of the room with an air of indignation.

Silence. A long silence. I decided to end the meeting.

"Well, we will be meeting every Monday at two and I expect you all to come. If no one has anything else to bring up we'll close for today."

I got up to leave and was followed by John, the man who wanted to go home for the weekend. He demanded an answer on the spot and said that I had promised to tell him as soon as the meeting was over. I asked him to wait ten minutes and went into my office and was surprised to find that I was covered with sweat. John followed me. He would have none of this. "You promised. You promised. Let me go home," he was shouting. I asked him to come into the office and Miss Barker handed me his medication sheet and his record. "Let me go home. I have an uncle who wants to see me. He's counting on me. Let me go."

I picked up his record and looked at the man. Somehow, sitting in the meeting he had looked threatening, but standing here he appeared grotesque and pitiful. He had a large purple birthmark which covered the right side of his face and neck and he kept trying to hide it with his spindly fingers. His spine was deformed and he listed to one side, his walk was uneven and he dragged his feet. He reached for my hand and said, "Gimme my medicine for home. Gimme it. Gimme." And just as suddenly he started crying and knocked over a chair.

"John, stop that this instant!" said Miss Barker.

"What do you think?" I asked.

"He gets upset a lot, but he does well with his uncle. He goes every weekend practically. No harm in it."

I wrote out the prescriptions indicated in his record, two tranquilizers, a drug to counteract the Parkinsonian trembling that the tranquilizers produced, some sleeping pills, and some liquid antacid for his stomach. He took them in his thin red hands and went downstairs to the pharmacy to have them filled and never even said thank you.

"Not bad at all," said Miss Barker, putting John's chart away.

I've been a good boy, I thought.

NOTES FOUND IN THE SUGGESTION BOX

Tell mother to visit me.
                    —Signed by an eighty-year-old man

Two eggs instead of one for breakfast.
                                        —Unsigned

The veil of heavenly spirits descends. Its presence is
near.
The work of the flaggelation is yet to begin
                                        —Unsigned

One million dollers
                                        —John

New razor blades
A bar of hypoallegric soap
Shoe polish
New shoe laces
New metal tips for my old laces
Pliers to tighten them
A leather craft kit to fix my belt
Spare pieces of leather
Needle and thread
Buttons, assorted colors
A dozen pencils
Six erasers
Pad of paper
Half dozen envelopes
A dollars worth of stamps,
Including two air mail
And one special delivery,
Woolen gloves
Silver polish to polish my watch
A subscription to *Vermont Life*
A bronze watering can
A chrome plated trowel
A large bottle of vaseline
Two boxes of Kleenex
Soft toilet paper
Bottle of Aspirin
A carton filter cigarettes

Passes to local sports events and movies
A stapler
A pencil sharpener, electric

—larry

I think that the person who is controlling my geni-
tals should stop doing so. He knows who he is.

—Unsigned

Shortly after I came to the ward Miss Barker retired,
deserting me, taking all her knowledge of the patients with
her.

Miss Stuart, her replacement, was the prettiest nurse
you ever saw, not really beautiful, but really pretty. She always blushed when you talked to her and would stare down
at her white shoes, her curly jet-black hair falling all over.
And she had a terrific figure. She was lovely. At twenty-three,
Miss Stuart had just taken the ward over from Miss Barker,
a comb-in-the-breast-pocket-type nurse who was easily twice
her weight, but very far from her five-foot-four of instant,
mix with water, loose Jello, anything-at-all sex appeal.

Miss Barker's weight, some two hundred and fifty
pounds, had taken its toll in daily punishment upon her arthritic knees. The bouncing, vibrating thud of her heavy
step was just as loud and shook the walls as much as before,
but it was much slower now. The patients always knew when
she was coming long before she reached the ward. The lack
of an elevator in the building was given as the main reason
for her retirement, but there were others. For all her good
points, she had begun to resist the changes that were forced
upon her and upon the way she had done things over the
years. She said that no one appreciated her and she had a
fight with Superintendent Larkin about her unwillingness to
try new programs. He kept his ground, she yielded only
tears.

The aides encouraged the patients to give her a little farewell party. Actually, the aides did all of the work and decorating and made sure that the patients were all in the same place at the right time. Some of the patients had been on the same ward with Miss Barker since she first came to the hospital and they had shared much of the past thirty-two years, but today she was leaving.

I wonder what the patients were thinking as they automatically formed lines of orderly khaki and gray and shuffled preoccupiedly to get the sparsely frosted sponge cake and diluted lime Kool-Aid. They did not seem to be aware, they did not seem to be hungry, but they were part of the party and they did eat the refreshments.

An aide from the chronic female service brought his guitar over and led the singing. He always led the singing at parties and special occasions for the patients around the hospital. He always used the same routine and sang the same tired songs. On weekends he made a few extra dollars by singing at childrens' birthday parties. "On Top of Old Smoky" got the best response—three out of forty-one patients joined in the singing. One old man pretended to move his lips and sing, but he was really imitating a young student nurse at his side. He imitated everything he saw. The rest of the patients found their special chairs in which they had sat so long for so many years that they had become life masks of their bodies.

Bert, a thick-lipped, drooling, mentally defective old man, frozen a child forever by an injury at birth, interrupted the singing again and again, shouting, "I remember when you came here. I remember when you came here." It was the only speech any of the patients made.

Miss Barker leaned forward and pushed on the arms of her red plastic chair, the yellow foam rubber bursting through a torn seam under the pressure of her weight, pulled herself up, and wiped a tear from her cheek. She blew her nose in a flowered handkerchief that she always carried in the pocket with the comb. No one seemed to notice that she was crying.

She turned to the window and stared blankly for a minute. She looked out on the rainy, cold day, the wet asphalt walks reflecting the sky, on young nurses laughing, holding onto their white caps, running to shelter on knees that they could trust and that she envied, their blue capes blowing in the wet summer wind. She looked at the building across the lawn where years ago she had begun and remembered how frightened she had been that first day. It seemed unbearably far away. Over the years she had made many friends. She had always found someone to eat lunch with. She had not been alone. She had shared her years with the patients. There was a fog bank sitting on a back field and a few lonely sparrows circling the gray afternoon sun.

She turned to the men she had cared for and said that she didn't know what to say. She tried to tell them what it all had meant to her, those long years that she had given, but the words would not come out. Some of the men just stared at her, the way they had stared at her for years. A short squirrel of a man stuck his head through the doorway and looked up at each corner of the ceiling and then went away to reappear every so often and repeat his ritual. Several men paced, one anxiously, one angrily, one pensively. Others talked to themselves or laughed, or, like one arguing with his voices, said, "No . . . no . . . NO, no, *no!*"

A tall man picked things out of the air. An old man soiled himself and interrupted her in the middle of her speech to ask her to help clean him up. In a corridor off the large day hall a man urgently rubbed the wall with his body. Old Bert, the defective interrupted again to say, "I remember when you came here," and ate the cake with his hands.

Someone turned on the television very loud. An aide ran quickly to shut it off.

Miss Barker went on: "I can never forget the wonderful trips and the long walks we took in springtime together."

A swarthy, gaunt man got up and started out, "I have to go the laundry. Can't be late."

"I will always remember you and . . ."

"Okay, D ward, supper," yelled a loud voice from the hall. "Oh, I'm sorry, I really am. I didn't know you were having a party."

But it was too late. Most of the patients had gotten up and were walking out through the open doors of the ward, which when she was younger and more receptive to new ideas Miss Barker had fought so hard to unlock. Many were already down the stairs.

She was now alone and was replaced. She wrapped a piece of cake in a paper napkin for later; walked slowly to the long steps, and, switching the cake to her other hand, reached for the bannister before her.

"I remember when you came," shouted Bert.

The voice startled her; she thought she was alone.

"You better hurry, Bert, or you'll be late for supper."

He went down the stairs, touching the walls with his hands, and disappeared beneath the landing. She started down.

For thirty-two years it had been no different. She treated them all alike, both permissive and stern. She loved them when they were tidy and scolded them when they were not. In many ways it was as if she were still bringing them up. She would say, "That's a good boy" or "Isn't that a bad boy!" to men who were old enough to be her father.

I must be fair to her and tell you that she honestly tried and never hurt anyone, but what was going on in their heads remained a mystery to her. What they needed, she felt, was a good rest, nourishing food, and a good, clean bed. It will be shown on the records that little about the patients changed and that time did nothing. Each year they just grew older and each year her legs got worse.

Such wonderful things were said about her.

"She's never thought of herself in all these years."

"She treats the patients like her own children."

"A very determined old lady. We'll miss her."

Miss Stuart was afraid to be her replacement. She had studied very little psychiatry and in nurses' training had spent only three short months working in mental hospitals and had tried to get away for coffee every chance she got. All the other hospitals wanted nurses who would take night duty and the state hospital was the only one that would give her every evening off.

The two nurses had met briefly on the ward, where they discussed the patients together. Miss Barker had seemed angry then and was very quick, hardly saying more than a word or two about each man.

"Borkum, been here, let's see, eighteen years. No medications. He sweeps the corridors each day. A sister visits every so often. He's no problem."

And they met for the last time at the staff tea. The older woman took Miss Stuart aside in a corner and told her: "Take care of my children . . ."

Miss Stuart was very uneasy before she started work and she scraped her new convertible on the way into the hospital. The first day was a blur of a hundred different faces, of a hundred different medicines distributed to stiff hands, to trembling hands.

"I'm Albert. Can I have milk instead of water to wash them down?"

No one really seemed to say hello, or even notice that she was there. She went through the day hall, from chair to chair, from patient to patient, introducing herself to them and finding that she was carrying on both sides of the conversation.

"I'm the new ward nurse. I think we'll get along fine, don't you?"

Except for Francis, who wet his bed, all of them responded to her as they had to Miss Barker—passive, silent, with no emotion.

After a while it was really quite easy. Checkers in the morning. You had to be careful not to win and to set up some of the patients and coax them into jumping you. Bingo or cards in the afternoon, and long walks on Wednesdays, weather permitting.

When she got to know their names, she could say to relatives, if any came, "John seems to be better this past week." The relatives would nod and say, "His father thought he noticed a change in him. Do you think he could be getting better?"

After a month or two she said, "They never look at me the way other men on the street do. I've never gotten the once-over. Whenever I thought someone was staring at me, I'd look again in a minute and find them staring in the same direction, into the same empty space."

She spent one year in charge of that ward, passing out pills or on the telephone calling down for supplies, looking for a wayward patient, making a date for lunch. She planned to leave to get married, to have babies that she prayed to God would grow up all right.

At Miss Stuart's farewell party the same aide would play his guitar and lead the same three patients in singing the same familiar songs. Her farewell speech would be short; she would not need turn to the window to gather her thoughts and put her feelings straight to say, "I have enjoyed working with you and hope that you all will feel better soon."

She would not cry. She would feel relieved that she would not have to see the men pacing to nowhere and talking to themselves. Bert, still drooling, would shout over and over, "I remember when you came here, I remember when you came," and eat his cake with his hands.

Four

My days were full of faces, flat emotionless faces, mute faces. My days were full of hands pulling and tugging at my clothing, begging cigarettes or loose change. There was always a demand upon me and upon my time. No matter how I arranged my obligations in the hospital I didn't have enough time to see patients.

There was an endless array of seminars offered by almost every department in the hospital: seminars in psychology, psychoanalytic theory, job placement, music therapy, art therapy, psychiatric nursing, and treatment—and there were grand rounds and case presentations as well. Each area had its own schedule.

If you wanted to give the impression that you were interested, curious, and worthy of higher things, you could fill

your day with seminars. With time off for a leisurely lunch
and an occasional hour spent with the nurses talking *about*
the patients, you could avoid seeing almost all of your patients except the two or three you had in therapy.

Therapy patients were chosen by each resident either
from the old patients on the chronic wards or from the new
ones on the admitting floor. A good patient for therapy was
one who would be willing to talk with you, meet with you
regularly, and make a commitment to work out his problems. The decision to take a patient was made between each
resident and the patient and had to be approved by the resident's supervisor, who had power only to make suggestions.
The resident had the final word. The term therapy was often
applied loosely to cover any interaction between a doctor
and a patient, but I saw it as a special relationship in which
two people struggle to make one of them more human. It
took months to find suitable patients.

The men on my ward were under my administrative
control. I was responsible for the mechanics of their existence, their medications, privileges, diet, and sleeping arrangements. If unusual difficulties arose, I was to make the
decision which would restrict, seclude, or tranquilize them or
affect them in some other way. Restriction meant taking
away a privilege, but since very few of my patients ever did
much to begin with, I seldom used it. I took a benign view
of my patients' obstinacy and, unlike some of my aides, especially Stan, I was unwilling to take away Jake Leven's job in
the greenhouse because he didn't always make his bed. I
never used seclusion unless a patient asked for it. Each ward
had a seclusion room, a room with only a stained and incredibly putrid mattress in it, which could be locked as a kind
of a maximum-security cell. I made a rule that the door
could never be locked and that the room was to be used only
by patients who were afraid they were going to lose control

of themselves. I suggested at one of the ward meetings that if anyone felt out of control he could walk into the seclusion room, sit, think, or read a newspaper in peace and leave whenever he felt better.

Tranquilizers were purchased by the hospital pharmacy by the ton, it seemed. Pharmaceutical detail men were always tracking down the residents in the hospital and squeezing themselves in between the doctors and their next appointment to hand out a reprint of a study about their particular drug and several pounds of medicine to try on "those especially resistant patients who are difficult to motivate." I knew about those kinds of patients. I had a ward full. I used drugs a good deal at first, mainly because all my patients were already on drugs. Miss Barker would greet me on Tuesdays with, "Time to rewrite the medication orders," and I would sit like a machine and write orders until my hands cramped. After a while I decided I would try to cut down on some of the medications. To my surprise, many patients showed no negative response to being taken off drugs and so I kept them off; the ward got a little noisier because more of the men were talking, but that was all. Other patients got worse and I either put them back on the same drug or started them on another. I found that there was very little difference among many of the drugs, and that the effects of some tranquilizers were more imagined than real. The worst thing about the drugs, I discovered, was that they offered a convenient way of dealing with an upset patient and upset staff. During a busy night when you have been running from one ward to another calming a staff angered about troublesome patients the easiest way of handling another disturbing patient is to give him medicine to quiet him. The staff liked medication because it was simple.

Sometimes the staff set you up. For example, Stan would provoke Willie into such a rage that Willie would start breaking things apart and then Stan would call me in and say, "Doc, you've got to do something about this guy because if you don't he's going to wreck the day hall. Usually a couple of hundred milligrams of Seconal does the trick." There you would stand, with a raving maniac of an aide pushing a patient to be destructive and telling you what medication to give. I reported Stan once to his supervisor but Stan only got worse, taking out all his frustrations on my patients and me.

Often the aides had little training for their jobs. Many on the evening shift were college students earning extra money as "baby sitters." They sat and did their homework on the ward after the patients had been safely locked behind them in their bedroom. Some of the students had no idea what they had gotten into, but there were a few who were interested and spoke to the patients. I suggested things for them to read to help them understand and went over some of the cases with them. They turned out to be among the best staff there, mainly because they had few prejudices about the patients and treated them as people. Some of them were terrified of noises in the night and insisted that the doctor come and take care of their ward problems so that they wouldn't be frightened. I could understand their feelings and I was sympathetic because they admitted they were afraid, and they had had no training or preparation. I found it more difficult to tolerate the trained hospital staff—the terrified social workers, the sadistic aides, the manipulating nurses, and the overcautious doctors—who kept patients locked up because they were afraid that their patients' failure would reflect upon their own inadequacy or because they just didn't want to be bothered.

I found that there was only one way to manage a ward of patients and that was to get to know them. It seemed like a very simple answer. If you know why someone is upset, you can help them understand and do something about it. It was not a profound solution. It was simply a matter of not locking up the patients or drugging them into submission or punishing them by taking away their only healthy activity. It meant that if you wanted to help them you listened to them and talked to them as real people, people to contend with, and that took time. You could never be sure if what you did would help and there were always those who found other reasons for your success, just as there were those who blamed you for the things that did not turn out well even when the cause was entirely unrelated to anything you had done.

I had decisions to make. How should I spend my time? People streamed across the lawns from the wards and from the outside and filled the offices. They wanted to be seen. Relatives wanted time and reassurance. Secretaries wanted time and dictation kept up to date. The hospital administration wanted an audience for important speakers. I avoided the seminars almost entirely. The patients had a challenge to offer, and there was a hunger I felt we could share. There was very little time left over—almost none—and so even though the senior staff might object, I decided to spend all of my time with my patients. I was playing an old hunch, a feeling of a former success, a memory from my past which suddenly seemed fresh and clear.

I only know him as "Crazy Harry." That's what all the children call him. He is a strange man who lives at the end of our street, who talks and laughs to himself as he makes his way around the neighborhood. Some child is always following him, laughing at him, making faces and mimicking his funny bouncing walk. On barrel day he goes back and forth across the street collecting what he thinks is worth saving from the garbage cans and storing it in the pockets of his enormous brown coat.

Children follow him and laugh when a bottle falls from

his hand and breaks. Many of the children have been told that "that man" will come to punish them if they do something wrong. If he makes even the smallest movement toward them they all turn and run away screaming.

He frightens me. He's very strange and aloof. He does very silly things, for which, if I had done them, I would have been punished. He doesn't seem to notice that we laugh at him. He doesn't seem to care. What scares me most about him is that no one seems to like him and that he's always alone. I am frightened to think that I could ever be like that and so I laugh when the others made fun, but secretly I am glad that I am not him and that they are not making fun of me.

One day after school I meet him coming out of a candy store. "It's Crazy Harry, run for your life," shouts my friend Paul DaSilva. Perhaps it is the warm spring's evening light, perhaps I misread one of Harry's funny smiles, but for some reason he does not look as wild as usual to me. He has on a bright plaid sport shirt, and it is the first time I have ever seen him without his coat. He reaches into a brown paper bag and pulls out a small wax statue of an Indian filled with orange syrup and offers it to me.

"Don't take it, it's poison. It'll kill you," Paul shouts from a safe distance atop a brick wall across the street.

Harry reaches out and holds the orange Indian in front of me. Is it poison? Will I die? He seems rather gentle and not terrifying. Could everyone else be wrong?

I take it. I reach out my hand and I take it! And like a man who has resigned himself to any possible consequences, even death, I bite off that Indian's head and swallow the thick, sticky-sweet orange liquid. I look around to see if I really have survived. I have survived, and have even liked it, although I prefer lime over orange.

Harry reaches into the bag again and holds up a red

wax soldier and, lifting it over his head, steps onto the street and waves it in a huge gesture to Paul, sitting on the wall.

"You want one?" he calls in an unexpectedly high voice.

Paul had slowly edged himself to the end of the wall, and when Harry speaks he jumps down and breaks into a run in the other direction. Suddenly I have doubts. It is a very strange voice.

"Here, you take it."

Harry hands me the red soldier and takes an orange baseball player for himself. "Save the wax when you're done. I always do."

I thank him and then go to find Paul, who is waiting for me at a lookout post he had established on someone's front porch. We sit together looking at the red soldier, but Paul will not take it. Harry is looking at us from in front of the candy store. We sit and watch him walk away down the street, amid the sounds of a ball bouncing against wooden steps and the high-pitched squeals of children playing hide-and-seek, and then some other children start to follow him and shout at him. I grow terribly sad watching him disappear in the distance, and for the first time I can remember I feel really lonely for another person.

From then on I said hello to him whenever he passed by. And once when someone called me Crazy Harry's friend I really didn't mind; in fact, I think I smiled.

I felt that same loneliness at the hospital, that same desperation and rejection. I wanted to try to get to know the patients, to get across that distance, to be their friend and to understand what had happened to them. I wanted to try without hiding my possible failure with the excuse that I did not have enough time, or that I did not try hard enough. I had no illusions. I did not see myself as a giant killer. I was only one person, but I *was* one and I felt I must try. I was not going to waste my time pretending I was too busy to help.

One of the first things Miss Barker had told me when I arrived was that I would do very well to stay clear of Willie. He could get very angry, even explosive at times, without warning and for no apparent reason. The day when he tore the day hall apart no one could approach him. The staff just watched helplessly until he ran out of energy. He never hit anyone even though he threatened everyone, and he was usually content to sit glowering in a corner, his corner. When he was on the hospital grounds he could usually be found sitting there, but he was fond of wandering away from the hospital. On even the hottest summer days he wore a heavy woolen sweater and a matching fisherman's cap. His clothes were always green and his complexion sallow.

"If you ever get a chance," Tom said, "take a look at that notebook he carries with him. He's always writing down things in it. I once saw it when he was in the shower. All crazy writing and strange words—like a different language. And formulas and numbers and funny shapes. Whenever someone gets him upset, he writes it down in that book."

I looked through his record and discovered nothing new about him, just the yearly mental-status exam by the state psychiatrist, who was fond of his ability to describe schizophrenia with the adjectives of psychiatrists of a generation ago: "A shallow, silly, confused, hostile, unrealistic, deluded, hallucinating, empty shell of a regressed, hopeless schizophrenic."

There was no comment about who he was or how he got that way. There were some notes about his medications; he had been given almost every one of the new drugs as they came out.

None of the drugs had helped; he had stayed the same. The admission note in the chart was twenty-five years old and had turned yellow and fragile with time. He had been only nineteen when he was admitted. There was a brief note about his parents having been killed in the Second World War, but it was a vague statement; the examining doctor attributed the incompleteness of the history to Willie's confusion.

Willie had a sister who had occasionally come to see him and his social worker, but she had stopped visiting when she married and moved to Ohio ten years earlier. The chart did not give her name. According to the record, he had always been like this: hostile, in a corner by himself, given to outbursts of temper.

I went back up to the ward with his chart in my hand, full of the desire to understand and help solve the mystery which had eluded so many before. I decided to try and talk to him—perhaps no one ever really tried before. I asked him to come into the office. He looked frightened, but he came. He looked up at me, waiting to see what I would do.

"I am the new doctor on the ward, and I am trying to get to know you better, to see how you are and if I can be of help to you."

He shifted in his chair and stared out the window. I looked in the same direction and commented on the fine summer day. He turned his head to the wall.

"I've been reading your record to try and understand your history better, but it doesn't seem to be complete and I thought you could help me fill in some details."

He looked straight at me, cold black eyes in a flat, emotionless face, a hollow face, a two-dimensional face, an optical-illusion face, a clown's face in black, a terrible face, perhaps a sad face.

"I can't find out why you came here."

A blue-gray mouth, a tense mouth, a biting mouth, a silent mouth.

"Do you remember?"

A fixed stare, a cold stare, an empty stare.

"You were nineteen?"

A gray, blue mouth, a clown's face in black, a cold stare.

"Your parents, they were . . ."

A scream broke through his silent face. The clown's face spoke in booming shouts: "Formula 37 is not for you! Tonight at twelve your death will be accomplished. You cannot outlive the writings. You defy what is written. You die and are smitten."

A cold smile, a trembling smile, an empty stare, a flat face, a silent mouth again, a cold room in August.

I shook at the suddenness, the volume, the voice, that voice, a broken-stick voice, a firecracker voice, a fingernail-on-the-blackboard voice.

"I don't understand what you just said."

An air of superiority, of condescension, of disdain, of disgust. A nod, a communication, a nod, a patronizing nod, he would communicate. His angularity dissolved, a softer line took over his face: he turned toward me, leaning back in his chair. Would he tell me something—or would he scream again?

With great contempt for me and all that I stand for he said, "How can *you* understand? It is not something that *people* are able to understand."

I noticed the book in his right hand for the first time. He had kept it behind his back until then.

"It is all in here. It is all written down. *You* would never understand it."

"But I would like to have that chance."

A moment of consideration. The book and hand disappeared again.

"The secret will die with me. You will not know it."

A long silence, a sad face, a glassy eye, a shaking hand.

"Can I go now?"

He got up and walked out. Miss Stuart, who had been

waiting outside and had overheard much of what was going on, walked in.

"How'd it go? You told me Miss Barker warned you not to mess with him. Are you going to die tonight? I must have been told that a hundred times in the past two weeks. Move yourself a minute so I can open the drawer behind you."

The next morning, I admit, I was happy to wake up, even though I didn't believe in magic; psychiatrists aren't supposed to. When I got to the hospital I went straight to the ward and called Willie over. We walked into my office together and I announced that I was alive and had survived the night.

He opened that enormous mouth of his and shouted at me: "The disperinative quality of decisions is densified and promulgated by scravative forces. Your obfigurative disjuncture is disparate. Formulae 6, 22, and 37 gamma apply; all condensify, codify, reapplicate, and disrupt. As a direct result, two disinclinative polarities, disintegrating structures, death is always a certainty."

"What about all these formulae, these secrets for understanding people?"

"Disperinative, idiot, disperinative."

He spelled it for me at the top of his lungs: "D-I-S-P-E-R-I-N-A-T-I-V-E"

And left the office.

Later, one day when Willie was away with the other patients, Tom asked if I would like to look at his notebook, which had been left behind. This was more than I could resist, and I opened up the book:

$$\text{"}37 = 65 \ z_3, \text{ semi log } 789.099 \text{ pi}$$
$$\text{Ch-11} = X - (N + 4.7 \ B')\text{"}$$

There were at least a hundred pages of these figures, sometimes written in a hand so small that you needed magnification to read them. And many notes—strange, comic, even, if they had not been so sad:

> "Tommy Tommy run.
> Liebste Kind, meine Kind
> Mamma's Kind, Papa's Kind."

And copies of soap and toothpaste commercials, pages upon pages of drawings, all of the same thing—two rocks, one larger than the other, leaning against each other.

I decided not to try and draw him out even though I felt I understood him. He had lost his family in the war and had constructed a world out of numbers to protect himself from that great hurt, and he drew gravestones on paper as a continuous memorial to his parents. I did not feel that I could help him and would only tear open old wounds without much chance of a better healing the second time.

Several years after I left the hospital I saw him stalking behind a rock in a park as I went driving by. He was staring into space.

A cold stare, an empty stare, a lonely stare.

My feelings, which were touched like my motivation, were both in the present and the past.

Arbie is one of the big kids on my block who terrorize me on the way to school. He always has two other fifth-graders with him, his henchmen, who knock books out of my hands or try to tear up the leaf that I am bringing into school. They have tremendous power over the four of us on the block who have just entered kindergarten and round us up and lecture us, tell us the rules, and shout the perils of disobeying them.

It is horrible to be stopped by one of them, and we try to find short cuts through back yards to avoid meeting them on the way home. The worst time is when they happen to catch you all alone.

"Aha! We caught you in Billy Sobelloff's back yard."

"We caught you dead to rights. It's off limits."

"Leave me alone!"

They hold me against a garage wall and then Arbie appears and walks slowly toward me. He makes strange gestures and cackles, "Die, die in your sleep at twelve o'clock tonight. Let him go, he's doomed anyhow."

They release me and I run. I run faster than I ever thought possible. Up the driveway. Across the street, through bushes, up the stairs, I stand pounding on the front door, tears streaming down my face. I run to my room.

"What's wrong? Tell me what happened."

I cannot speak and am too afraid to talk about it anyway. I stay in my room till supper and then eat very little. I stare at my parents and watch them eat. I am terrified.

"Where are the hands when it is twelve o'clock?"

"They are together straight up, together, like this."

"What's wrong?"

"Nothing."

I take my sister's alarm clock from her dresser and bring it into my room and stay up to watch the hands move over the numbers. What is going to happen? I sit and numbly wait, firmly convinced that there is nothing I can do but watch the hands point straight up and then, somehow, die. The numbers become a dim blur and the next thing I know it is morning.

I am alive! I am really alive! I gulp down my breakfast and leave for school. I am going to show that Arbie a thing or two. He was wrong. I am alive.

Dr. Pellegrini became my friend. He was an unusually gifted man who had what seemed like a direct pipeline to the secret lives going on beneath the surface in even the most difficult patients. He had been in charge of teaching for years and would demonstrate his interviewing techniques in conferences, leaving the residents feeling hopelessly inadequate. That was not his intention, but the result of seeing a true master at work. He was warm, persistent, and very intelligent.

"So, Bob. You have decided to be different, I hear. You don't go to any of your social-service meetings or study programs. Word gets around. You are getting a reputation."

"What? I don't understand."

"Well, according to the rules, if you aren't in a seminar you can't be learning anything of value."

"I guess I have really been getting involved with the patients."

"How much time do you spend with them a week?"

"I think about forty hours."

"That's quite a lot. I think it's important to get involved and to try and help patients and I wouldn't tell you otherwise, but you aren't in some private office in the suburbs with bright young people as patients who sit and talk to you, an easy load."

"I know."

"I'm sure you do, but I don't think you know what a letdown you are in for. There has been a study done where the best men in a department treated patients just as sick as yours. They weren't residents, Bob, they were full-fledged psychoanalysts."

"I've heard about that."

"Have you also heard about the results? You know, none of the patients they treated got better, even after two years of intensive treatment."

"Does that mean I shouldn't try?"

"God, no. You must try. But—I hate to say this—you must be prepared to fail. Even after your very best efforts.

You'll watch patients get better at first and then when they hear that you are leaving, you'll see them go downhill and some of them get even worse."

"So what's the answer?"

"I'm not sure that that is a pertinent question. The question is, really, why are you trying? What is it that makes you try? What is it in you that makes you want to help these people? You have to understand this in yourself. If you don't have a good reason, under pressure when you are most needed you won't be convincing and the patients who trust you will feel cheated and betrayed. And that's the worst thing you can do. If you let someone get close to you and you cannot follow through and you hurt them it will be very difficult for anyone to ever reach them again." He leaned back in his chair. "If you know why you want to help, you can use that understanding."

"I don't know why I'm trying. It just seems so wrong not to. How can I walk past a patient who really has problems and wants to talk about them and instead go to a conference to discuss a review of recent drugs? Especially when I have already read the review? Some of those seminars are like coffee hours."

"Mine, too?" Pellegrini was being playful.

"No, not usually." We both laughed.

"It's all right. You don't have to come. A word to the wise: Dr. Glickman and Dr. Charpentier do not like you. They find you a threat to their little world and they run to Dr. Larkin over everything."

"I can't stand either of them."

"Well, stay out of their way. What you are trying to do is hard enough. You *will* see more in the patients if you try to get close." Pellegrini looked up over his horn-rimmed glasses and smiled. He was getting a little gray, a little overweight, a little old.

I had a very strange feeling watching Pellegrini take out a cigar, light it, and blow the smoke in the air. "I have the feeling that in some way I am trying to find a part of me that was lost," I said.

"I don't understand," he replied.

"I just have the strangest feeling that somewhere, sometime, a part of me was lost in this place. I have the sense of there being something missing, a feeling of incompleteness."

"How do you think you can find this by getting closer to the patients?"

"I really don't know. I just have the feeling that I want to understand, to get close . . . this sounds crazy, but to get close to a very old mystery."

"About whom?"

"I don't know."

Pellegrini stared at me with a worried look. "Old mysteries are those that have remained unsolved for a long time. Such shadows are hard to move."

But I find it harder not to try at all."

Five

The chronic service gave me a hollow feeling. I was beating my head against a wall. I was walking through a wax museum and trying to make the figures move. I found myself alienating my staff, losing contact with my friends, trying to understand how to get close to patients who refused to recognize my existence.

What was this place doing to me? Often the harder I looked for a hopeful sign, the crazier my patients seemed. Sometimes I was convinced that no one would ever be cured and that all I was doing was watching the dark process eat away all that was left. I resolved to confront their tormentor. I would find a way in. I had to find some door that opened, some window that admitted light.

There were times when I felt sure I was crazy to do

what I was doing, to sit for hours in some corner of the hospital greeting a new patient with a hundred pleasantries in hand only to have each one summarily rejected without even a shrug or an acknowledgment, leaving me feeling empty and useless.

And yet I couldn't pity them. I couldn't. Some of them were so hostile, so contrary, so stubborn, that they would fight just for the pleasure of not yielding, of not yielding to anything. And I would try to understand why they felt that way, why they acted the way they did, and what it all meant.

Besides the administrative patients on my ward, I had other patients whom I would see more frequently in intense sessions, in psychotherapy. It was on these hours that I found myself placing most of my hope when my ward appeared dismal. Some patients refused to allow you to get close enough to treat them.

Linda, a thin sylph of a girl who hadn't turned twenty yet, came into my office and looked around wide-eyed and full of suspicion. She stared at me for ten long minutes, refusing to talk to me or to answer my questions. Then she got up suddenly and opened the door and said, in a dramatic whisper, "Ah! Beware! Use caution and stand back. I will not be enticed. You ask me why I cannot trust you and I laugh at you. I just laugh at you! You extend one hand so gladly and say you want to be my friend, but what is in the other hand hidden behind your back? So beware! To trust is to die and I have died enough. I will remain in darkness, but at least in darkness I will live. Though you be the only light on this dark stage, I will not play moth to your candle."

And with the gallant flair of a lady-in-waiting she left and never spoke to me again.

She was honest. Most painful was the patient who would come and play at being treated. Ed was like that—he toyed with me, gave me the illusion of hopefulness at the critical times when he perceived that my interest was waning. He really had no intention of trying.

Even though Ed had been on the chronic ward for five years, he was so much more active than the other patients there that, in my greenness, he appeared to me to be full of hope. Because he was only twenty-three, I felt that time had given me an advantage and I began to see him three times a week in intensive psychotherapy.

In many ways he was an unusual young man. In spite of the fact that he was so distracted and preoccupied with his fantasies during his last two years of high school that they were a total waste, he managed to get a good education and could give a remarkable account of himself in a surprisingly wide range of subjects. He was always reading books, magazines, and papers he found on the ward. He loved the *National Geographic* and would spend entire afternoons dreaming his way across the colored pages.

Someday he would get to Tahiti, where he could avoid the stresses and pressures of life, where he could hide from the pain that had turned him against the world. "Nobody in Tahiti has problems," he said.

Some of our sessions were like pleasant geography lessons in which together we would survey some distant hill of sand from a shaded coconut grove. He would describe the native women on the lonely atoll walking out onto the beach to meet their fishermen. Life was serene! One had only to reach up to pick a meal from the nearest nodding bough, which would seem to thank you afterward for lightening its fruity burden.

During his hours in therapy Ed would stretch out his hands and spread his fingers apart and then reach into the air like some giant spider. Suddenly he would dart his tongue in and out like a snake in one of the fantasies he was always talking about. At other times he would sight down his arms to his fingers as if they were the muzzle of a gun, stop suddenly, wince, and then smell his fingertips as he blew the smoke away. He repeated this over and over again as if he were entirely unaware that he was doing it as he talked to me about Polynesia, the meals in the hospital, his weekends at home, or the new nurse on his ward.

Ed had had a succession of therapists who thought they could help him. One of them, a resident from Indonesia, once said something to him that he didn't like and Ed had never forgotten it or forgiven him for it. His anger with this man knew no bounds, and he would build elaborate fantasies of how he would slowly destroy him by the most painful torture imaginable if they ever met again. He could not remember what that doctor had said to him.

Sometimes when Ed was silent he would make horrible contortions with his face, especially with his mouth. He would grimace and grind his teeth together, making a gnashing sound. Then he would start punching the seat and say, "Johnson, that sonofabitch. What a bastard!" Johnson was a black aide who had been rough with him three years before while attempting to subdue him when he had lost control of himself. He could never get this man out of his mind and in almost every meeting the anger would bubble to the surface. Very often when he became angry at me he would go into a tirade about Johnson.

For the first three months of therapy Ed kept all of his appointments and was never late. He was courteous, polite, and filled the hours with every pleasant story that came to his mind. He would challenge me to ask him questions about geography.

"Ask me to name three rivers in New Zealand. What are the states which have serious geologic faults in them? Where are the highest waterfalls in Bhutan? Describe the

Tasmanian countryside."

He would answer his own questions and put on a spectacular and entertaining show of his knowledge. He would tell me what a good doctor I was, what a warm and kindly and understanding psychiatrist I had been to him. If only I had been there when he first came in he would be out now, he said. Gradually he ran out of things to say and we were left with a lonely atoll and a cruel, heartless black aide as our only topics of discussion.

I asked to hear more about Ed's family and suggested that things at home had not been as rosy as he had described them to me. He rebelled at this, but I persisted. I brought up other unpleasant things that he had mentioned—for example, his fear of failure—and pointed out his anger at the world. He said that he was angry at no one except Johnson and "that stupid Indonesian with his stupid look. You could tell he was a moron just by looking at him."

The period of grace was over. He came late and sometimes missed his appointments entirely. Once, in a reflective moment, he told me that he despaired of his youth and wished that he were older so that he would not be bothered by the forces that pulled him apart inside. Yet Ed wanted to be cared for and was disappointed in me because I was unable to change him.

"If I were older, I would be settled. I would be a mature man. The Cardinal says that a man is not mature until he is thirty. When I am thirty these stupid problems will have disappeared. I won't be in a place like this. When I am forty, I'll be out in the world, traveling somewhere with a bevy of girls. Beautiful girls in sarongs with their breasts showing."

One night Ed ran away from the hospital and went to Boston harbor and watched the ships riding at anchor in the swells. He found an old artillery emplacement from the last world war, two musty bunkers with a sealed tunnel between them. He lay on the grassy bunker listening to the water lapping against the shore and watched the ships into the night. In the growing chill of evening he went below to the old door that sealed off the bunker, knowing somehow that there would be a room beneath where he could sleep. He struggled with the door but it would not open. He found a huge rock and crashed in the door with it, and in the warm darkness of a forgotten passageway he slept for two days. "It was so peaceful and calm. It was as if the world had stopped outside and I was safe from everything."

When Ed finally left the bunker and stood in the glare of the sun, he had the strange feeling that he had been reminded of something he had seen before, something that had happened to him a long time ago, but he could not remember it or describe it. He felt that he wanted something, but he was sure that I could not give it to him.

We grew farther and farther apart and his fantasies of the South Seas interrupted my questions with increasing vehemence and hate. He would permit no explanations and would allow me no freedom to speak. Soon I became, in his eyes like all others before me, stupid and useless.

When I tried to tell Ed that he was angry with me, he cut me off by shouting, "The German submarine, wounded from a long and bitter voyage, goes aground on the silver, coral beach. And the captain, the only survivor, mortally wounded, runs for the trees on the distant shore, leaving a trail of blood behind. His blond hair is blowing in the wind as he climbs a palm tree to the top. And the crackle, crackle, crackle of giant man-eating crabs, nearly wild from the smell of blood he has left, is heard as they converge on the beach to get him. Slowly they climb the tree after him and tear at his flesh with their razor-sharp claws and kill him. Snap, snap, snap."

He got up and opened the door and looked at me for a moment. There were thousands of miles of empty beaches between us and many islands that we would never find. He gritted his teeth and fired a volley from his finger and said, "Snap, snap, snap!" and blew the smoke away. He turned sadly, I think, I think he turned sadly . . . and walked away.

He ran away from the hospital that night and I never saw him again, but learned later that he had done this in the past with each therapist and would probably reappear at the admitting room of the hospital the day that my residency at the hospital ended and I was to leave. He had done that before, too. But he was on an open ward. Patients were free to roam from an open ward.

It is hard to do. It is very hard to try and find out why, to understand, to sit in an uncomfortable chair across from someone who refuses to talk to you, who doesn't bathe and picks his nose and wishes you were dead and would leave him alone. It is very hard to get close to someone whom society has trained you to avoid since you were a child.

It is very hard to be understanding when sometimes you really don't understand, when the patient fills up the entire hour with the most boring details of the most trivial things in his life, putting you to sleep and far and safely away. The only thing that happens then is that the patient proves a point known only to him in a language all his own, and you get confused. Sometimes you admit that you are confused and ask the patient to clear things up, but usually the admission is a victory for the other side—not for the patient, but for the other side of him, the dark side. And you struggle to bring that side into the light and make the darkness go away. It is very hard to do.

Whenever I got involved with a patient I would feel a loss if therapy went badly, but I could not help but get involved. I could not help but find myself caring about people. Dr. Glickman, my supervisor, continually cautioned me about keeping my distances, about not getting too close, and yet in the same breath he would tell me that the patients' main problems were not trusting and not getting close to people. It was such a transparent inconsistency that I would not buy it.

"Come on in, Robert," Glickman said, opening the door to his yellow-tiled office in the basement. It was a cold, uninteresting room without even an attempt at decoration. A broken Morris chair stood opposite a heavy steel desk and a swivel chair with a torn, fraying green cushion on the seat that had been worn thin by countless hours of Glickman's heavy frame; it was starting to give up some of its brown foam-rubber filling. Above his desk was a small window through which I could see the feet of several patients who were shuffling by on the walk outside. It was a dirty, unpleasant office.

I hated coming to see Glickman for supervision once a week. He seemed to wait for me to say something he could jump at. He had an addiction for pointing out my errors— not for correcting them, just pointing them out. I never learned much from him, but unless I was found to be grossly incompetent by the senior staff I did not have to worry about my residency.

Glickman was almost a hundred pounds overweight and his suits were always wet with perspiration, even in the winter. He was always squinting and had a very annoying tic that periodically tightened up the left side of his face. Besides his appearance, there was something very peculiar about this man that bothered me from the time I first met him. He ran several wards and occasionally gave a series of talks to the new residents. Very few attended. He also had some patients in long-term therapy—very long-term therapy, some as long as fifteen years. All his therapy patients were practically mute; one or two were on my ward on the chronic service. There were about eight in all, and he spent some twenty hours a week sitting with these burned-out human beings—doing what, I could not imagine. No one ever heard any of his patients say very much. I suppose it must be very safe to sit with patients like that. It gave Glickman a kind of martyred-hero self-image. He was always saying things like "You don't really understand the therapeutic process until you have had a patient in therapy a long time —a very long time. Then you will learn. Then you will see." He was intolerable. Worse than that, he was terrified of active patients and tried to steer me away from younger, more verbal patients.

"Well, how is Ed getting along these days? What new tricks are you getting him to do?" I had told him the week before that I thought Ed was going to leave the hospital. He knew that, and he probably had heard that Ed had left.

"I'm not sure how he's doing."

"Why don't you call his home and find out?" Glickman reached into a desk drawer and took a handful of English toffees out of a can, unwrapped them one by one, and swallowed them without chewing. "You see, Stevens, you were wrong in pushing him like that. The proof of the therapy is in the strength of the alliance."

"I confronted him with very obvious feelings."

"You shouldn't have. He wasn't ready. Why do you have to rush things? A delicate patient like that might not be ready for a confrontation for years. Just because you are only going to be with us for a few months doesn't give you the right to go ahead and rush things." Glickman began to smell his fingers, another of his habits.

"I only pointed out that he was angry with me."

"Only? Why, I have a man in treatment these past eight

years who is just getting ready to realize that he sometimes gets angry with me. You know, I think that you have a great deal to learn. First of all, you look upset and anxious, Stevens. Are you? You can't fool me, you know. Stevens, there seems to be a lot wrong with you; your work reflects it. How are things in your personal life? I'm sure that something is terribly wrong there. There just has to be."

"My personal life is my own damn business!"

"Not when it affects the way you handle *my* patients." Suddenly they were *his* patients. "Not when it affects your professional judgment."

"You are certainly making an assumption. Why does there have to be something wrong with my personal life? Why does there always have to be a deep-seated reason for everything you don't like?"

"Getting a little hostile, aren't we, Stevens?" He got some more candy from the desk.

"Whenever there is something you disagree with, you can't come out and just say that you disagree with it. No, you have got to destroy the other person by saying that there's something wrong with his mind."

"Remarkable. Just remarkable. You know how projective you are being, Stevens?" He started to get busy with some papers on his desk.

"You haven't cared very much for the way I have done things around here this year, Dr. Glickman, and you are entitled to your opinion, but you have no right to say that the way I handle things is always the result of a neurotic conflict. Is this the way you are with your patients? Christ, you must drive them crazy! Aren't they entitled to any unanalyzable activity, or do you put labels on everything they do?"

"What was your father like?" he said, having obviously shut out every word I had said.

"I don't believe that this is happening. This is like a

scene in a very bad movie. 'What was your father like?' You know, if you are serious, if you really are serious, God, I can't even talk."

"I mention your father and you can't even talk. Mmmm."

"This is insane. Look at the two of us. I come to you for supervision, and you sit waiting for me to fall . . ."

"Nonsense. You must trust people." His face jerked wildly.

". . . and I get in a fight with you over a patient. And the reason is, if you look at it, because you are threatened by me."

"Oh, come, come now. Really, Robert, I just want to help you. Why, Greg Charpentier and I were just talking about your good intentions at lunch today. We both feel that you want to help, but that your enthusiasm is misguided. Innovation for innovation's sake, upsetting the staff and the patients—and for what? You can do pretty much what you want here. You know that. No one is going to step on your toes, but you have to develop some common respect for other people."

I suddenly felt as if I were insane. The eyes of this jowly man never looked directly at me. He saw me as another sick person. He had given me that label and now he did not have to listen to what I said or consider me seriously. By adopting the position that all my comments were the product of a constellation of problems that I did not want to discuss, he could dismiss whatever I said against him. He could benevolently forgive me for my hostility, and my failure, and see himself as generous and patient. The ideas I had would die in the air as I left the office. My failures with my patients were the reflection of something going on inside me. As far as he was concerned, he was right, I was sick. The matter was closed for discussion.

He sat, waiting for an answer from me. What did it mean to be normal? What did it mean? If it were this man making that judgment, anyone with whom he disagreed was sick, was abnormal. I could imagine him speaking in front of his PTA some evening as the authority on mental health in his community—all by virtue of the fact that he was a psychiatrist—and people believing him! He loved authority and could only act from that position. If you agreed with him it was fine, but if you disagreed then it must mean that your neurotic defenses had managed to get in the way of reason. Only *he* had the power always to see things as they really were.

What did it mean when I looked at a patient and judged him? How many times did my own feelings of being threatened color my judgment and make me dismiss what my patients said to me as part of their illness with no need for me to take it seriously? This was the worst pitfall, the most seductive trap of all. Was I treating my patients as human, or was I just like Glickman?

I had been taught that every feeling I developed toward a patient could be interpreted as countertransference and was suspect. If I liked a patient, I was told not to let those feelings get in the way. If I disliked a patient, I must cope with those feelings. Glickman was frightened by me because I told patients that I liked them and told them when they got me furious, and I meant it. I learned to use my feelings, not hide them. To my surprise my patients, did not go wild; I did not become inexorably tied in psychic knots. We developed some feeling for each other. That is, sometimes we did. Sometimes we just sat and the feelings and the efforts seemed one-sided, but I did not allow myself the luxury of blaming all my failures on the patients' inadequacies. Therapy could go badly because I was mistaken and it could go well because I was effective. I did not enshrine what I was doing with the magical term "the Therapy" and I did not see my-self merely as an instrument.

It is much harder that way. Glickman was one of the most frightened people I had met. He was trained as a psy-chiatrist, but he hid behind patients who never questioned and some who never spoke. Unlike Pellegrini, Glickman did not have a private practice. He saw only chronically ill, insti-tutionalized patients.

"Dr. Glickman, I do not feel that we can work to-gether."

"Come, come. I'm sure with a little outside help . . ."

"It just won't work. We have what they call a personal-ity clash."

"Well if you must see it in those terms, I feel sorry for you."

"I will find another supervisor."

"You have to get Superintendent Larkin's permission before stopping with me and changing supervisors. I doubt if he'll let you, by the way."

"I have just stopped. You can tell Larkin."

I left the office and as usual, sitting in the corridor with his arms pulled up to his shoulders, frozen in motion years ago, sat one of Glickman's patients, waiting for his weekly appointment. Drooling and gesticulating, he stared straight ahead. Glickman called, "Come in, Tony." Tony did not move.

Six

After my first month at the hospital I stopped tossing and turning in my sleep and was no longer afraid to climb the three flights of painted green stairs to the ward. The old men standing in the shadows and the stony people who lived out their lives on the landings no longer startled me. I could predict with confidence and sureness who would be sitting in which chair; that Stanley Slotkin would be loitering in the hall and stop me for a cigarette as I came in; that Marcus would grab my hand in his and shake it, not wanting to let go. It was his way of telling if you were real or if you were a hallucination.

Depending on the time of day I came to the ward, I could anticipate what would be going on. From two to four o'clock three old cronies would be sitting in the corner at their afternoon card game with Tom, one of the aides. They never spoke, they just played, and I never saw them speak to each other after a game. When Tom was off they did not play. The red-haired, red-faced man who was always pacing when I came in never looked up. Miss Stuart was always attended by the same court—a brain-damaged old man who was always pawing at her, and two younger patients. At first I thought they found her attractive, but I discovered that they were only interested in helping with the afternoon snack because they would be able to get more for themselves.

What once appeared so strange to me, so bizarre and removed from meaning, had begun to take on an order all its own. This new world of frozen time was simple, perhaps too simple, too uncomplicated. In its peculiar way, its odd, horrible weirdness, it was entirely predictable and chaotically ordered, but it was ordered.

Here I was the intruder, I was the one who was unpredictable, for I might stop and try to speak to one of them and ask what they were doing and what it meant, or why they just sat, and what they thought about when they were sitting. The others could be trusted to be inert, to keep to themselves and their allotted place in time and space, but I was meddling, intrusive, and nosy. I suppose that by their cloistered standards I was a rather disagreeable fellow, and a newcomer at that. The average patient on my ward had been there before I was born. When I was just beginning to discover the world, they had already cut it off and confined it to this narrow room and less.

Whenever I stopped to speak with one of them I felt as if I were competing with some powerful force for their attention. Threatening voices, voices warning them of danger, voices accusing them of past transgressions interrupted the conversations we had. Some patients formed allies with their voices, which reassured them that I would soon be gone and would bother them no more. Some would freeze in grotesque positions, their arms extended at right angles; others would clutch their bodies and their clothes, and they would stay that way until I was safely gone.

Fear does strange things to you. I learned to identify patients by the sound of their footsteps before they came into view. Poulos always dragged his left foot, Riley stamped every fourth step, Peter shuffled in his worn slippers. I knew how some of them wheezed, how some of them grunted, sneezed, panted, and groaned. It became very reassuring to recognize a sound in a poorly lit corridor.

Their beds in the huge dormitory room told more about them than they could tell themselves. Some beds were incredibly wrinkled. Some were never made at all. Rosary beads and crucifixes took up as much space on O'Keefe's bed as the blankets and pillows did. Over his bed (he was lucky to have a corner bed) were pictures of the Virgin and the Savior, and his night table had three statues of the Infant of Prague. Some patients slept with newspapers in their beds, some with their wallets or with pictures taken in another time and place. And some beds (Miss Barker had pointed to them with great pride before she left) were so neat that they didn't fit my understanding of the men who slept there.

Orlando, a catatonic man in his forties who stayed in the same position for hours at a time, had the most beautiful bed of all. His mother visited him every week and brought him little things to make him more comfortable and herself less guilty. He had a special mattress, a baby-blue quilt, foam-rubber pillows, and a rubber sheet, because he wet the bed every night. If he appreciated her kindness, we never knew. She always tried to tip me—for the good job I was doing with her son, she said.

Every bizarre thing, each disorganized sound, each appalling sight on the ward became catalogued and ordered, and in the immense sadness of it all I began to feel at home.

The hospital was a giant stage upon which a countless number of routines were performed. Every stratum of hospital society had its routine, always the same; only the players changed. Even the staff had routines of their own.

Every morning the student nurses would hunt around the day hall and pull patients from their dark corners and chairs and march them into the large gymnasium with the sureness that only young people can have, knowing that time is on their side. Some of the patients refused to go. One would go so slowly that by the time he got there the exercises were over, completely discouraging the student nurse assigned to him.

The staff took turns leading them through fifteen minutes of calisthenics. We made it a game, a hopeless game in which the stiffness from their endless immobility was our adversary. We played "Simon Says" but never told anyone he was "out" because we were pleased if someone even bothered to play. One man imitated everything "Simon" did, even when the game was over.

Many of the patients remained waxen and rigid, but some moved their arms in what looked, on first glance, like some sort of exercise. But if you looked at them when it was all over, when they were led back to the hall, you would see these same patients moving their arms in the same grotesque patterns they did when they were sitting in their seats in the corners.

At other times Miss Stuart would throw a large leather ball around to patients standing in a circle—more at them, it seemed, than to them. They always looked surprised when the ball came their way, no matter how much warning was given. The ball would hit them, bounce off, and roll away as if they were merely extensions of the wall they stood before.

Stan, one of the aides, a muscled ex-Marine, would try

to get the younger patients to work out with weights, but they just looked at him or, more accurately, looked at the place where he was standing, and did not seem to understand what he was doing. It was the only thing Stan did well.

Sometimes the staff would break into a spontaneous game of catch and there would be a lot of running and laughing. Stan would single out a pretty student nurse and pepper her with the basketball, and then she would run and shout and squeal. It was great fun. The patients would stand waiting for it to end, showing little feeling. Bert would walk up to the staff and say, "You're playing ball. You're playing ball." We let him play, but his coordination was so poor and it was so frustrating for him to try that he always gave up. The happy smile he seemed to have when he was watching would give way to a scowl and a very sad face as the fact that he was different seemed to become apparent even to him.

Those fifteen minutes formed a break in the day's routine for the staff more than for the patients, for whom the days were really never broken and for whom time had become an endless exercise.

No matter where the players came from, even if they were only visitors, they soon fell into a pattern. Billy Riley and his mother were no exceptions.

She came every Tuesday at three and hadn't missed a single day in the twenty years that her only son had been in the state hospital. It had become part of her life's routine. She always took the same bus and had gotten to know the driver. He even waited for her if it was raining. She never failed to come. She always got off one stop before the hospital, did her shopping at the delicatessen—Tuesday night had been delicatessen night in her house for years. Her husband could count on that even though he never visited the hospital.

Billy would meet his mother at the far gate and, stamping his foot every fourth step, he would carry her bags to the patients' lounge in his building. It was a ten-minute walk and most of it was uphill. He grunted under the weight of the bundles, which always contained the same things and weighed the same from week to week. During the entire walk they were silent and she would look around the grounds wondering why the patients acted the way they did and dressed so funny. Why couldn't they be well behaved like her son? It always puzzled her.

They would sit in the visitors' lounge for precisely an hour and never say a word. She would look out the window and watch the smoke curl from the chimney of the hospital power plant and wonder where it disappeared to. Billy would stare at the floor and count the vinyl tiles in the lounge. When he reached about four hundred the hour was usually up and it was time for her to go.

Billy would watch her put her gray and yellow coat over her squat frame, take a compact out of her pocketbook, and fix her face. Then he would pick up her bundles, walk her down the stairs, and stamp out to the front gate. He would stand, anxiously watching the traffic, as she crossed the street, and she would wave—a short wave—from the other side of the street.

He would watch her greet the bus driver, who also knew her by name and asked her how her son was doing, and wave to her again as the bus drove away.

Then he would wait until he had counted four hundred automobiles moving in the traffic before he went to supper, assured of her return next and week and the week after that.

I seem to remember that it had always been this way, that the people in this place were difficult to move, difficult to reach.

Sometimes when I was small we played catch on the street that ran along the hospital grounds and spent as much time watching out for automobiles as for the ball. Although I can throw the ball far enough, I have poor control; in fact, I am pretty wild.

I throw the ball to a friend with all my might and watch it soar some forty-five degrees off course, high and beautiful, over the iron fence and down through a maple tree to land on the grass of the hospital lawn.

Immediately there is a chant, "Robert's got to go in and get it. Robert's got to go in and get it." The fence is too high for me to climb. Under the tree, very close to the ball, is a man lying on the grass watching us. I call to him, "Could you please throw our ball back?" He doesn't answer, but just lies there staring at us. "Please throw our ball back." Still he does not move. I will have to go in through the front gate all the way back here to the side and out again. It is a quarter-of-a-mile trip to get something less than a hundred feet away.

I always avoid that sidewalk with its strange pedestrians and now I have to walk the entire length of it by myself. A fat lady in a housedress and a man's sweater asks, "What's your name, sonny?"

Her friend shouts, "Where do you think you're going?"

"For my ball."

There are people who seem frozen, as if they were playing "statue."

People talk to themselves and to the people carrying bundles who get off the bus. Cars nose into the gateway and honk, chasing shuffling people out of the road. I am bumped and touched, and I break into a run as soon as I reach the grass.

I approach the ball and the man, and I slow down as I near the fence. Why didn't he throw it back? Why didn't he answer? He watches me as I get closer and nods as I pick the ball up and throw it over the fence to my friends.

I turn and run to the gate, to the sidewalk and its parade, and then up the hill to catch up with my friends, who are just going over the crest. Stopping, out of breath and looking down, I can see that man lying in the same place. Why couldn't he throw the ball back?

I must have thought of that a hundred times since. I always wanted to know why he did not throw the ball back . . . didn't he want to? Didn't he care? Why did he just lie there?

The routines that were hardest to break were the routines where nothing happened, where the only movement was the passing of time, the changing of seasons. The chronic service was a repertory theater of many old plays given to a captive audience in a silent, dimly lit house.

For six silent years they had shared only the space between them; the same room, the same tacky brown walls, the large, heavily screened window opaque with two years' accumulation of dust, and the same gummy-wet ceiling traversed by insulated gray pipes that hissed and banged. It seemed to be the only communication between them. Four metal bed frames, chipped and rusty, with four scratched metal night tables at their sides divided the space between them.

Yet the space they shared was separate. Each of the four had his own corner, each his own chair, each his own world, four worlds in one room. If they ever spoke to each other, no one ever saw it, and patients who might see them talking would have no reason to tell about it.

They were like four statues in a studio. The artist, having grown tired of working on them, had abandoned them somewhere in the process of creation. Four blocks of stone with the barest outline of recognizable human form. Seeing them for the first time, one might have said, "If only a little more care or time or energy had been given, they might have been finished." Four forgotten works in a state of decay, decaying still.

Richard was corpulent and jowly. For days at a time he would sit on the edge of his bed and stare through the space between him and the others. He left the room only for meals. Fifty, perspiring and ruddy even though he got no sun or exercise, he watched specks of dust floating in the sunbeams, for days on end measuring dust.

Arnold believed himself to be the only one on this earth, who (through strange circumstances at his birth known only to an albino midwife who had suddenly and mysteriously disappeared soon afterward) was endowed with special telepathic powers that allowed him to look out on the universe to see and to know and to receive communications from the cosmos. These powerful and vindictive forces, if he proved worthy and patient enough, would some day reward his suffering and the endless ordeals with which they tested him, and would pronounce him rightful king and master of the earth. He sat, awaiting communication, looking through the same bright patches of floating, glittering dust to the sun and beyond.

Irving had been in hospitals of one sort or another almost all of his adult life. His family tried to make sure that their only son, that last great hope for that proud family name, would have the best care, the best hope and chance for recovery. His file in the commissioner's office bulged with letters, memos, and requests, and filled five large manila folders. There was a standing joke in that office whenever a new secretary was hired. She would be told, matter-of-factly, that she had only one file to type up before she could to home, and then they would hand her Irving's file. But for all his family's letters—well over a hundred—and good intentions, although his creature comforts had increased (he had an electric blanket), three decades had passed and he had become only more quiet. He sat, slouching and wheezing, his blue denim shirt hanging out of his trousers, wiping his nose on his sleeve, slouching and wheezing away the time, away the years, away his life.

Of the four, Ben was the most active and had achieved the most before he arrived at the hospital. He had gone to college and received his degree, entered the world and taken a job in sales for a plastics manufacturer. He had married a pretty girl against her parents' wishes and fathered three children, a daughter and two sons. He had shouldered responsibilities and bought a home, an automobile, and a trailer for the summers in New Hampshire at the lake. His wife played bridge, his children grew up, his friends increased and some were even a little jealous of him.

But in spite of all this Ben had remained a lonely man. Surrounded by the trappings of a home, he felt empty, unfulfilled, and hollow; there had been no setbacks, and he had been a good provider and a good husband. (There was one weekend in Cleveland when he slept with a buyer, but he pretended to himself that it had helped make the sale, and he could live with it.) Something was wrong; no matter what the situation, he could see only its drawbacks. Each new child to feed and to share with his wife he saw as a loss. He always seemed to be remembering something taken away and not replaced.

One morning about ten years before, Ben had refused to go to work and had stayed in bed for three weeks. He hadn't been able to bring himself to venture out of the house. And in a scene that was destined to be the worst his children would ever remember, the doctor and the police had been called, had struggled with him, and had taken him away.

Slowly he gave up his ties to the world and extended his hand only for pills without bothering to look at the face of the nurse who handed them out. Slowly he restricted himself to his building, then to his ward, and finally to his room. And he stayed there, in his room.

After years of being stagnant, of not moving, of resisting even the kindest approach, he began to make an effort, a small effort, to do things for himself. He made his bed, went to meals without being reminded, and even did little chores on the ward. None of us was sure why, but after years of doing nothing he was moving. He was assigned to a workshop on the hospital grounds repairing old mattresses, and his work supervisor once reported that Ben even seemed to enjoy it, seemed to be a friendly, efficient worker and helpful to others in the shop.

His wife, who had lived on relief since shortly after he came to the hospital and the money from the sale of the house and trailer was gone, had visited him faithfully every Sunday. She tried to cheer him up and tell him the news: "I understand that Howard and Bonnie's little boy is getting a scholarship to college this fall. . . . Susan has a job at the dry cleaners, so we get a break on cleaning now."

But he never seemed to listen and just stared at his feet week after week. But then, finally, he began to listen to her, and plans were mentioned for him to go home for a weekend. He liked the idea, he said. Finally, even though his wife was anxious about his return, she agreed and I wrote out a pass for the weekend.

He went home. It was a different neighborhood. He had no friends, and he felt uneasy, remembering that it was his illness that had displaced his family, and he tried not to let his wife see that he noticed that she was covering up for his failures.

"It's a shame how fast things wear out. You no sooner

get something than you have to replace it."

He knew it was his fault, and every faded dress, every empty cabinet reminded him. They had supper together Saturday night. The children were distant and cool, and when the oldest returned home from visiting a friend with their dog, the dog snarled at him. He started to cry and his daughter, Susan, became angry and embarrassed: "Is he going to stay and act like that, Mother?"

"You should be ashamed of talking like that."

The noise and the clamor, the coldness and the distance, proved more than he could stand, and in the morning when the children were getting dressed for church, they could hear him crying in their mother's bedroom. A neighbor had to be called to take him home to the hospital.

He came back Sunday morning just before lunch, unpacked his things, and reappraised the space he had shared for so many long years. Miss Stuart was surprised to see him, but commented that he had a peaceful look about him and that the visit home must have done him some good, and then went about her routine.

The others sat (they always had), measuring dust, awaiting communication, slouching and wheezing, as he took a rope from his bag, untangled it, and threw one end over the dusty ceiling pipes.

Measuring dust, awaiting communication, slouching and wheezing, as he made a slipknot and pulled it tight to see if it would hold.

Measuring dust, awaiting communication, slouching and wheezing, as he climbed onto the bed.

Measuring dust, awaiting communication, slouching and wheezing, as he made a noose and tied it around his neck.

Measuring dust, awaiting communication, slouching and wheezing, as he clenched his fists and took a deep breath.

Measuring dust, awaiting communication, slouching and wheezing, as he jumped.

Measuring dust, awaiting communication, slouching and wheezing, as he jerked.

Measuring dust, awaiting communication, slouching and wheezing, as he agonized.

Measuring dust, awaiting communication, slouching and wheezing, as he died.

Measuring dust, awaiting communication, slouching and wheezing.

They were discovered at lunchtime, the living and the dead, motionless all four, measuring dust, awaiting communication, slouching and wheezing, and hanging dead, sharing in silence, as they had always done, the space between them.

When Miss Stuart told me, I felt my face become numb. I suddenly could not breathe. My legs felt weak. Ben! I slumped into a chair. Had I been wrong in letting him go home? He had done so well, so many real gains in the past few months. He had wanted to go home to visit. His wife had been frightened by the idea, but that was common. I had seen that before. How could I have known? Why did he kill himself here in the hospital? I was suddenly angry because no one had talked to him when he came back. Oh, but Miss Stuart had talked to him. She had spoken with him and he had seemed fine to her. Why hadn't his roommates said anything? Ben had known they would not. Should I have kept him here and not let him go home? I was unsure of everything all of a sudden. Somewhere there must be hope. Should I have kept him?

I tried to find a way to break these endless routines, but many of them had been so ingrained, so fixed, that there was no place to begin. There was no crack in the surface to force open. And in the case of one man there was no hope for improvement, no hope at all.

I first saw him on a ward that was always locked but I have never understood why he was there. From birth he had been both deaf and blind and in one institution after another. He had never been held, never loved. He had not been abandoned, he had just never belonged to anyone. Who would keep him?

"Besides," his mother had said when she gave him up forever twenty years before, "I have four healthy ones at home who really need me. This one I can't take care of. It wouldn't be fair to the other children. Besides, I wouldn't know what to do."

In those twenty years he had had no visitor.

"What would I do if I did come? Besides, he never even knew me . . ."

What does the touch of a hand mean to him? What tactile memories does he have? Has he any language, any thought? He tells the time of day by the touch of people leading him to meals. Each of his thirty-five years is the same.

He knows the breeze, the dampness, and the cold. In winter he is walked across the grounds and can feel the crunch of snow beneath his feet and the weight of the extra clothing he must wear and so he tells the time of year. When it is fall he smells the burning leaves and in summer his arms are warm. His time is like a shallow present, lacking perspective and sense.

He sits in an armchair in a corner, laughing and crying, sometimes both at once, and rubs his legs endlessly in a fixed, repeated pattern. Sometimes he extends his arms as if to catch a fly. His hands jerk violently and the motion stops.

He appears to hallucinate constantly, laughing, grimacing, and grunting. But about what? Rumblings in his stomach? His skin tingling from a shower turned on too hot?

Sometimes, in their miscellaneous violence, he is jostled

by other patients. If, in his random reaching out, he happens to touch a hostile patient, he might be badly beaten, without ever knowing why.

How does he comprehend this world? He knows only pain and its absence. Whether it is real pain or pain created by his mind, any form to fill the void, he cannot know.

Occasionally, without knowing, student nurses new to the ward and new to psychiatry sit and talk to him. After a while, when they begin to wonder why they are not getting any response, they appeal to the aide, who tells them that he cannot hear or see. Then they usually get up and walk away. Once a student nurse took his hand in an effort to be friendly. He jumped up and, thinking it was the aide's hand, his dinner bell, he started rapidly across the lounge. He tripped over a chair, fell, and cut his head.

He needed six stitches and laughed with a painful grimace and winced with each one as it was put in. When the job was done it was too late for him to go to lunch and he had to settle for milk and crackers alone in the nurse's office. But he was alone in the cafeteria, too. He was always alone.

No one but the aides were allowed to touch him after that. Perhaps that was best. I do not know. With his prematurely gray hair, his grotesquely distorted face, and his flapping arms, I am still haunted by him.

I am haunted by him and I am haunted by the other old men who hear and yet are deaf, who speak and yet are mute, who see and yet are blind. I am haunted by them as much as I am by my own futility in trying to help them.

In the fading soft summer evening's glow, the men on the locked ward sit on their bench perches on the caged porch. Twisted, rusting iron bars stretch their flaking brown arms from the stained cement ballustrade to bury themselves in the ivied wall above, a human aviary.

Some stand, some sit, some sleep. Others forage for cigarettes along the wall or in the pockets of their dreamy neighbors. A bearded man without pants gawks angrily at the sun as it disappears into the orange grass.

Now there is a flutter of activity between two white-haired cranes over a disputed chair. A lean bird grown vague has fallen into the wrong nest. Rights are asserted and the stranger is beaten away.

As evening approaches the air grows still in the after-glow. The pigeons, free in flight that day, fly home to their nests above in the leafy shadows of the wall, and the attendants call their flock home from the caged world of the sun.

I decided to organize a work-incentive program on my ward to motivate my patients, to get them to respond to something, to respond to anything. It was a simple program; perhaps it was even a little childish. Patients were rewarded for staying clean, for doing chores, for working and helping around the ward. Miss Stuart was doubtful and hesitant about trying the new program. She was straightening her uniform in front of the mirror in her office and admiring herself, talking to my reflection.

"If you think that Cleary or Hotchkiss or Ryan are going to do anything for any reason whatsoever short of saving their own skins from a fire—and even then I have my doubts—then you need a psychiatrist more than they do. What good has all the time that you have spent with the people on this ward done? Really, Dr. Stevens. I mean, you've just about taken out everyone's tonsils. You spoke to Willie and he got worse. Now he just sits in the corner all the time swearing at me when I go by. You decided to push Mr. Segal and insisted that he work in the upholstery shop. Now all he does is stay away from the ward in the cellar somewhere. I can't see where that has been any help."

She turned around. "If you ask me, this work program

is not going to work. Let's face it. I don't like it and I'm not going to do something I don't like. I think that it is a waste of time and energy, and I can find many better things to do. Robert Stevens may be a nice guy, but he is going to burn himself out and get hurt besides. Now I'm going to shut up."

"All I'm saying is that the patients need something to motivate them, to get them moving again."

"Again! What's this again? When did they ever move?"

"Don't you think some of them can move?" I found myself shouting.

"Sure, and they already do things. The manics clean the place. Very nice and very fast. They are the only ones with the energy to push the other people. Did you see Larry out there this morning getting old Clarence to move? It was beautiful, but Dr. Stevens, you can't be here twenty-four hours a day to make them do things. As soon as you leave they'll all slip back into their old ruts."

Miss Stuart poured herself a cup of coffee and offered me one. I refused. I was furious.

I tried to set some machinery in motion. I divided the patients among the staff and asked them to try and get the patients to wash themselves and do chores. Although I made suggestions for handling difficult situations and was always available and willing to help, any change from the established routine was seen by the staff as destructive and undermining.

And it seemed so—to everyone but the patients. The staff members were accustomed to being overburdened with a load with which no one expected them to succeed. I limited the duties of each person on my ward by setting realistic goals and by so doing I created a situation that was threatening to them. For the first time, Stan had something specific to do. Something that could be judged. Tom liked the idea at first but preferred to limit his interaction to playing cards in the afternoon. Everyone had found his own game, his own way of keeping apart, from getting involved and becoming dismayed at the hopelessness of the place. Talking to the patients, asking them to do things, asking the staff to help, was called "pushing." It would have been acceptable to the staff if I had pushed only the patients, but as soon as I asked the staff to feel, to act as people, I ran into a brick wall. My own staff was ready to undermine me. At least Stuart was honest. The two aides just smiled and nodded when I suggested something and then said they would do it, but Tom's enthusiasm was gone, and Stan rarely helped. Usually he would go to the nursing supervisor, Mrs. Angoff, and make up some sort of story about my pushing them or the patients too hard, being too unrealistic, expecting too much.

Nursing supervisors, being what they are, were always ready to criticize and moralize. Mrs. Angoff was a small, thin lady, who thought she knew everything and was completely sure of herself. She had two secretaries, and dictated long memorandums on every idea she had and saved all the memos in a wall of olive-green filing cabinets. Her office was so neat and symmetrical that I became aware that I was sitting straighter in my chair to fit in when I went to see her. It was our first confrontation but it was only one of many that she had had in each of her twenty-five years at the helm. She spoke rapidly and with great emphasis.

"Well, I see we are having some of our little difficulties in understanding the duties of the staff, Dr. Stevens. You young doctors always have so many good ideas. I've seen hundreds of you and I've yet to see one who was willing to get in there and do the hard work necessary to make a program work. The same work you demand and expect of your nurses. No, you fellows manage to put all the blame on the staff. You think that we are your servants or something, that all we have to do with our time is to make things easy for you. I don't suppose you know how many separate medicine orders are carried out on your ward every day, Dr. Stevens."

"About two hundred." I knew it would be the only comment I could get in. I was drumming my fingers on the desk —just like Willie, I thought.

"See, you do know. And I bet that you know how long it takes to fill out the slips and prepare the trays and make sure that each patient has the right medication. Well, where do you think the extra time for carrying out your ideas is coming from? Where do you think the funds for staff is coming from? You and I both want the very best treatment for our patients, don't we? The *important* things first. First, Dr. Stevens, is the medications. When that is done and the ward duties are finished, then you have a right to demand time, but not before."

I wanted to run to the order book and rip all the pages out and let them float over the grounds. Every time I tried to discontinue medication on one of my patients I would warn the staff that he might act up, but in spite of this they would complain to the other residents on call at night. Because of the pressure on the resident on night call he would not have time to investigate staff complaints, and the medication would be started again. For my ward staff, medication was the answer to everything. It was the answer because it put the patients to sleep, and sleeping patients do not cause trouble.

This was a difficult point to get my staff to understand. When patients got better they became less passive. They asserted their rights. They took an interest in outside events in the world and wanted to watch the conclusion of a movie on television even if it happened to be bedtime. Something outside themselves became important. To me it did not seem to be such a revolutionary issue or a difficult one. I did not think it was fair to punish patients with medicine just because they started to act like people again and were sometimes obstinate.

I was not alone in trying new things. Other doctors at the hospital tried.

Dr. MacNeil, a man in his fifties, had left his lucrative general practice to become a resident in psychiatry. He had a charming if simple country-doctor way about him. Years of listening to complaining ladies masking their depressions by talking about their bad backs and nervous stomachs had convinced him that since much of the time he was already playing the part of a psychiatrist, he should get more training. His major tactic with patients was to suggest some diversion to rechannel their energies into some neutral area. He was remarkably simple and disarmingly practical.

"What these patients need is a more active social life. This place is so dreary that it would drive anyone crazy. They get plenty of understanding from us. What they need is companionship from members of the opposite sex. I think we should plan a dance for some Saturday night and invite patients from the rest of the hospital."

His staff and his patients were very excited. Patients in occupational therapy were set to work on decorations. Greenhouse workers were consulted about the flower arrangements. Kitchen workers joined with the dietician in planning the refreshments. And in his ward meetings Dr. MacNeil discussed the choice of hosts and hostesses with his patients.

Early Saturday evening the nurses and aides helped fix hair, check fingernails, tie the bows of donated ties, iron creases in shining pants and pleats in faded dresses. They checked at the last minute to see that all flies were buttoned.

The Grand Promenade revealed a splendid array of costumes, coordinated more by size than color, modeled by ancient mannequins arranged boy-girl in two lines. The staff and their wives chaperoned and received the garrulous, the stiff, and the silent with the gracious dignity and decorum that suited the occasion. Some patients made flamboyant curtsies or courtly bows, which were returned with regal smiles. Others just stared as they were presented, and shuffled by, trying to keep in step.

Hand in hand they were led around the hall. An excited woman in a yellow flowered housedress began to skip across the floor in time to music that had not yet begun. Some stopped to brush imaginary creatures away. Some turned suddenly into frozen statues of flesh or grimaced at a partner who was not there.

The music started and the punch was served. The phonograph records borrowed from a staff member's daughter were so loud that they startled many of the patients and the music was often too fast to follow, but no one seemed to notice.

Some danced together. Some danced alone. Whenever staff members danced, the patients applauded and smiled, more because the staff was taking part and showing that they were human than for their skill.

A bloated, red-nosed woman walked up to Dr. MacNeil and said, "Dr. MacNeil, I saw you dance then. I saw you dance with Mrs. MacNeil."

"That's right, you did, Lucy."

Larry, manic, still carrying his broom, came up to my wife, Anne, and me and asked, "How come, doc, you didn't take Miss Stuart to the dance, doc? You're supposed to take her, you know. Any fool knows that. Can I cut in on your date for a dance? I used to be a good dancer. You wouldn't believe it, lady. Hey, I got to run and sweep up that mess in the corner. Don't worry, doc, I won't tell Miss Stuart."

The last of the coffee, the last of the cake. A last dizzy twirl around the orange and green crepe-paper hall, a last

high-pitched silly laugh, a last suspicious sneer. The enchantment was over. It was ten o'clock and time to go. The gaiety
was over and the chaperones became shepherds to lead the
patients back to their wards for their evening medications
and then off to bed.

Some of the younger men on the staff laughed at Dr.
MacNeil and saw him as an incompetent buffoon trying to
make up for the silent damage caused by the passing years
with a few minutes of dancing, but he had lived longer and
his kindness allowed him to see the remnants of the people
beneath their masks . . . people in masks dancing in the
night. . . . It was eerie and somehow it was familiar.

Halloween past, and I am dressed up in a skeleton costume with my sister placed in charge of me. She takes me to
the houses on our block, makes me go into each one and
show my disguise to the neighbors, who pretend they are
frightened.

I make the rounds, fill up a small bag with candy, and
am deposited back on the porch steps by my sister. Having
completed her duty, she is free to go with the older children.

My porch is a strange outpost on the bizarre. The light
has grown dim. There is the sound of broken glass somewhere in the night, of a trash barrel being rolled, the unwilling hostage for whom no trick-or-treater had been paid ran-
som.

The figures that pass on the street are older children,
their faces painted with lipstick, outlandish amounts of
rouge, and burnt cork. They are stuffed with pillows, pregnant with down, and they laugh to frighten the dark.

When they pass my secret reviewing stand, they gesture
or growl or twirl in their mothers' old dresses and hats.
Larger boys dressed in their fathers' clothes peer out from
beneath huge hat brims at me and chase me up the steps. A

dozen fists are clenched in mock anger, and hands frozen into taunting claws paw through the night. Nothing seems real—neither the players nor the play. The only thing familiar is the stage.

Friendly hands coax me inside, help me out of my suit, and wash my face, and I am left to the darkness of my own room to conjure up memories of what I have just seen, and shudder at my own costume hanging on the closet door, waiting for the morning to make things real again . . .

It seemed that no matter how hard I tried to gain ground on the emotional chaos that had taken over my patients' lives, the result was much the same. From the very first step I took on my ward I would be greeted by an old routine. As soon as I turned the corner and walked onto the floor I was met by Mr. Myers. If he was not there, I was probably in the wrong building.

Mr. Myers stood all day at the door of the ward with his hands neatly folded behind his back, nodding and smiling at other patients and staff as they came through. He was the best-dressed patient in the hospital. Each week his wife would visit and take his shirts home with her and leave a bundle of clean clothes. His pants were always neatly pressed and he never went anywhere in the hospital without a tie and jacket.

When new visitors came to the ward, they would think he was some sort of official, perhaps a guide, in any case someone more normal and more alert-looking than the other patients looming just behind him. Often they would ask him questions. If they did not, he would walk up to them and in a pleasant but firm voice say, "Won't you please sit down? On the seat there, yes. Good. The manager is out just now, but I will see what help I can be to you."

Visitors and sometimes patients would sit down because

they were so overpowered by him or wanted to avoid making a scene. Schizophrenics believe in what they are. In a very professional and matter-of-fact way, gleaned from years in the trade, Myers would quickly remove one of the visitor's shoes. Before most people realized what had happened, he would be examining the shoe and commenting about the arch, the lacing, the stitching, or the style. He would hunt in the lining, find the size, and quote it, and would then say: "I don't like the way that one has worn at the toe. You see? The instep is a bit off, too. I do wish you people would spend a few dollars more initially when you buy a shoe. Good shoes cost money. You get what you pay for. That's all there is to it."

Defensive and feeling sheepish about their shoes and usually too self-conscious and too polite to offend this nice man, the visitor would squirm and uneasily tolerated him.

"I think we have just what you want in stock."

Then he would clean the shoe with his hand and suggest that his customer try it on for size, pronounce it a perfect fit, and excuse himself for a minute while he took care of another customer.

Just beyond, in the corridor across from the day hall, dressed like a railway engineer, stood Merrill, a man who had lived his life before coming to the hospital according to a rigid schedule. Merrill controlled the world inside and out by keeping that schedule alive.

Merrill had been a railway conductor most of his life before he retired. He couldn't adjust to an unscheduled world that had no place left for him, and he spent all his pension checks buying tickets to ride his old line. One day he began to call out the names of towns along the way and would not stop; and then he came to the hospital. He rarely spoke. He hated to speak, but when you passed him you heard a soft murmuring sound that began to fill the narrow space of the men's room on the hallway where he usually stood:

Dum dum dum dum dum dum dum dum dum
Dum dum dum dum dum dum dum dum dum
Dumdumdumdumdumdumdumdumdumdumdum
Dumdumdumdumdumdumdumdumdumdumdum
Dumdumdumdumdumdumdumdumdumdumdumdum
Dumdumdum Dumdumdum Dumdumdum
DUM DUM DUM DUM DUM DUM DUM DUM DUM

And if you came closer to him, he would go faster and get louder:

DUMDUMDUMDUMDUMDUMDUMDUMDUM
DUMDUMDUMDUMDUMDUMDUMDUMDUM

And if you tried to speak with him, he would shout into your face:

DUM DUM DUM

Each one louder than the next and each one more distinct, more threatening, more threatened. Red-faced, he would shout, his prominent blue veins sticking out on his nose and his eyes popping with the pressure of each dum.

If Merrill was in a good mood, he would mutter softly to himself and, with a claw hand that had fixed long ago in a cold, relentless grasp, he would reach out and place it on your arm and give you a small but forceful tug that would startle you no matter how many times he had tugged at you before—and you would have to look up at those bulging eyes.

He would remove his hand and mutter again. It was impossible to understand him, and if you asked him what it was that he wanted he would become silent. After the tenth time this happened, and if you were angry and demanded to know what he was after, he would suddenly shout:

"Tickets, Springfield, Urbana, Lexington, Marlboro, Chicago, New Haven, Hartford. Dum dum dum dum dum."

And he would build.

"Springfield, dum dum dum dum dum dum, Urbana, dum dum dum dum dum dum, Chicago, dum dum dum dum dum dum."

And he would hold tight onto the brim of his tattered engineer's hat as if to keep it from blowing away.

"DUM DUM DUM DUM DUM DUM."

And he would slowly walk down the hall.

If you listened closely from the end of the hall, it sounded just like a train dying away.

"DUM DUm Dum dum dum d-u-m d—u—m d—u—m."

On the lawn outside, the story was no different. Even though the patients might show more animation and speak more words, day in and out they did the same things.

On long, green, slatted benches on the south side of the building the ladies of the chronic service take the sun. Some of them lie in the same position for hours without moving until the shadows of later afternoon crowd them off the lawn.

An old woman, always in black, sits counting her fingers and forgetting her place when she switches hands. She stops and returns to the first to begin counting again.

Mary Jane Elizabeth Susan Alison Martin, if you haven't heard until now, owns all the benches on the hospital grounds and tries to collect rent for their use. She places her three hundred pounds in polka dots on the edge of a crowded bench and elbows and pushes herself to the middle and frightens the others away.

Two young prostitutes, their hair always in rollers, toothless and drawn before their time, sit smoking and laughing at the other patients who approach them.

"Go away from me. Oh, go mind your own business? We have better things to do than talk to you. Come on, beat it, or I'll have your doctor put you in seclusion."

"You have no right to talk to me like that. I don't like that."

"Oh, why don't you drop dead? Will you? Leave us alone. I bet this one's a frustrated les. Don't you? Look, dearie, why don't you run to the nurse and tell her your nose is running?"

Occasionally a relative or a friend visits with one of them outside, and the unvisited ladies, like beggars spotting an easy touch, uncovered by one of their number, gather around and, armed with tortured hungry faces, whine away all the stranger's loose change and tobacco.

When a patient brings nature into his rituals, nature becomes lifeless. The mechanization and dehumanization that have destroyed the patient make him take what is beautiful in nature and make it cold and artificial.

Every spring and summer when the large hospital lawns covered themselves with dandelions from fence to wall, he spends the entire day gathering yellow and wrapping it into newspaper bunches, many huge bundles each day, which he brings to the ward bulging and falling, leaving a wilted trail behind him, scenting the corridors.

Other times, when he cannot find paper, he stuffs them into the pockets of his swollen overcoat, filling it out like a fabric balloon. He covers all the tables and chairs on the ward and while he is at supper the nurse throws them away.

The market for dandelions is not what it used to be.

I have just picked a dandelion bouquet for my mother. She seems to be very impressed and very grateful. I watch her fill a drinking glass with water and stuff it full of my flowers and place it right in the middle of the kitchen table. As soon as they are arranged I run out to the back yard and gather another bunch. I can't resist. After a while she begins to lose interest and tries to discourage me by discarding the wilted ones. And even though I knew that this would eventually happen, I am just a little hurt by it.

Some patients were usually left alone and what was found to be comfortable was allowed to be. Difficulty occurred only when someone from the outside world arrived at the hospital and intruded, someone who didn't understand. It was then that the silent, hidden barriers that we had taken for granted appeared in the open. It was then that the oddities and strangeness of the patients seemed even more bizarre. It was as if we had lost some of our sensitivity to the patients' bizarre ways, that in being there we had become used to the things that terrified strangers.

For years Mrs. Casey had been a member in good standing, properly and regularly attending, of Saint Michael's Sodality. When one of the younger members suggested that the women visit members of the church—"our fallen brothers," she called them—who happened to be in the state hospital, Mrs. Casey, as was her custom, seconded the motion. It was passed with murmurs of anxious doubt and excitement. She was one of the first volunteers chosen to make the trip to the hospital.

Mrs. Casey wore her gray tweed suit that fit loosely over her fragile frame. She brushed her gray hair back and checked in the mirror to see if she had on too much rouge.

She went to the briefing at the hospital and sat in the back of a crowded, overheated room filled with the other volunteers, gossiping about their daughters' coming marriages, new babies, and apartments. Father Devlin was the priest assigned to the hospital, and because my ward had many Catholics and most of them had not responded to him either, we had become good friends. He always wanted to help and had encouraged local parishes to send volunteers. I agreed to say a few words about the hospital and answer questions.

He introduced me to the crowd of thirty middle-aged women with the kind of remarks that only clerics seem capable of making. "Now then, ladies," he began in his brogue, which he had intensified for the occasion, "Dr. Stevens is going to tell you about *our* hospital and *our* patients. I might say before you come forth and smother the poor doctor with all your *very* important questions, that Mrs. Stevens has asked me to announce that he is a happily married man with a growing family." He smiled at me. "But if you pay attention he might tell you about some unmarried doctors your daughters' age." The ladies laughed that peculiar warm laugh that a priest gets when he does or says things that make him sound worldly.

My talk was short, perhaps five minutes long, and there were no questions at all. I sat down, and Father Devlin thanked the ladies again and again and then a woman described their duties to the volunteers. Mrs. Casey did not hear a word the speakers said and had to come to the front after the meeting was over to find out where she should go. We walked around the grounds on a tour for a half hour and not once did she lift her eyes above her sensible walking shoes.

When Mrs. Casey was finally assigned to her building, she walked directly toward it, staring straight ahead, avoiding the peculiar smiles of the patients that she suspected were directed at her. I started back to my office. She was to report to the treatment room in my building and she found it at the end of a long hall lined with idle lounging patients who were sipping coffee and arguing and looked very strange to her indeed.

"Lady, you got a cigarette?"

"Hey, where's my change? This Coke machine is broken. Hey! Where the hell is my Coke?"

"Goddamn, no good bastard psychiatrists. Goddamn, no

good psychiatrist bastards. Bastards. Bastards."

The door was open and Miss Stuart was arranging medicines in little paper cups. Mrs. Casey introduced herself to Miss Stuart and asked if she was Catholic and went right on to talk about Saint Michael's. Miss Stuart, she learned, went to Immaculate Conception, and Mrs. Casey promptly upbraided her for going to a place where the confessors were supposed to be so liberal and easy-going, not like at Saint Michael's. Miss Stuart said something about not having gone to confession in years and wrote some notes in a large brown notebook.

"It's always nice to have a volunteer around this place," Miss Stuart offered. "Very few people come to visit us in this building—mostly relatives coming to get Social Security checks signed or to make visits on birthdays or at Christmas."

"Miss Stuart," Tom shouted into the treatment room, "Herbie fell in the shower and really did a job on his forehead. Cut it terribly. Looks like a five-stitcher."

"Bring him in and put him down here."

Herbie came in dressed in a torn bathrobe with fresh blood stains on the front. He was wild-eyed and suspicious-looking. Miss Stuart wiped his cut with a saline compress and then placed some gauze pads over it.

"Would you hold this down tight over Herbie's forehead while I call the doctor? I'll only be a minute," she asked her new volunteer.

Mrs. Casey was frightened and hated blood. The very sight of it made her feel sick to her stomach. Even in the familiar surroundings of her own doctor's office she had trouble when he took blood for tests, and it was all she could do to keep from fainting.

Herbie had come from the front wards a decade ago. In spite of the hopes that were raised, the family that cared, he had gotten worse each year and had retreated more into his

world of fantasy. Here people were no longer people; he saw
them as animals, the hospital as a zoo, and himself as the as-
sistant keeper. He was fond of telling the other patients how
much he liked his job, how much he enjoyed the daily routine even though he claimed that he could never get used to
the smell.

To him, the aides were members of the cat family and
he was fond of checking their paws to make sure that they
were free of burrs; often he made a nuisance of himself. He
had not been visited this year except for his birthday, and
that was during the winter. It is very warm today, he must
have thought. So who was *this* looking down at him?

"What winged, feathered creature is this wiping my
bloody brow? Gray feathers, skinny bird. What coop did you
come from?" he shouted.

Mrs. Casey started and trembled, afraid to back away
and remove her hand for fear that the horrible blood would
start to flow again. "I'm helping out," she tried.

"You're helping yourself to my blood, vulture! I've seen
you carrion vultures act before. Sitting in the dark, just waiting for someone to die."

"I'm from Saint Michael's."

"A Saint Michael's vulture with the God bird's drop-
pings from the cross. A Christ cross. Crisscross bird. Crotch-
ety-crossed vulture."

Without thinking, she crossed herself.

"Crisscross bird. You proved it. Flap your wings."

"Oh my God. Now, now. Just relax. Stop. Please.
Nurse!"

"The gray bird wants the white bird for dinner tonight.
Dinner birds."

"No, no. My God, no. Help! Nurse!"

"Birds of a feather flock together. Winged bird. Sing
bird."

And he broke into a hideous cackle and started to jump

up and down on the shaky litter, making clawing motions at the air with his hands, defending himself from imaginary blows.

Mrs. Casey was holding the compress and could feel the lukewarm blood staining her fingers. She had to get out of there. Herbie leaped to the floor, slipped, and landed, bleeding freely from his cut, blocking the only door.

"Help!" she screamed, and screamed again, and finally didn't stop. Herbie was rolling naked on the floor, growling like a lion, when I came in.

"The gray bird is trying to kill me. She attacks helpless people and feeds them to Saint Michael birds. Save me from the bird!"

"Oh my God! Oh my God!"

"Herbie, cut it out! Stop it, just stop it."

Herbie pointed to her with a bloody finger and whispered in a loud, hoarse voice: "Bird, bird, bird!"

She was crying, and in her confusion blew her nose in the compress she had been holding and got blood all over her face. When she realized what she had done she panicked and began to scream. It seemed forever before she calmed down. We talked to her, held her hand, walked with her.

"Home, I want to go home," was all she said.

I patched Herbie up. It took eight stitches. Someone called a taxi for Mrs. Casey and the nurse stayed with her until it came.

When she climbed into the taxi, still shaky, still crying, Herbie came screaming from behind some bushes where he had hidden himself, pointed at her and in a hoarse whisper grated: "Bird, bird, bird!" and ran shouting after the car till it disappeared through the gate.

There were some patients who got better and left the hospital. I think two out of seventy left my ward those first four months.

Because John had gone home every weekend to his uncle for so long, I suggested that he try staying overnight during the week. He got a job at a car wash near the hospital, wiping the back windows of the automobiles when they were done. Gradually he gave up his bed in the hospital and I got Dr. Larkin to sign a special pass that allowed him to have lunch every day in the hospital cafeteria. It was his only tie left.

Larry, the manic patient on my ward, was the other man who went home. He and I had become good friends. Actually, it was inevitable, because I always felt indebted to him for talking during that first ward meeting. Larry had been in mourning for his parents for years and covered it with a flimsy manic shell, which broke when Miss Barker retired. He became very depressed and angry with her for leaving, and all of his old hidden feelings about his family came through for the first time and were able to be discussed.

"You know, doc. This is odd. I don't feel high any more. I mean I don't feel great all the time."

"No one does, Larry."

"Yeh, but, doc, it's different. I don't feel bad, either and I don't worry about dying. I just feel like me. You know, I haven't been able to say that in years!"

It was a real improvement, and Larry went home and to work again. I gave Miss Stuart a hug. "It really can happen," I said.

By and large, I came to see that what I could do was to replace an old routine of the patients with a new routine of my own. I no longer thought of these chronically ill patients in terms of cures; I was developing new standards.

There were victories (we called gains victories), but they could only be seen as victories by us. They would have been laughable to an outsider. A forty-year-old man finally

picked up a broom after breakfast and swept without being
told to. He had been reminded every day for six months, but
one morning he did it alone. Somehow we intruded upon
the special space that was reserved to his psychosis, the part
of him that was alone with him when we put on our coats
and went home.

We owned a piece of that now. He had interrupted his
chaos with the thought: I just ate, now I must sweep. This
was a victory. This was an inroad. The language of sweeping
would earn status and praise, a better room, and a weekend
at home.

There were triumphs when a patient learned to trust
and began to give up his mask during his hours with me and
talk to me as a real person. And when I could see that the
hours with me were eroding away the barriers and becoming
as important as the time when I was not there.

"Dr. Stevens, I think I dreamed about you last night. Or
did I wake up and remember what you said? I'm not sure.
I'm confused. It was all yellow. The boat was all yellow. And
you were rowing it. And we were towing a coffin and . . .
hey, you remember all this. I . . . you recall you were rowing . . ." Jerry looked at me and rested his black hands on
mine. "You don't even have a callous there. You wanted me
to get out of the boat. I can't swim. You knew that! You
wanted me to get out of the boat and open the coffin. . . .
That's right. Remember?" He sat back in his chair and
looked at me intensely and appeared to be recognizing something.

"No. You told me I could swim. And I swam! . . . I
opened that coffin and it was empty . . . wait. . . . No, I
had to piss and got up . . . went to . . . I went to the bathroom and pissed and then I remembered what you said yesterday. I . . . you're right! You're right! I do feel like killing people, sometimes."

"And *me*, too!"

"Yes, when you say something I don't like."

There were conquests. One man always talked of suicide. Each time I said to him "I'll see you next time" I was never sure I would. He called me on the phone one evening.

"Dr. Stevens. It does make sense. I know this really sounds crazy, but it does make sense. I mean it doesn't really make sense to stay alive. We're just going to die and there is no God, no afterlife, but it makes sense to see other people and be in the world. I know this doesn't sound sane."

"No, go on, go on."

"It's just a feeling. No reason. I mean the reasons for killing myself are really no better than the reasons for staying alive. There may not be any sense in my life, but there may be sense in life itself, and because I'm part of that it makes sense to find the part of me that is worth living for."

"God, that is beautiful."

There were victories, eating with utensils, using the toilet, showering, shaving, being sociable and friendly for the first time in years. There were victories (we called gains victories).

Seven

In spite of all its frustrations, I found treating patients within the framework of a long, intense relationship to be the most rewarding part of my training. On the chronic service I spent many long hours with the patients, but it was not treatment in the formal sense. I tried to understand them and to find out what their problems were, if they were willing to talk about them, but usually there was very little I could do. I went through all the stages of trying to help—changing medicines, recommending work therapy, doing additional psychologic and neurologic examinations and medical workups to determine if there was any possible chance of there being an organic cause of their problems. Most of these studies were in vain, although I did discover two cases of leukemia during my first week on the ward, and debated with myself whether leukemia was worse than mental illness.

I had always felt at home with patients; although sometimes I was anxious and often confused and bewildered, I was usually comfortable with them. There were exceptions. Mr. Gordon called himself by the name of the French poet Pierre Charles Baudelaire, and had so confused the staff that his official folder in the record room was filed under the poet's name rather than the name Gordon. I was amazed when I saw this and insisted on doing something about it. I decided that everyone should call him Mr. Gordon. At least the staff should know who he really was.

"Stevens, you're Stevens? Sit down." A tall, immaculately dressed man towered over me. He was close to seven feet. He put his hands on my shoulders and with a single push sent me flying into my seat. He leaned across my desk, put a hand on each arm of the chair, and began. "You are under some mistaken notion of my identity. You call me Gordon. Who is this Gordon? Show me Gordon! I don't know any Gordon! Do you know a Gordon? Show me Gordon!" He could bellow! "Show me Gordon!"

"You . . . are Gordon," I said, calling on every bit of bravery I could.

"You are crazy. Ha. Look at these," he said, emptying his wallet out on the desk in front of me. A dozen cards and forms fell from his hands, each plainly marked with his pseudonym—a driver's license, a medical-society identification card with another alias showing that he was a doctor, a card that said he was a member of the Massachusetts Bar Association. "Where is this Gordon? You are some kind of mistaken fool. There is no Gordon. Do you hear?" he shouted. "Do you see a Mr. Gordon on any of these cards?"

"I see a very unhappy Mr. Gordon standing and shouting at me right now. A man who is so miserable he wishes he were someone else."

"There is no Gordon. There never was any such person. If there was, he is dead. Look at this." He pointed to a tooth in his mouth and drew on my pad a diagram of a tooth with some sort of device in it. "See, this tooth is a very special dispenser that I had built. It releases 1.23 milligrams of opium extract into my bloodstream every three hours. Now you show me where there is a Gordon."

"I said you are Gordon."

"You are a fool. You are a fool," he exploded. Then he ran around the desk, threw me up against the wall, pulled my tie as tight as he could, and dragged me out to the stairwell. He somehow picked me up and threw me down to the landing. My glasses flew off and shattered against the wall. I was dazed, I could see only a blur. He leaped down the stairs after me. I was lying on my back with my neck against the wall, looking up at this enraged monster.

"Show me who is Gordon."

I lifted up my hand. Three aides had come to the top of the stairs, and a crowd of stiff patients had formed. "You are Gordon," I said. He started at me again, but did not hit me. Instead, he ran past me, down the stairs and out of the hospital. My neck felt wet and I touched my head and found that my forehead was bleeding. I was stunned and beaten. I had tried to help Gordon see himself, I wanted to help him leave this place. My head, my poor bleeding head.

"Well, Lions, 1—Christians, 0," said Stan, handing me my broken glasses.

"Lions, 1—Christians, 0," I repeated in disgust. "Thanks for your help, Stan. What the hell were you waiting for?"

"Look, fooling around with Willie is one thing. Mr. Gordon can kill you. It doesn't say anywhere that I have to save you. You leave him alone, he'll leave you alone. Everyone with any smarts learns that."

If Gordon refused help and was difficult, there were nevertheless some patients who accepted help and got better. Ricky was twenty-two when he came to the hospital. He had been in isolation for several months and had gradually deteriorated. He had become upset every autumn on the anniversary of his mother's death even though he felt that he did not know his mother and couldn't remember her face. He became very confused this year and could not stay at home. I first saw him one night when I was on call and making rounds on one of the back wards. He was a handsome, thin young man with a Cheshire-cat grin.

"Who are you? Are you who? Who you? You hoo. Hoo hoo. I like you. Do you screw? Who do you screw? Screw you monkey. Dipity-doo. What's new? Are you new? Are you blue? Do you blow? I know you blow."

"I'm Dr. Stevens."

"I'm Dr. Livingston."

"How long have you been here?"

"Since prehistoric times, before my mother was born. Do you know my mother? She's a good shit."

"Why are you on this ward?" I pointed to the bars and the locked doors.

"I just wanted to see you, so they let me in. How are you doing? Are they treating you good? You eating well? Ha ha."

He was really funny, and personable, and I laughed. "What . . . is your name?"

"John Milton, you've heard of me. I'm a swinger."

"How do you manage to keep your sense of humor in a place like this?"

"Oh, I'm just a visitor. I'm only staying a while. I'm visiting you, as a matter of fact. Just the facts, please."

We sat down in the lounge off of the day hall. "Is there

a doctor following your case?"

"No. Can you recommend one? I have this terrible neck ache. See?"

"Really, what is your name?"

"Ricky Kelly. One of the Mama Kelly boys. I remember mama. Do you remember your mama? I bet your mother is dead. You poor fucking bastard. My mother is alive and well in South Boston. That's for sure. You want a cigarette? I'll bum one for you from the aide."

"No thanks, Ricky. I'd like to come by tomorrow and look at your chart and get a better picture of what's happened to you and then talk things over with you. How does that sound?"

"It sounds like a man talking words."

I saw Ricky twice a day for the first month and then four times a week for the rest of the year. More and more he was able to speak about his longings for a mother and how cruel and ungiving his father had been to him. I had him transferred from the locked ward to an open ward; he had been placed on a locked ward originally because he ran away so often, not because he was dangerous. It was felt that his prognosis was very poor because other attempts at treatment had failed, but we got along well from the start and I frankly enjoyed his sense of humor. Even though some of the remarks he made were crazy and confused, he managed to generate a great deal of warmth, and we settled into a close and highly productive relationship.

Ricky had blocked out a great deal of his past and had no memory of his mother. It was as if he were forced to go through a disorganizing sense of loss every year because he refused to remember her and her death. Every year his confusion grew worse and every time he seemed more vague about what had happened to him.

"Hey, look at this, Dr. Stevens." Ricky took out his wallet. "This belonged to my grandmother. No shit. She gave it to me. This is a picture of me and my grandmother. She's an ugly bastard, isn't she? Would you believe it, she still washes the floor on her hands and knees? The whole world could fall apart and she'd still wash the floor. I'd rather eat off her floor than her dishes. It'd taste a hell of a lot better, too."

"Who is the lady holding the basket?"

"An aunt, I guess."

"Which aunt?"

"Huh?"

"Which aunt?" I repeated.

"Which witch is the witch that watches other witches."

"Is that your mother?" Ricky looked at the faded picture and screwed up his face.

"Naw, she'd be an old bag now."

"She would have been young then. Pictures don't age."

"You're right. Hey, she's not bad, you know. That couldn't be her. Look at this one. That's Ginger."

"A cocker spaniel?"

"No, he's really a zebra, we dyed his fur. I hate stripes."

"Who is this?" I pointed to another picture that had fallen from his wallet.

"That's some lady who used to clean house for us. Hey, can I see your wallet?"

One thing that had been stressed during supervision with Glickman was that a psychiatrist must have anonymity in order to be effective. If a patient knew too much about you, I was told, he would be unable to project his fantasies upon you. That was only one of many precautions that Dr. Glickman warned me about. "Reveal nothing of yourself. That way you can be sure that everything you see is the patient's and not contaminated by external events."

But I felt that Ricky had spent too much of his life in fantasy and that seeing me as a real person would be more helpful. Besides, I thought he would get a kick out of it and I wanted him to know about me. I took my wallet out and opened it.

"How much money do you have? Only four dollars. No shit. Oh, one of them is a five. Who's this? I know, it's a kid. A fat kid. Your wife must really stuff the old food down her gullet."

"It's a boy." I laughed.

"No offense. Better to be a fat boy than a fat girl. Who's this?"

"My wife, Anne."

"Not bad. She really your wife?"

"No, she's a zebra. I had her skin dyed."

"You don't like stripes either? Aha, who's this?"

"Oh, that's a picture of my mother and brother and me at the beach."

"Old man dead?"

"No, he took the picture."

"Is he dead now?" Ricky looked anxious.

"No. See, here's a picture some years later."

"A sailboat! Do you own it?"

"No, it's an uncle's." Ricky was holding the pictures up, getting a better light, admiring my two boys, looking at a picture of my brother David and his wife and two kids.

"You have a nice family there, Dr. Stevens," he said, and for the first time his face looked nostalgic, quiet, almost contemplative.

Ricky was extremely sensitive, and if I was five minutes late he would be ten minutes late for the next hour. If I went on vacation, he would run away from the hospital and go to a resort, entirely without funds. He hitched rides with hearses, moving vans, and cattle cars. He loved to walk and would sometimes be returned by the police from twenty miles away. We became good friends. We liked each other, and I continued to see him intensely. I was determined to help him.

I learned something very important from Ricky. I learned that I could be myself when I was with patients and did not always have to play doctor. I began to let patients see enough of me so that they could call me their friend and have it mean something. I grew able to tell a patient who I was and become as real to him as I demanded he be with me. It only seemed fair.

There were some patients who could not tolerate this kind of intimacy and others who sometimes used what they learned as weapons against me. I made adjustments for these more guarded patients, who were often content to call me their friend when a medicine I gave them seemed to help or because I seemed interested in their problem.

I could not accept the image of a passive omniscient psychiatrist. I felt it was too artificial and was designed to protect the doctor more than the patient. It provided a convenient way for evading pointed questions. It was a cloak of silence that did not fit me. If patients were to learn a more honest way of feeling, it had to begin somewhere. I felt that setting an example was a good place to start.

Although I was more open with patients, I continued to see a great deal of transference. That is, patients would sometimes attribute feelings and attitudes to me that were mainly imagined. I believed my openness with patients helped solve some of the difficult problems about which I had been warned. With the openness sometimes came trust. My patients were able to say I *seemed* a certain way rather than insist that I *was* that way. Since they knew me, reality was harder to deny.

It was more difficult for me to be open, and took more energy. It made me feel with my feelings about the patients and be honest with myself. It felt so much more real. I knew it was worth it.

If individual therapy was a challenge, group therapy was a circus. More than once I felt as if I had been thrown to the wolves and was expected to survive in a den of glowering schizophrenics.

My old friend Alan and I met twice a week, when I took notes during his group-therapy session and he took notes during mine. We tried to cover our inadequacies as best we could, but it was much harder to do in front of a group of eight or nine people than with just one, because there were so many more persons trying to figure you out.

After each session we went out to discuss it over coffee, and for a few months we picked each other apart, saying things like "I wouldn't have said this" or "I wouldn't have said that." Finally we settled down and really tried to understand what was going on in each or our groups.

One day his group was especially confusing. Some patients were storming in, others were rushing out. Some were carrying on conversations with themselves, with us, the dearly departed, the Holy Ghost, and W. C. Fields.

Alan had a manic woman, Rhoda, in his group who talked the entire hour. It made no difference to her whether anyone else was talking or not. She dominated every moment of the session and kept other patients from talking about their feelings. She would get up and walk around, put her hand on Alan's shoulder, tell us how cute he was and how much she liked him and how loyal she was to him, and then proceed to scream at him and call him every name she could think of.

Susan was a dimpled, blue-eyed, freckled blonde girl who had been very active and difficult to manage when she first came to the hospital. She either talked about having been mutilated when she was born or broke out into gales of uncontrollable laughter.

Carla was always filthy and greasy. She would do nothing for the entire hour and then would walk up to Alan as if she was going to make a great pronouncement, lift her hand up, stand silent and at attention for about a minute, and then sit down again.

Veda was a gap-toothed young woman who was unable to express her own feelings at all. She would play follow the leader when anyone else said they felt something and throw fuel on whatever fire the others had started and then sit back and watch the others with a faint and knowing smile.

"You're a goddamned son of a bitch of a doctor. You just sit there at the head of the table. King shit and all. Well, I don't have to put up with you. I'm a member of two groups. You didn't know that did you? Well, if things don't get better in here doctor doctor, *doctor,* I'm going to take all my business elsewhere and, if you ask me, when I go this place will be pretty dead. Pretty dead. Look at them. Stiffs." Rhoda had begun.

"Tell that person in the hall to stop dropping that spoon. She always stands out there during one of our meetings," Veda shouted.

"Oh, gracious Mother of God, Holy Mary, Mother of God, Holy Father," said Susan, and started giggling.

"Holy shit. Look, smart doctor, I'm serious. You give me some special attention or I'm cutting out," continued Rhoda.

"What kind of attention do you want?" asked Alan.

"Well, isn't that nice! Look, group. Ha! The good doctor is talking today. Get your questions in early," said Rhoda.

"You want me all for yourself?" Alan was fencing.

"Wouldn't that be sweet. A little dark meat might clear

that big Jewish pecker of yours out." Rhoda was in good form.

"I was slashed and murdered before they even let me suckle. They cut me up with a knife. Look, I'll take off my dress and show you. They cut me up where I piss." Susan started crying then laughing. "Look!"

"You want to try a different taste, huh doc? Tell old Auntie Rhoda all your hangups. Come on, girls, he's receptive today!"

"Holy father of waters. The air is the firmament," Susan gurgled.

"I'm gonna get that spoon from her." Veda stood up.

The silent one comes to the front of the room.

"What do you want, Carla?"

Silence.

"Carla, why do you come to the front all the time?"

"They cut me right where I piss." Susan lifted her dress. "Look!"

"Too bad they didn't cut you where you talk." Veda loved it.

"Isn't that horrible to be cut like that? I was just a baby. Ha ha ha ha. Do you want to see the scar? I still have a hole down there."

"Come on, my little Jewish doctor. Let me take you to my house and I'll make you some southern fried blintzes. Did I ever tell you how I seduced a professor of anthropology from Yale?" Rhoda had had two years of college, and she had a quick mind.

"If she doesn't stop it with that spoon . . ." Veda walked to the door.

"Well, if you don't want to come, I'll ask your recording secretary." Rhoda got up and went to the back of the room and sat down by me. "Oh, I love blue eyes. My people don't get blue eyes without monkeying around—and even then it's

not a sure thing. Black eyes sure, but blue eyes . . . what's
the matter, secretary, can't you talk?" Rhoda was after me
now.

"Holy, holy, holy." Susan was crossing herself.

"Look, my smart little doctor. Obviously you and I are
the only sane ones in this place. Let's cut out and make it.
Your friend Stevens with the pad of paper can sit here and
take notes. You can come back and read them later. I'm going
to sit here until I get an answer from you!" Rhoda sat down
on the table.

After the patients finally left, Alan and I just stared at
each other and then broke out laughing. We put our arms
around each other and laughed. We couldn't stop. It was
chaos, nothing made sense, not even our being there to see it
all. What was the sense of this disorder? Eight patients gathered around a table each week and were asked to share their
feelings and ideas, the only possessions some of them had.

They rarely communicated anything meaningful. They
talked around the point or underneath it, if they bothered to
talk at all. Usually they just said words with no intention at
all of saying anything. They hid from each other and sometimes from us, even though we were supposed to be skillful
at finding out what they really meant. Sometimes, as on that
day, it was just impossible.

We sat through group-therapy sessions, listening, trying
at every opportunity to show the patients what they were
feeling, what was important to them, and what they must be
feeling about us. At the end we could not be sure what we
had accomplished. Some patients formed attachments—some
always do—and in breaking them, they grieved for some earlier loss in their lives.

Some denied the purpose of what we were doing, but
others came faithfully each week. There were some patients,
very few—in fact, only one of Alan's and one of mine—who

did get a great deal out of being in a group and of the chance to have a second family. The others called the sessions "classes" and tried to stay at a distance to keep from getting hurt, and they tried to forget about us as soon as we left.

Miss Dowd (no one ever called her by her first name) was a member of my therapy group that met every Tuesday at three. I had invited her to be a member before the meetings began, and she had said she would rather not, that such groups were meaningless and a waste of time at best—but she came, and was always on time.

She always sat in the seat to my left, silent, rigid, and red-faced, as if she had taken a big breath and was determined to hold it forever. She was at least fifty pounds overweight and the year before had had a serious heart attack. All I knew was that for the eleven years she had been in the hospital, attempts had been made to get her out. Many times she had been at the point of being discharged, but each time, just when she was about to leave, she had suddenly fallen apart, into a hundred depressed pieces.

Laconic—she hardly even nodded, but she always had a curious smile, secret and self-satisfied. I'm sure it was the face that she put on when she was too terrified to talk. Time passed, and after many months, although she still remained silent, she seemed in touch with everything that was going on, nodding agreement, smiling or scowling, and usually appropriately. Aside from the brief account in the records, I did not know much about her. She knit beautifully and sold her work, and each year put aside several hundred dollars, her nest egg. Yet she said nothing, nothing at all.

One day in the spring, buses arrived to take the patients in her building to see the spot where the Pilgrims first landed. The others had left without even mentioning a word about it. Glad to be gone, I thought. She was the only one who stayed.

"The others have all gone to Plymouth," she said. These were the first words she had spoken to me since the group began. "I tire of traveling with so many people. A lot of them talk nonsense most of the time. It gets on one's nerves. I've done my share of traveling. After I graduated from college, I saw all of Europe. In my junior year I was Phi Beta Kappa. I majored in languages, Romance languages. It was hard to find work then. I took a position as governess for a wealthy family in Cambridge.

"They had seven in help. That's right, seven. I alone ate with the family. Two lovely boys they had, so bright and eager. It was a pleasure to teach them.

"We would summer on the coast of Maine. Such a beautiful place, twenty-five rooms, right on the ocean. And the flowers! Roses right down to the waves. And the lovely cool breezes, pity the poor people sweltering in the city. And the lights from yachts across the harbor at night, the sounds of parties carrying over the water. Lemonade on the grass, badminton, laughing, the sun!

"In the winter we would go south with the birds. In those days when you had a winter suntan people would really stare at you. Why, it was almost sinful—luxury in the heart of the Depression. Such a happy home—the parties, the gaiety, the visitors.

"The boys grew into handsome, fine young men. Oh, you should have seen the beautiful girls they escorted. Before going out on an important date, they would always run to my room and I would make a last adjustment of their tie or collar and give the final approval. It was wonderful. They were such fine people, understanding and kind.

"I left when the boys were in their teens. They wanted me to stay on but mother had a terrible heart attack and I came home to run the boarding house. Oh, you can imagine how dull it was by comparison. About once a month or so the older boy would send me a letter. You remind me of him in a way. He's a doctor now. I forget where. In pediatrics.

"After mother died, she had always been sick, the poor dear, I sold the house and was determined to teach, but these attacks started and began to get worse. The first year after I came to the hospital I learned that the boys' father and mother were found dead in their garage. A double suicide. Who would have thought it? It was in all of the newspapers. I have the clippings upstairs."

Her eyes glistened as she stared out through the maple trees. She described her childhood as if she were looking through a steamy window—a rich uncle who had ponies, and how she cared for them, snowy Christmases in Vermont, raking the leaves with her father in the fall and the wonderful smell they made when you burned them, pretty dresses and doting aunts, and schoolteachers who marveled at how bright she was. If I only knew, she said.

When the other patients returned, again she would not talk and became as silent and withdrawn as before. After about a year, just before what was to be our last meeting, she had another one of her attacks and came into the meeting from a room in seclusion determined to say goodbye to me. She was so drugged and unsteady that two aides had to help her. She swore and flirted with me at once.

"You no good. Oh God! Why are you leaving? I won't miss you. I'm going . . . I'm going to plant a great big kiss on you before you leave . . . Oh. Ha, ha. Oh." She started to cry.

She emptied her handbag on the table and rummaged through an incredible mound of treasures and finally found the farewell card she had bought and forced the others in the group to sign it. She handed it to me. She was the only one who had not signed it. When at the end of the session I stood up to leave and watched the others rush to the door to meet their friends or argue with the vending machines, she collapsed into tears and started pounding the table with her handbag. It would take more than a year of treatment to help her, but because her attachment to me was so great I felt that she would be unwilling to work with anyone else in the future and that the chances of her ever leaving were slim. After trying so hard to build trust, I was betraying her by leaving and I wondered if I had done more harm than good.

Working with patients and helping them make plans reminded me of a time during my childhood when I spent a great deal of my days with a sad, frightened boy.

Gordie was my friend. He was very different from the other children in the neighborhood and had been kept back several times in school. He was very gangly and very tall for his age and towered over the other children in the class, who were three years younger and were always making fun of him.

Gordie was always getting into some sort of trouble, especially with fire. He loved to sit and watch my father burn things in the wire incinerator in our back yard and would push long sticks through the grate. When they caught on fire, he would try to burn everything in my back yard and I would end up spraying the hose all over. It was always a mess.

Gordie would fall in love with the sound of a familiar word as if he had never heard it before in his life and he would run around screaming the word and using it in the strangest ways. Then I would begin to use the word the same way to show him how silly he sounded. It never made sense but it was always funny.

Gordie lived two blocks from us in Nantasket during the summer in a very large white house with red shutters and flower boxes, right on the edge of the water. One day I got the idea that we should build a raft and try to sail around the harbor. There was plenty of driftwood on the beach and what we needed we could scavenge from under neighbors' porches and back yards. We collected empty bottles and returned them for the deposit money, and bought a large assortment of nails.

Gordie was very strong and dragged all the wood to one place on the beach and I tried to put them together into some sort of raft that would float. We worked on the raft for almost two weeks. As it neared completion, Gordie grew more and more upset over what would happen when we launched it, and he started to worry about drowning.

We finished it at low tide one afternoon and I decided that we would test it early the next morning. When I came down to the beach I found Gordie sitting on the sea wall, looking at a pile of charred wood that had been our raft. We never left the land; it was part of being Gordie's friend.

Therapy was unpredictable. Just when things were hopeless the light sometimes shone through, sometimes only for a moment, leaving you in stunned darkness. Sometimes it lasted. You could never be sure. If the patients' defenses were not strong enough to hide their problems they had other ways of irritating me and getting me angry so that I would get lost in my own feelings and keep away. It could be a confusing muddle trying to stay on the track, controlling my anger and trying to be helpful. It was especially difficult when I had sat through many boring hours in which nothing seemed to happen and expected more of the same.

Well, here she is, finally. That funny green hat, off and on the hook. The coat, off and up. She's perspiring. Must have run over. Fifteen minutes late. I wonder what the excuse is this time? Last week she said she was the only one in the coffee shop who knew how to run the coffee machine. What did I say to her? I don't remember. The handbag—always sits with it on her lap. So, shall I make the first move today or let her talk? That funny look of hers.

Poor Melinda, hallucinating again. Her eyes are darting all over. Her hands are so sweaty she leaves prints on the handbag. What's going on with her today? Is there something I don't know about? Something must have happened.

"Melinda!" Doesn't hear me. "Hey, Melinda, excuse me for intruding. Remember me?" Well, a little smile out of her. "What's wrong today?" Just a shrug. "You look upset." Why should she be upset, she says. She's just as happy as she could be. So, since she's talking, she might just as well go on and tell me about her thyroid troubles.

A person with thyroid troubles might easily have problems. Did I forget that there is a history of goiter in her family? That crazy family of hers. Oh good, now a rehash of her thyroid operation when she was a teenager. God knows what they might have left in her. It's a possibility. Oh, and I'm incapable of understanding how difficult it must have been for a teenage girl to be operated on in those days, not like today. Today is going to be like this—a lot of talk going nowhere.

"But Melinda, you've know all about these things for years. Why should they be getting you so upset now? Perhaps it's something a little more recent?"

Oh, her niece is having a birthday party next month and she won't have anything to wear. She won't be invited anyway. Like last year. Look at her shake, she's absolutely terrified. What's going on?

"Have you had any visitors since our last meeting?" Damn it, I shouldn't have said that. I shouldn't. Here it comes. I should have known that for a year no one has had the decency or respect to come and visit her. All this anger! Out of the chair, pacing the floor, staring out the window, playing with the blinds, writing her name in the dust. Still at it. I might as well make myself comfortable. This will take at least ten minutes. She's in rare form today. Stamping her feet. What a temper tantrum! What did I say? What did it mean?

I'm an ingrate, an experimenter. Who would listen to all this if it weren't for me? Oh, that's beautiful! Why was I late twice in a row last summer? She's dragging out all of the old skeletons. This is incredible!

Where is all this anger coming from? Still pounding her hands. What a strange thing. Here she is, a grown woman, so angry at someone or something that she barely can stay glued together. She can't even talk about it, all she can do is bury it somewhere, so she walks around with a chip on her shoulder and starts hallucinating. Then she comes in here with the usual amount of vagueness, I brush the chip off her shoulder, she makes it so I have no choice—and bam! All the old crap, all the anger that she ever had is thrown right in my face.

The funny thing is that when this is all over, I won't know one bit more about what is troubling her than I did before. She won't be able to tell me. Still at it. I'm a dirty bastard because I will leave this place and make money. Good place to jump in.

"Perhaps your feelings about me aren't so clear-cut as you think."

Oh, the don't-tell-me-what-I-think-routine. What an hour!

"Well, you said I'm a bastard for leaving. What would I be if I didn't leave?"

I am a bastard and a shit besides. She's really getting into it. It's so incredibly artificial, so childish. Come on, Melinda, drop a clue, tell me who I'm just like. Back in the chair.

Oh, now it's the adjust-the-hemline bit, just like the first month of therapy. She wants to see if I'm looking. What if I'd look, so what? It's what she's trying to get me to do, the tantrum will really get going. She has to make everything so sexual. I mean, why can't she say, like a normal human being, I like you, doctor, but I get angry at you or I'm angry and upset today. "Good," I would say. "Glad you could tell me about it; let's find out why." She can't be that direct. No, she has to set up a trap—aha, I caught you looking up my dress, you pervert psychiatrist—and then let me have it. She can't tolerate any closeness without making it come out all sex.

It stopped. She stopped. Quiet. She's absolutely silent. Looking out, seems calmer. Those damn eyes jutting about again. Voices, I bet. Voices, voices, voices.

"You seem troubled, Melinda."

Oh, brother. Head in the sand. Must be very loud voices —they've stopped too, I guess. She's looking right at me. Very sad. Very, very sad face. I bet if she weren't crazy it would have been a pretty face. When did her father die? No good, last May or June. Birthday? No. Maybe something, though?

"Melinda, was there a special day this week, an anniversary or something?" Huh or what is all you can say? Hey, you're not even looking at me.

"I said, was there an anniversary this week?"

Her parents' anniversary. That's it! "Which one would it have been?" She's counting . . . thirty-five. "And this is the first one since father's death." Yes it is . . .

She looks like she's going to cry. I don't believe this. After forty-five hours of talking about utter nonsense she suddenly has a real feeling. "You really miss your father." That did it. She is really crying. Honest-to-god tears. Nothing crazy about this. Look at those tears. Do I have a tissue I can give her? "Sure, take one of these." Have a box. You can have them all. Cry.

All that anger. It is at him for dying. That's it. The being alone and like a child. She couldn't tolerate knowing that, though.

"You sound as if you have felt very alone and empty these last weeks."

More tears. I'm going to sit back and just let her cry and keep quiet. Let her do it all. She's telling me about him. What a nice man, but he didn't have much insurance. His bad habits were really so small and she was so cruel to him. How she and mother ganged up on him all the time. How good he was to her when she was a kid.

Well, it's almost over.

"Would you like one of my cigarettes, Melinda?"

Let's see, where are my matches? Here they are.

"It sounds like you haven't gotten over the loss of your father yet, Melinda."

She nods. She agrees.

"Well, we have to stop now. I'll see you next week."

That hat and coat. She isn't waiting to put them on in here. Can you believe it? She is actually starting to grieve for him. She's left her pocketbook. That's probably her knocking at the door now.

"Yes, Melinda. Here it is."

I think she's going to make it. She's going to make it.

Do not be too hard with me, but there were times when I laughed at them, but then there were times when they were terribly funny, moments when, even behind the best professional face that I could conjure up, the best mask of indifference I could put on, I fell apart laughing.

There was Josephine, large, round, and completely

crazy. She had been in a state of confusion since her admission and tore the ward apart every day like clockwork, hunting for something. She would leave piles of clothes strewn all over the hallway and take beds apart in her search. I would find her in my office, which had no lock, hunting through pads of blank paper, turning my chair upside down to read the writing on the bottom.

"Josephine, what are you doing?"

"What does it look like? Out of my way."

"Josephine—hey, watch those books! Josephine!"

"I'm watching them. They're falling. Why should I watch them?"

"What on earth are you looking for? Tell me and I'll get it for you."

"Plymouth Rock!"

"What?"

"Plymouth Rock."

"Plymouth Rock?"

"Yes, you've seen it?"

"Yes, but it's in Plymouth."

"Well, it's not supposed to be. It's supposed to be here."

"Why do you want it?"

"I want to go home for Thanksgiving."

"So why do you need Plymouth Rock?"

"The Pilgrims had it and they had Thanksgiving."

"Josephine, it couldn't possibly be in that drawer."

"Why not?"

"Because it is twice as big as the entire desk."

"That was years ago. Get smart. Out of my way."

I admit that I had some favorites and that I frankly disliked others. No matter how hard I tried, no matter how I explained away the reasons behind their disagreeableness, I found that I was always meeting with some patients at the extremes of their hostility and the limits of my endurance. Bryan was a vicious paranoid who had once been in law school.

"Well, why do you want to talk to me?"

"The nurse told me that you were upset last night."

"She did, huh? What else did Piggy tell you? Did she also tell you that you have a big nose? That pisses me off. You know, you're a real asshole. You're worse than that, you're just plain shit."

"You certainly get angry when I mention feelings."

"You certainly get angry when I mention feelings. That's a good line. Did you get that out of one of your medical books? How come if you're such a great doctor you're working in a crap hole like this place?"

"And just what are *you* doing here?" I was getting angry.

"Oh, very clever. I'm here collecting names of the stupidest doctors in the United States, but after seeing you they all look smart. Do I have to stay and talk to you?"

"I can't make you," and I just didn't want to.

"You bet your ass you can't."

There were patients, because I liked them so much and couldn't bear to think of them as that sick, that I thought of as healthier than they really were. Sometimes I granted them privileges too soon and encouraged them to do things they were not ready for and felt bad when things did not turn out as I had hoped.

Melinda started to do very well. In a few short weeks she had begun to open up and put together the pieces of a fragmented past. Her family visited the month after she started to improve and what they saw they did not like. Melinda's role was to be the weak sister in her family. They took her out to dinner and began to undermine the gains she had made and told her that she shouldn't waste her time talking to me about her father because he had never loved her anyway. Having torn her apart, they left.

I never saw Melinda in my office again, only on the wards. She would not move. She never spoke to me again. The cocoon she had spun about herself had sealed out the entire world. If she recovered it would not be because of the sessions I had with her from that point on, trying to bridge the silence. It would have to be someone else's triumph. It had become my failure. I felt as if a part of me had died.

I began to see time as the great and major healer and began to wonder just how much I was worth and to doubt if what I did made any difference. I watched patients with whom I had struggled for months one day give up in spite of how much I cared, in spite of how much I gave. I saw patients who refused to talk with me at all and who spent each day just sitting on their beds get better and leave the hospital.

Time seemed also the great destroyer, killing chances to go home, killing hope, loosening ties, making the acutely ill chronic, making the caring and concerned lose patience, swallowing up people in the jaws of years.

There were times in the cold, damp walls of the place, in the endless paperwork covering my desk, in the steady stream of patients filling my ward who didn't seem to get better and didn't appear to want to, when I counted the months and calculated the time when at last I would be out of that madhouse.

How I longed to sit in the comfortable out-patient clinics next year, in my second year of training, and discover neurotic conflicts in patients who were polite, appreciative, and kept their appointments.

I stand on a hillside in deepening shadows, looking at people trapped in a maze below. I see them gliding in dusky walkways or standing frozen before a fading sun. If they could only call out and tell me. But from the labyrinth there is only silence.

Therapy is like moving an eclipse that somehow got stuck. How do you move a shadow when everything is dark?

Eight

Arriving on the acute service was like a breath of fresh air. There were patients who talked, who argued, who moved and did things. There were patients who had come to the hospital only a week ago and who had problems that could be solved. There were patients who would some day go home.

On the chronic service I had measured success in terms of transfers to old-age homes where my patients could die in comfort. For those few who went home it was an effort, directed as much against my feelings of hopelessness as it was against the process that was eroding my patients and grinding down their years without opposition. When I finished my six-month rotation on the chronic service Jerry Bieberman took over my ward. The acute service contained wards to which patients were sent directly from the admitting floor. Unless a patient was returning from running away, he was formally admitted, no matter how many times he had been in the hospital before.

My ward on the acute service was one of thirty women, of noise and of confusion, where windows were broken by apples or fists and furniture was smashed against the wall. It was full of emotional outbursts, of crying, of yelling, of screams in the night that sent us all running to see who was being attacked. It was a ward of young girls who chewed gum and talked about boys and slashed their wrists (not too deeply) because they wanted a scar to show.

At my first ward meeting I barely had time to introduce myself when a smiling woman with long bleached-blond hair knelt in front of me, crossed herself, and said, "Father forgive me, for I have sinned against you, against the covenant with Israel."

"Jesus, Mary, you're crazy, but I love ya," shouted a short, chunky fifteen-year-old prostitute, her hair up in pink plastic rollers. A judge had sent her to the hospital for evaluation after she had started to swear and throw things in the courtroom. She bounced over and tore Mary away and then returned to establish a cross-legged vigil at my feet.

"Okay, you can begin now," she said to me. "I'm Margie. I'll help you win them over. Don't be afraid. Okay, folks, let's hear it for the new doctor, yea." Some of them started to applaud.

"Hey, he's cute. Are you married, doc?" a sultry-looking woman shouted from the back. "I bet you're really hung."

"Okay, Barbara, cut it out," said a voice, apologizing. "Barbara's boy-crazy."

"And girl-crazy, too," commented a lady without bothering to look up from her knitting. Barbara reached for a chair to silence her accuser.

"Okay, okay, I was just kidding," said the woman, patting her yarn.

"On with the meeting," said Margie. "Come on, let him talk. Go ahead."

"Doctor, God bless you," said an older woman in a brown knitted suit who gave the impression that she could talk forever if given the chance. "I'm not crazy. They all think I am. But I'm not! Get me out of here, doctor. I just know you believe me. I know you can get me out if you want to. Please, doctor, please help me. You're the only one who can help. I know that you're a nice doctor, nicer than the other doctors here. You're more understanding. You're considerate. I can tell by looking at your eyes. Please help me. God bless you. God bless you, doctor."

"That was Mrs. Ziegle or Ziegler or something," offered Margie. "She's a royal pain in the ass." Then Margie turned to Mrs. Ziegler and shouted, "You're a royal pain in the ass aren't you, honey? Anyone else here sick of her?"

"What a mouth," said the woman knitting, never looking up.

Mrs. Ziegler didn't seem to notice.

A hand was raised by a frail, black-eyed, black-haired girl, about twenty-two or three, I guessed. "I . . ."—a long silence, chairs moving, little jokes being told, people walking about—". . . I forget," and she sat down.

"She always does that. She's a waste of time. Don't call on her again," said my new-found friend at my feet.

"Someone has been stealing my things."

"Mine, too."

"That's right," Margie said. "Someone is stealing. You better do something about it. I mean I never saw anything like this until I came to the hosptial. People stealing from me, Jesus."

"Let's have a dance with the boys across the hall," said Barbara.

"Barbara, sit down," said the woman knitting.

"Jesus, Barbara, show a little respect for the doctor," said Margie.

"Respect, look who's talking respect. She charges, doc. I do it for fun." Barbara started across the day hall.

"Barbara, you're a pig. You're going to have to do something about her mouth, doctor. You get me so angry, Barbara. One of these days . . ."

"You'll what? That shut you up. You all saw her shut up." Barbara said her piece.

"I don't know if I should say this, because I really don't know how appropriate it is. I'm really so much better-educated than anyone here that I doubt if I'll be understood. I've been taking notes on everything that is said." This strange character, a thirty-year-old dowager with an air of condescension, a patronizing smile, stood serene and aloof, pushing up her glasses, which kept slipping down her nose.

"Jesus Christ. There she goes again. That girl's always taking notes. She's got dozens of notebooks, haven't you, Gwendolyn?" Margie shouted.

"Let *me* speak. You've had the opportunity, which you used admirably, I might add, to show what a vulgar slut you are. You haven't said anything worthwhile as far as I can see. I have it all down here. I'm making my report out. I know who said what," Gwendolyn continued.

"If she doesn't stop writing down every word that I say . . . Look at her. Would you cut out that goddamn writing? Jesus!" Margie was wailing.

"If you let me finish, I assure you that it's far more important than anything your simple brain could offer."

"One of these days I'm going to tear your eyes out and shove that pencil down your throat." Margie seemed to be taken with her own voice.

"Because Margie really wants it up her ass," Barbara got in one more jab.

"If you notice, doctor, she threatens everyone. I suspect *one of these days* she'll be placed in maximum security. Now then, you can see your duty, an intelligent man always can, and if you're really intelligent, you'll do that now. Have her confined. Now then, I know who's been stealing," Gwendolyn went on.

"Come on, smart ass, tell us," shouted Barbara.

"I shall make my report in the morning. You can't rush me."

I looked at this anxious, sweating woman, her hair pulled tightly back, her glasses fogging up and slipping to the tip of her nose as she wrote down everything I said as I began.

"Ladies, I feel a bit lost my first day over here. First of all, I don't know your names. Perhaps if you introduced yourselves when you spoke you'd make things easier for me."

"I . . . I . . . ." the reluctant black-haired girl began.

"Don't call on her!" warned Margie again.

"Hey, he *is* really cute." Barbara patted her breasts, gave them a heave, and winked at me.

"I've been listening. I have it all down. I know the significance."

"Why don't you take a flying fuck for yourself," shouted Margie.

"There will be no fornication. There will be no fellatio. There will be no cunnilingus. There will be no sex, no filthy significances. No lesbians in my bed. Keep your hands to yourselves, ladies. I know, I keep the notes. I know who manipulates me."

"Vot a filty mind. And she's got a college education. Can you believe det, doctor?" asked a gray-haired woman, shaking her head.

Margie added, "Gwendolyn goes on like that all day long. You know what she said to me? She said I jumped into her bed. Sure, I've gone to bed with men."

"Loads of men, huh, honey?"

"Barbara, shut up. But I've never gone to bed with a woman. Jesus, certainly not her."

"I know what you are whispering about. I've written it all down here."

A fat Italian woman stood up and said, "I want to know just one thing. One thing. Where are my children? Tell me that one thing if you're so smart, doctor."

"There will be no number one."

"Where are my children?"

"No ones, no ones at all," Gwendolyn persisted.

"For two cents, I'm going to punch you in the fucking mouth." Margie was on her feet.

"There will be no fornication."

"See what I mean, always like that." Margie was threatening to swing at her.

"Things are getting a bit rough," I said. "I think that everyone should have a chance to speak, but one at a time."

"No one at a time. There will be no gang bangs."

"He's so cute when he domineers women." Barbara was beckoning to me with her finger.

The woman with the blond hair genuflected at my feet again.

"Come on, Mary, get up. This isn't church."

All over there was a bustle, whispered conversations. Some patients bummed cigarettes; others refused to give them. My head was swimming. After an hour, when the meeting was over and they had left for lunch, some stopped to press for special privileges or for visits home, or to tell me their names and that they wanted to speak with me in private when I got the chance—or, like Mary, to stay at my feet and pray.

Everywhere I turned on the new service there was something to see. There was an excerpt from a life tragedy in every corner of that ward. From the moment I walked through the door I saw a panorama of the human condition.

In a corner sitting darkly, stretching her dress into a tent, watching parades of patients conspiring, craning her neck to hear whispered sounds, distorting her face and the noise of the room. In a corner darkly sitting.

In a corner thinking darkly, who poisoned the flowers and stole the birds' song? Who tore off my petals and left me to wither? Before noon took my childhood away? In a corner darkly thinking.

And just to the side, another nameless woman whispers her lament to her hands. "Did I see my love walk by my door tonight? Was he behind the curtain in the hall? A man on the bus today looked just like him, but he got off before I could make my way to the front and pay. I am not sure. This morning in a cloud I saw his face, a sweet, good face. And I heard his name spoken in a whisper by two jealous women in the yard behind the fence. But look at this old shoe I found in the bushes, I think it was his. He had a pair just like this to wear when he worked outside. I am sure he is near and someday will return, but I must always be looking out or I will miss him. You wait and see, he will come back and take me with him, and when he does these long years of waiting will be repaid and we will walk out together arm in arm."

Another woman looking puzzled, standing in front of the fireplace, muttering. "There's a secret passageway behind the mantle clock where strangers enter in the dark of night to rummage through my purse. They know exactly what they're doing and, wasting neither step nor breath, they stand and watch in heaving silent shadows, while scarcely moving, I pretend to sleep. Tomorrow they will not believe me and will tell me that it was just a dream. And I will take them to the mantle and with both my hands explore the wall and space behind the clock and find only my handprints from the day before."

As I turned the corner to the patients' bedrooms, I looked through the doors to see who was inside. The day was gray and cold and the muted light silhouetted a young girl on her bed.

"Snow," Lisa thought, "snow. Have I been here so long? It is snowing!" She shuddered and looked through windows nearly opaque with dirt and grime. (If the housekeeping staff was questioned as to why they were so filthy, they would shrug and say, "You can't clean a window that's covered by a metal screen unless someone unlocks the screen first. You go unlock the screen and I'll clean it.")

The gray morning was turning white. Black ribs of bushes and trees were losing their battle to the snow and were barely visible. Lisa ran her fingers through her stringy brown hair and sat cross-legged on the bed looking out, holding her head in her hands.

"The world outside is becoming silent. Everything is slowing down. It was like that. It was just like that last spring, everything becoming muffled and distant. God! That's March, one; April, two; May, three; June, four; July, five; August, six; September, seven; October, eight; November, nine; December, ten . . . ten. Ten months I've been here. Ten months.

"And what happened to me? Tell me what has happened! It isn't real, it can't be. It isn't, that's all there is to it. It is a game, but I haven't been in it. It's been played around me. I feel like people have been dancing around me in a circle shouting.

The words. I don't understand the words. I think I

know what they mean, but they begin to lose their meaning to me. They become nonsense sounds. Like they're made up. Hospital. Hos . . . pee . . . tal, hosss . . . pea . . . pih . . . peh . . . tal . . . tall! Horse be tall. Whore's beatle. Hos . . . be . . . tal. Oh, I am crazy. I am, I am, I am."

Lisa reached forward to the metal screen and peered through the frozen grime and wiped some away with her fingertip to make a streaky clearing on the filthy glass.

"Oh, it is snowing. Ten months. Ten months! I'll be sixteen in January. That's next month. Look at the way the window pane and the snowy grounds come together. They are both flat and merge. It's just a picture. It is snowing over everything inside here too.

"When was it I came here? March twenty-third? Oh, I don't know. It was just becoming spring then, all muddy, bright and warm, but . . . there was something wrong. Yes, something was terribly wrong. I couldn't think. My mother was going to kill me. I . . . oh God. Ten months!

"We were in Schenectady, yes, to be with Dennis and Aunt Jessie, and the doors slamming and the fire in the stove and the screaming and the yelling. Everyone was doing something with their hands, sending signals, beckoning, God yes, and tempting. The house was dark, just candles, Jessie crying and having to sit in that horrible living room with Uncle Harry there." She pounded the bed with her fists.

"I hate gladioli. I hate them! I hate them! I had to sit there. All of the relatives crowded together, patting at each other and yelling with their mouths closed, 'Harry, Harry, Harry.' Yes . . . oh, God."

Lisa buried her head in her hands again and then covered her ears. She clutched her Orphan Annie doll and kissed it.

"Oh, and Dennis, tears running down his face, and the smell of perspiration. And mother squeezing my hand to comfort herself, hurting me.

"And someone I didn't know. A fat man, sitting in the folding chair next to me, he kept bumping me with those awful fat legs of his. A button on his shirt was open and I could see the hair on his belly. I wanted to throw up. He was sweating like a pig. I suddenly wanted to open his shirt and lick the sweat and I gagged. Ugh. That's so horrible. What's wrong with me? What is wrong with me?

"I went numb and started to tingle, my head was swimming and then all these bad thoughts wouldn't go away. I wanted to lick Uncle Harry's face and put my hands in the coffin and touch his private! They wouldn't go away. I stood up and screamed, 'He's moving, he's moving, he's moving, he's moving.'

"I ran out screaming, 'Eyes! Eyes!' Everyone's eyes, mother's, especially mother's. They could all read my mind. They knew. I ran out. I ran and I ran.

"I didn't go to the cemetery. No I didn't . . . I think . . . some yellow waiting room, some hospital . . . everything was growing silent. Everything was getting smaller and fading out. People were being covered with something and were fading away. I stood and watched myself. I was dead! I was dead! And I watched myself scream through a long, black tube and the echoes. Oh!

"Is it really ten months? The clear spot on the window is fogging up. The sun is frozen behind it. Oh, Annie, my heart is broken. My face is wet with tears. Why doesn't mother take me home?"

Lisa was in therapy with Alan, and in the past weeks before I came to the ward she had begun to make progress and to consider what was going on in her life. Alan felt that she would require years of intensive treatment, but she was beginning to talk to him and there was hope. On the acute service it was important, to insure consistency, that the pa-

tients' activities, medications, and privileges were acceptable
to their therapists. Unlike the patients on the chronic service, almost all of these patients had hope and many had en-
gendered hopefulness in some doctor who took them into
treatment. Most of them would never be healthy in the usual
sense of the word, but they had never been really healthy to
begin with. But they could get better and many, like Lisa,
would get better and go back out into the world again and
function.

Some of the stories took time to unravel. The first day I
walked through the ward during visiting hours I saw a man
in the back hall, a strange little man who seemed somehow
to be as much a part of the place as the women who lived on
the floor.

I could only guess his age—not that he was so old, really,
but in his late fifties he gave the impression of having already
lived out what was left of his good years. He was not a
patient, and yet every day during visiting hours I saw him on
the ward, standing like some prehistoric creature, shifting his
weight from foot to foot, peering from beneath a long, vi-
sored leather cap that even on the warmest days he wore with
the earflaps down even though they did not reach his ears.

He waited for a patient of mine, Miss Pepper, who
claimed that he was her only living relative, and he was
quite cooperative. Miss Owens, the ward nurse, said, "He
just signed her commitment papers for us without even saying a word. He just scribbled with a shaking hand. A cousin,
I was told. He never misses a day."

"How kind," Margie's social worker remarked, seeing
them together. "So devoted, so attentive."

When the two were together, they stood in silence.

Miss Pepper was fifteen years his senior, but looked even
older. She always wore the same wrinkled, striped housedress, and her hair was always falling down, even though one

of her repeated mannerisms was to pat it into place. It never stayed. When she spoke it was gibberish, a mixture of French and English and words she made up because she liked a particular sound. Her favorite cry was "Doobie, doobie," and she would repeat it over and over. Whenever a stranger came to the ward she would paw at him incessantly as he walked through.

She seemed to get better after a few months. She became quieter and would sit all day listening to the television, when it happened to be working, and staring at where the pictures came from when it was not. Plans were made for her to go home with her cousin for a weekend, and the two of them drove off in an old automobile he had borrowed from a friend.

When she came back the next Monday, she came back screaming. In fact, she screamed for two or three weeks. She was worse than she had ever been. We could not talk to her, she could not listen. She scratched us and tried to push us away.

When her cousin came after staying away for a while, she pointed her finger at him and screamed, but it was all garbled. He stood as always, staring ahead at nothing, silent.

"What happened that weekend?" I asked him.

He lifted his eyebrows, spread his pants pockets, pouted, and shrugged his shoulders. He never came again.

A young nurse from Quebec, Miss Dufy, had taken over the evening shift on the ward, and like the others before her she had to put up with Miss Pepper's endless screaming. There were occasional moments of lucidity among the animal cries that kept the other patients awake, but they were in French.

During one of these outbursts, Miss Dufy discovered that Miss Pepper had been her cousin's unwilling mistress but that he had finally abandoned her. He had always wanted to be a father, Miss Pepper had said in French, with a surprising amount of sympathy and guilt, but she had proven barren to him. He had been fair, he told her, giving the doctors so much time to find out why she couldn't have babies. He had given her every opportunity, every chance, but still nothing had happened. She had failed him for the last time.

Miss Pepper seemed better. She talked a little, of simple things. Although she was still afraid to leave, in time plans were made.

Through the winter she watched the rain falling and hid from the sun, and sat in the day hall patting her hair in ritual reassurance.

The ambulance men came, and while we tried to reason with her and to tell her that the nursing home was the best place for her, that she would have more freedom and better food, they had to carry her off the ward. Angry and confused as she left, she screamed: "Doobie, doobie, doobie."

I was becoming something of an unpredictable figure myself, spending time with the patients when I should have been with the social worker, spending time with the patients when I should have been in conference or writing short, inadequate notes into the charts. I never had time to write long notes and I found that no one ever read them.

Somewhere, hidden beneath the surface, the patients had a humanness that I delighted in uncovering. I tried to find something about each patient on my ward that I could identify with, something that would bridge the gap across the horror. I made a nuisance of myself telling the nurses things like "Did you know old Mrs. Kellman taught Greek civilization at Vassar?" in my efforts to extend the humanness I had found and expose it for others to see. Perhaps, if I must be honest, it was to make the patients less hopeless for me to deal with. I became convinced that if someone thought you had been human once, it was reason enough to be treated that way again, even if no one could remember the last time you responded to a direct question.

Nine

The acute service was different. I had the feeling of motion, of the pulsation of life and reaction to things. I could see people being transformed from wild, chewing beasts—from madmen—into people. I had the feeling that I was doing more. I interviewed all the patients on my ward within the first week, something that had taken months to do on the chronic service. I began to see every patient on my ward in individual therapy as soon as they came up to the floor. The telephone never stopped ringing, and I enlisted the aid of relatives, social workers, and Father Devlin to make things easier for my patients so that they could return home. I called employers, I called friends, I called anyone who could help.

Often the problems that brought patients into the hospi-

tal were related to fights in their families, and I found myself playing the role of referee. At other times unwanted
pregnancies, abandonments, anniversaries of important losses,
deprivations, and death sent my patients to me.

I listened, I advised, I held, I comforted, I shared, and I
understood—sometimes I understood. Most of all I watched a
process of people who had suddenly fallen apart and were, I
hoped, coming back together. I saw my role as helping them
to see what was really upsetting them and to cope with feelings that they could not understand so that they could solve
their problems. They did get better, but I could not be sure
if it was really because of me, if it was my efforts that produced the changes. If I looked closely after their symptoms
had cleared, the fragility that appeared, the tenuousness of
their improvement, would make me hold my breath. And
after discharge, when a patient returned for his outpatient
visits, I was never sure what I would find when I opened my
office door and looked into the waiting room.

There were cures, whatever that means—long periods of
remission—but that took years and trust. And even when the
cause was known and the patient understood, you could
never be sure what you might find when you opened the
door.

"Dr. Stevens, the new admission is here. Erika Popolo or
Popolovono or something. It's a foreign name, anyhow."

"Can you understand her?"

"Well, I can understand the words she says, but not
what they mean. You know, the usual." Miss Owens was my
new ward nurse, an experienced hand with such things. We
got along famously. She was black and was always telling me
that I was a credit to my race. She would sit knitting with
the older patients, and they confided in her. She found out
more than I did half the time and was my confidante and in-
former. I looked over the new patient's record and then went

into my office to see her.

Erika had entered the hospital screaming, with the flag of Lithuania pinned to the front of her flowered housedress, talking about the powerful electric beams that were torturing her and how, after so many years of hiding, the Germans had once again found her and were trying to punish her for escaping during the war. Her last tie with her family was gone. Her only son had just moved away with his bride of one month and she was left alone, remembering the past and its fears.

Day and night she roamed the ward, belligerently searching each reluctant patient for hidden weapons and contraband, explaining in broken English, "You donno dem. You donno vot dey do. You donno vot I see in der vor. You donno. Belief me. You got no idea. You could never be sure. So I trust nobody."

She refused to take her medicine and could tolerate speaking for only a few minutes at a time, but once she did tell me that she wore the Lithuanian flag to protect her from the Nazis.

She remembered how, in order to get a half pound of sugar, as a confused and hungry young girl, terrified and dirty, she had slept with five German soldiers one after the other in the rain behind the sandbags near their tank. She remembered the terrors of the German occupation of her homeland, how she avoided being a hostage during the reprisals for sabotage by marrying a gangly German soldier, a miller's son from Pomerania, and how, on leaving the church, she was spit upon.

She used her pass to cross the border and then go to Sweden and safety, but not comfort. She learned in a letter from her brother that her parents had been killed in the bombings, and she never heard from her brother again. She could never return home. She bore her Pomeranian son in anguish without knowing if his father was still alive. And she remarried without bothering to find out, but feared that he would someday return and take the child from her.

Her second husband was killed by a hit-and-run driver just two months after they came to America. He left no money and she had to go to work in a factory and leave the baby with the landlady. All day at work she worried about her son. Had someone kidnaped him? Had they found out about her past and taken her son as a hostage? When he went to school she worried about the traffic and the rough older boys. She was afraid to teach him to speak Lithuanian because it might give them away, but she spoke so little English that as they grew older they understood each other less and they grew apart. What the war could not take away from her, her new homeland did.

She had been able to tolerate the horror and grief she had suffered at the hands of the Germans because she did not feel it was directed at her, but when her son left, he left her, and he left her alone.

Each day in the hospital she became less angry and seemed less afraid, and each day she would lower the flag on her dress until it hung like an apron below her belt. The lower it got, the clearer her mind became, and she no longer felt pursued by Nazis or other machines.

One day she suddenly appeared to be very much better. She had put on her shoes instead of the tattered pink slippers she had worn during her hospital stay. Her dressing gown with the flag on it was replaced by a surprisingly stylish suit. She demanded to speak with me about discharging her.

"I am finished here, now. I go home!"

"What has happened so quickly?"

"Vot is so quickly? You got your life in front of you. You donno vot you got dere. I ain't gonna be here, doctor, ven dey bury me. I got tings to do. So you'll excuse me?"

"Perhaps you can tell me what started all this?"

"Oh, such a story. To tell you the trut I think it had something to do vit the vater in dis place."

"What about problems in your life?"

"So ve all got problems, notting new."

"You don't want to tell me."

"Dere is notting to tell . . . so that's all."

She really did look better, and so I checked with her foreman at work, who said he would be glad to have her back. She returned to her empty apartment and to her job in a factory cutting, stitching, and grommeting little flags of her adopted country, leaving me to ponder what made patients better.

I was always willing to let patients go home whenever possible. I had seen the damage that institutionalization had done to the patients on the chronic service, reducing them to dependent automatons and so humanizing them that the disease for which they had originally been hospitalized was no longer a problem. Also, I felt that it was terribly important to let patients act of their own free will even though they might go out and do something that people thought crazy. I had begun to doubt whether anyone had the right to limit someone else's freedom merely because they were odd, and the destruction of someone's self-confidence and initiative by overly restricting them in the name of judicious caution was no less a crime.

I realized that this attitude was bound to get me into trouble with people like Glickman, but I was my own boss on the acute service, and some of the senior staff, like Pellegrini, encouraged me. The conflict that lay beneath the surface was that I felt that much of psychiatric practice had little effect on the course of a disease in a positive sense, and that many patients got better on their own. That did not mean what I did was not important, because it was, and I believe that many patients would not have gotten better without my help.

At the hospital psychiatrists, using laws that they had helped to write, could virtually imprison people because their behavior was bizarre or irritated others. If I had placed restrictions on people when I could have let them go without endangering themselves or others, I feel I would have committed the greatest of crimes. I decided that it was better to send someone home too soon, risking a relapse and return to the hospital, than to destroy their confidence and hope by keeping them there.

My social worker, Susan Lundgren, thought I was impulsive because I sometimes accepted what patients told me as the truth. She wanted a complete family history and an interview with as many family members as possible before taking a stand. I felt that she was too rigid and sometimes confused the importance of facts with the number of facts. Sometimes patients returned my confidence in them by acting sane and, if they were harmless—even though they were crazy by anyone else's standards—I sometimes let them go home. The will to get better is precious.

Susan had an office in the basement two doors away from Dr. Glickman. She was the best-looking social worker in the hospital and apparently had recently lost a great deal of weight, because someone was always telling her how great she looked with all that weight off. She had dated Dr. Rosatti, my predecessor on the chronic service, and apparently came out of what had been a very thick shell under his tutelage. In spite of her exterior changes, she remained somewhat constricted, but for all that she was very nice to look at and argue with.

Her office was filled with travel posters and straw flowers, and she had a purple donkey hanging on a string that I discovered was a piñata from a recent trip to Mexico. "Well,

Dr. Stevens, how is old Speedy Gonzales today? Do you have
any patients left on your ward? You've been there almost a
month now. What's the story? Dr. Stevens, would you mind
getting your feet off of my desk?"

We would talk about the patients' families and what we
felt was going on. She had been angry with me when I first
arrived because I was taking Rosatti's place—displacement of
her anger at him, I once thought.

"I understand that Elizabeth Barry is back in the hospi-
tal. Well, you don't know much about her so I'll fill you in
on her family, and then you should talk with her therapist.
She's been here a lot, and I know her husband very well.
You *will* talk to me before you do anything rash with her.
Won't you?"

"I promise."

"Good boy. I'd like to know what you think of her.
She's really a wild one. Your feet, Dr. Stevens."

"What?"

"They've somehow found their way up onto my desk
again."

When Elizabeth Barry came on the ward she was bi-
zarrely dressed in brilliant colors and her entire face was
painted with rouge. She was silly and talked about things as
they happened to come into her head, sometimes laughing
when it wasn't funny, telling me how she had been rail-
roaded, how her family had gotten rid of her, how they had
stolen her son and for all these years had schemed to keep
him away from her.

"My son has come and gone. The family took him away
today. What can I say? I can't say anything, and that's the
truth. They pull all the strings. String me along and tie me
up. Are you untied? Have you ever tried to untie yourself?
You never know what you can do until you try. Who said
that? I said that! That's who said that! I'm a goddamn poet.

I used to be a model. Now they're all dead and buried. The past is gone. You can't bring a dead horse back by crying over it.

"Well, what can I do for you today, doctor? Would you like me to show you my marriage certificate? I have it here somewhere. Let's see, lipstick. I need some more lipstick. Where's my mirror? Do you like my smile? I have perfect teeth, except this one. See it? It's been recapped. Would you like me to recap my past for you? Oh, I could tell you stories. I used to be a size seven. That's some tale. Tailor-made clothes, the best of all possible worlds."

It was hard to make sense of her garbled words, but when Elizabeth was pleasant she had a certain charm, if one could overlook her long gray hair flying all over and the rattling chatter of her teeth (she wore dentures), which she clicked in anger when something displeased her.

When confronted with facts she did not want to hear, she would stand up on her chair and shout "The willies, the willies!" and clap and wring her hands. Then she would laugh wildly as if she was trying to drown out the sadness of the news she was hearing.

Elizabeth Barry was a garish figure on the ward, and her hideous laughter would startle and frighten the visitors and staff in the hall whenever she walked by. Sometimes she painted a smile with her lipstick that reached from ear to ear, covering her cheeks, her mouth, and her teeth.

Her therapist over the years, Dr. Chookian, a warm and gentle man, once discussed her with me.

He said I would find it hard to believe, but years ago when Liz (he called her Liz) was in her twenties about the time he first met her, she was the loveliest thing he ever saw, features fine and delicate, bright blue eyes, exquisite taste in clothes and the means to buy them as well. Liz was easily led and very easily hurt.

She was a high-fashion model and worked in New York in the forties. "She got fifty dollars an hour, in the forties. Imagine! She was a beauty, believe me," he said. It would brighten his day just to see her. He told me how she loved large-brimmed hats—picture hats, he thought they called them—with a full dress the same color. "Oh she was lovely, a picture. You really can't imagine what she looked like."

He told how Elizabeth became terribly depressed and excited at the same time after the birth of her first and only child, a son. She let herself go and began to put on weight. She stayed around the house, didn't go out at all. She said that she was no longer useful to anyone and began to hate the baby.

"Her husband, have you met him? Oh, a handsome, striking-looking man. I suppose a playboy of sorts, a run-a-round. When Liz began to lose her looks—I guess she put on over a hundred pounds—he started to look around and meet other women."

Dr. Chookian told how her husband had asked for a divorce, claiming that Elizabeth was too sick to take care of the baby. She had fallen apart completely and had come here, and she stayed for six years. "I don't think she ever saw the baby even once that whole time. It was really criminal. Finally, we had the hospital attorneys get a court order so that she could regain custody and she gradually got better. She went outside again and worked as a secretary, but she was never her old self after that," he added, looking very sad.

Chookian's voice became choked as he told how her face had become flat and pasty and how she had tried to disguise it with her knowledge of make-up, but had so distorted what she tried to do that she looked even more terrible, like a caricature of a human being. "You know, like now." Chookian looked near tears.

He looked down at a pile of old journals, slipped into a

reverie, and was fingering the pages looking far away when I left his office.

After that when I was with her I tried to find the old enchantment, but it was no use. She still looked gray and rubbery, and I could not imagine what she must have been like before.

After a few remarkably simple telephone conversations with her ex-husband, arrangements were made for her to see her son on occasion. Her husband was extremely willing to help and during one phone conversation even started to talk about old times and how good things had been before she got sick, when in the background I heard his second wife angrily remind him that it was time to start getting dressed.

Elizabeth responded so well to her first visit with her son in over a year and improved so much that she returned to work from the hospital the next week. Things were going so well, in fact, that we were discussing plans for her to go home again within the month.

It was strict hospital policy that any letter written by a patient should be read and approved by his ward doctor before it was mailed, to keep threatening or harassing letters from reaching relatives and to keep the relatives' irate letters to the state hospital and the department of mental health to a minimum. Because Elizabeth worked outside the hospital and could write her own letters at work and mail them outside, it was impossible to read her mail. One day my secretary, Mrs. Braverman, handed me one of Elizabeth's letters that had been returned because of insufficient postage. It was written in pencil on white lined paper and was addressed to His Royal Highness Prince Philip, Buckingham Palace, London, England. The postmark was three days old. The letter read:

"Dear Prince Royal Phillip,
      If you wonder why you didn't see me on your last visit to America, it is because I am here in this

place where they are keeping me so long. So if you
didn't see me, it's no wonder. Therefore, I can't
blame you for not dropping in to visit. I'm writing
you because you're Greek too and a Mason. You
will understand a Greek girl. You know how they
treat Greek girls. And don't worry if you didn't see
me, because I'm all right. I'm just fine and I understand why you didn't come. I'll be outside next
time, so I hope to see you again. Please give my
personal regards to your wife, the queen, and all
the kids. You have a very nice family.

Yours truly,
Elizabeth the Pirate

I never mentioned the letter to her and discharged her the
next day as planned.

She left the hospital, talking about all the right things—
her plans about work and about visiting her son and having
him visit her some weekend—and concealed the hidden gran-
diosity which was bubbling below. As she walked down the
stone steps to the lawn her large pink ceramic earrings glit-
tered and tinkled about the shoulders of her yellow and purple striped dress. I smiled and wondered how it felt to know
that, no matter what people might think of her or how cruel
they might act toward her, down deep she was a pirate and a
friend of princes.

As I got more and more involved with the patients, I
had less and less time to myself. My friend Alan met me one
day walking across the lawn.

"What the hell are you always doing? Body Beautiful,
your nurse, says you don't answer your phone except in an
emergency. What the hell are you doing with your patients?"

"I don't know, just talking with them. Yesterday I sat
on the floor with a girl who hadn't seen a psychiatrist in
three years and was living camped inside her dress spread like
a tent, and . . ."

"And you cured her with a wave of your magic wand and out popped Dr. Glickman, who said, 'I've been trapped in the body of a dirty schizophrenic lady for years and you set me free, God bless you.' And now he's running the entire chronic service."

"You are really too much. That's just how he sounds, Al."

"No, *you* are too much! What are you really doing? What are you trying to prove? You aren't exactly scoring points with the powers that be, you know. Who are you going to get to write recommendations for you? Wouldn't it be nice if you had someone to recommend you to a private hospital staff? Some of the guys who teach here have a lot of pull and would send you private patients once you got into practice. Your absence is less than fondly missed from all the teaching conferences. You got one point on your side—Dr. Pellegrini likes you. But you want to spend your life working at a place like this? What the hell is going on? I mean, it's good to get enthusiastic about things, but you're overdoing it. I don't want to sound crass or anything, but you know you won't see patients like this in private practice so the whole experience is just academic. Even if you did see patients like this they'd never be able to pay their bills."

A patient walking across the lawn started toward us. I had approached her many times on the ward to try to speak with her, but each time she had walked away. She stood in front of me, blocking my path, not saying a word.

"Come on to lunch. I'll pay."

"Go ahead, Al. I'll be after you . . ." She stared at me for about ten minutes and then walked away.

The families of the patients were as interesting as the patients themselves. Much of the time I could predict just by looking at a group of visitors who belonged to which patient.

Once a visitor asked me, "The usual auditory phenomena that transcend equal thoughts—by that I mean the equalizing feeling thoughts that do not get freely expressed—do you think that could be the cause of some mental problem?" and I knew at once it was Gwendolyn's father, who was just as confused and obscure as Gwendolyn. Sometimes, as with Louise's family, the upsetting family members followed the patients to the hospital and tried to undermine what I was doing.

Louise—handsome black leopard lady running from her Pentecostal home with a handbag full of cigarette stubs. Policemen come looking for her children in the night. Shopkeepers watch her with a knowing smile and children on the street become silent when she approaches. Buildings lose their shape and the moon is angry. Windows cannot be seen through, they only reflect the people behind her. The sky is swimming and the sidewalks grab at her feet. Everyone knows her story and wants to punish and torment her. Footsteps in the corridor grow louder every night and when she sleeps, she feels the breath of animals behind her bed.

The first time she came into my office she looked at the walls and the floor. Before she sat down, she looked behind my desk and behind a print of Van Gogh's sunflowers.

"What are you looking for?"

"You know."

"I really don't."

"Don't play smart with me. I know when I am being recorded."

"There is no recorder here."

"Well, then, answer this question. Where is the intercourse machine? Where is it? Where do you keep it? I hear the footsteps in the hall when they drag it to my bed. The drugs you give me keep me powerless to move, but I still can hear the people setting it up on wheels, checking the pistons, running the motor. I'm no fool. You have to make them stop because it is driving me crazy. Why do you let them do it to me?"

Louise was pregnant with her fourth illegitimate child. Her overpowering mother came each day, Bible in hand, to promise a visitation of grief upon her and her sorrily conceived child. Louise would sit or hop back and forth like a sparrow at her mother's feet, or jump from chair to chair, cocking her head, looking to each side, growing more restless with every verse the old woman read. She could not sit still, but her mother always held her captive until the visiting hour ended.

Then Louise would begin her nightly search for the intercourse machine and offer prayers in lipstick on the bathroom mirrors and walls and write psalms on toilet paper and stuff them into my mailbox, pleading that I stop sending the machine to her at night and let her live in peace.

Other families were so disorganized and sick themselves that they saw nothing wrong in what the patient was doing or what he thought or believed. Angela was from a family like that and I saw her admission to the hospital as an event purely of chance. It could just as well have been any other member of her family, and under the stress of a restricting hospitalization—a confinement with the loss of civil rights— they would have acted just as psychotic, just as hostile, just as strange.

The world is against Angela and against her mother and her sisters, too. It lurks behind moving Venetian blinds and stares out, planning ways to deceive them. Members in a subtle plot study every movement they make. Supermarket clerks survey their shopping lists and make special notes on the side of the cash register. Even though they look so polite, appear so helpful, bank tellers scrutinize their family accounts and make errors on purpose to test Angela's vigilance.

No matter where they go or how carefully they conceal their plans, the family is sure to find a knowing stranger waiting for them and following them with his eyes.

Angela was in a convent for eleven months. Her confessor called her overscrupulous and complained that she confessed too much. Angela questioned the piety and sincerity of her superiors and found contradictions in her Bible and suspected its author. Was this really the word of God or a trick to test her faith; should she believe in it or would her trust prove her to be unworthy? Had Isaiah been rewritten?

At vespers she would turn her head and listen to the others pray. Were they praying against her? Did they have a code? Did they say angel when they meant Angela? Did they know of her impurities? Had her confessor broken his trust?

When she became certain that the peculiarly personal sermons were directed at her, she began to pray alone at night in the chapel and ask for directions, for she had begun to feel uneasy with others and was unable to concentrate on her devotions.

Angela was not doing well in the convent and she returned the kindest offer of help with a cold stare and a hard, biting lip. "There is nothing wrong with me," she would say. She accused the others, but was always so guarded and cryptic that no one knew what she was talking about. Gradually the others returned her coldness and she became desperately alone and isolated.

One evening during the prayer before supper, she accidently brushed her spoon from the table. She was not sure how it happened. She hadn't meant to do it. Perhaps she hadn't done it at all. A dozen irritated faces glared at her and she grew cold inside. Perhaps it was a sign? Only those who were not praying sincerely would have noticed it. So the spoon told her who was impure and who she should not trust. She clutched it to her heart and offered a silent prayer of thanksgiving. At last *He* would show the way.

She began to drop the spoon at meals, at meditation, and at mass, and it revealed in time that only she was pure and all the others were angry and jealous of her. It became very difficult for her, and her family came to take her home. She took the spoon, her relic, with her.

"What are they trying to do to us now?" her mother asked when they drove away.

At the very first stop on the way home Angela showed the powers of the spoon, and when success could not be denied, her mother crossed herself. Angela was the keeper of the spoon, and it was never again questioned.

Angela was the liveliest member of the family and the only one who was not resigned to being persecuted. She alone struggled against the angry shadows that played on her bedroom wall at night. She had called the police every day until her spoon showed that they, too, were in on the plot. Her letters and pleas to the authorities gave her away and the police surgeon signed her commitment papers. Over the protests of her mother, she was taken away to the hospital.

The spoon never failed her. She walked around the hospital grounds wearing a hooded cape and dropped the spoon again and again to see who became angry with her. In time even the most unsuspected would be shown for what they were. Her family came to visit and fed her rumors about the patients on the ward and the doctors' evil plans, and told of the poison in her soup. They planned the week together and decided whom Angela should test and smiled their smiles of contentment and pride, still marveling that she had been chosen.

If families intruded upon the lives of some patients, the absence of a family provided the most painful hurt. Hannah had come to the United States the year after World War II ended, and in the years that followed she did very poorly and spent much of her time in this mental hospital.

She had survived Auschwitz, had somehow lived through that nightmare, through that pestilence of hate and famine. But she paid a price of lingering guilt and constant fear that somehow managed to find the thread of a loss, of abandonment in everything around her. She had stood on the railroad platform holding up her crippled father, helping him walk. A German officer had put his hand between them and sent her to the left, to work as long as she was healthy and to be used in barbaric experiments when she grew too weak; he sent her father to the right, to his death, to become a haunting memory of a man limping away among the confused and frightened, a memory that never left her.

Hannah had been in group therapy for several years as an out-patient. When her group ended, she was unable to tolerate the loss of the other members and the leader and she grew despondent and cold inside. She had no living relatives and the only person who cared about her was an upstairs neighbor who feared that Hannah would kill herself. She did not want to go to the hospital "to live in a barracks," as she called the dormitory, but she became more and more confused and eventually arrived on my ward.

Dr. Charpentier, a member of the senior staff, was Glickman's best friend. He was a very unpopular man who had tried his hand in the world of private practice but, finding that he was unable to make a living, had given it up for a position at the hospital as a research fellow. Other doctors just would not refer private patients to him and those patients that did come to him did not stay with him. He saw himself as a very important man, but gave his feelings away by demanding obedience to his every wish, even when he had no authority to make demands. He had a federal research grant to be in charge of a study of antidepressant drugs in which some patients would be given an antidepressant, others a mild tranquilizer, and others a placebo. He needed a certain number of patients for his results to be statistically valid, and he had ordered every resident to place on the study all new admissions who were depressed.

Before I had even seen Hannah, he had already written for a research drug in the order book and placed her on the study. I was boiling. He hadn't consulted me. Neither the antidepressant being tested nor the tranquilizer was considered particularly effective, and I would not have given her either of them. I felt that Hannah, who had endured cruel experimentation during her life, did not belong in any experiment. Any truth that might be discovered would certainly be colored by her responses to being experimented upon. Further, Charpentier insisted that all the patients on the study remain in the hospital for a minimum of ten weeks, and I felt that this restriction would be seen by Hannah as an imprisonment. I had just interviewed Hannah when I walked into the nurses' office.

"Miss Owens, may I have my order book?"

"You've seen Hannah already? You're gonna love this. Dr. Charpentier has just written an order on her." Owens hated Charpentier because he felt a need to point out to her what a liberal he was and how she "was a model for other black girls to look up to."

"That bastard . . ." I began.

"Oh, I'm going to have to shut this door. I can see that. Just a minute, sugar, and you can yell or scream or whatever."

"He didn't even ask me. He has no right to do anything except read my order book, unless it's an emergency. Hospital policy! Is this an emergency?"

"No but if it were, honey, you sure don't give placebos in an emergency."

I wrote a very readable note in the order book in big letters that covered two lines each: "Discontinue all orders on this patient. No orders are to be written on this case by anyone except Dr. Stevens, unless directed to do so by him over the telephone. He may be called *at any time* at home for clarification, telephone 444-5671. New orders follow . . ." Then I wrote the usual hospital orders and started Hannah on the medication she had been taking and had done well with three years before.

"Let me see that. Oh, boy. Oh, brother." Miss Owens sank back in her chair.

"Clear?"

"Yes sir, you're the boss, boss."

"Questions?"

"What's your blood type?" She laughed as she started copying the orders.

"You think I'm going to have some problems?"

"Sugar, you already *got* problems. You're the doctor on this ward as far as I know. The nursing manual says that I do what you say, providing I don't feel it's against my best judgment. So what you say makes sense. I just follow my orders and tell Charpentier that you don't allow nobody to look in your sweet little order book. 'Cept me. 'Cause I'm a credit to my race."

"Any other problems cooking on the ward?"

"No, but I can start a small fire in a closet if things get too dull. You go home and get a good night's sleep. Tomorrow is gonna be your big day. I have a feeling."

I returned home to my apartment and looked for Anne and the kids. No one was home. Then I remembered that Anne had taken the kids to visit her folks in Connecticut. I had completely forgotten. The house was full of little notes —to leave the laundry out, to skip the milk order, to look in the refrigerator. A platter of fried chicken became my consolation and companion for the night. I couldn't call my in-laws because the lines were down in a rainstorm. I would see them on Saturday. I did not want to think about tomorrow.

Anne had never let me down. I tried not to bring my problems at work home with me, but sometimes it was impossible. When Ben hanged himself I had felt so guilty and unsure of myself that it had taken a week for things at home to return to normal. I was tense and moody, but Anne was always there. She was a good listener and really cared about what I was doing, not just because I was her husband but because she was interested. The only time she ever got upset was when I didn't know what I wanted. Sometimes she had the only view of me that I found worth depending on.

I could always forget myself with Michael. Although he was only four he was great fun to romp and play with, even if he did hit below the belt sometimes. Jeremy was two and although he was bright, he was not much for extended conversations about anything. Michael and I tolerated him fairly well, we thought. And Anne tolerated us all. I would have given anything for Jeremy to spill something on my lap at supper.

I turned on the television and dozed off and on during the evening. When, finally, the late show ended, I awoke with a start, showered, checked the locks twice—something I had never done before—and went to bed, feeling the empty space beside me.

Ten

A very rainy, gray April morning, and I overslept. It was already seven-thirty, and I was supposed to be at an appointment with Ricky Kelly at eight. I pushed the button on the shaving cream can and the lather missed my hand and landed on the floor. I tried again and covered my face with a mask of white foam and then turned the light on. As I uncovered more and more of my face with the razor and began to see myself in the mirror, I remembered the day before and I remembered Hannah.

Charpentier had probably spoken to Glickman and made some plans to talk with me. I did not want to go to the hospital. I did not want to talk with them. I did not want to be questioned about my sincerity, my mental health, my personal problems, my attitudes toward research. I did not want to hear what everyone thought of me, who looked in my direction with great alarm, who seriously questioned whether I should be a psychiatrist. I did not want to be treated like a little boy.

No time for anything to eat. Doctor who-is-it in the paper says that breakfast is the most important meal. A vitamin pill, the bottle's almost empty. Coat, where's my keys? My keys to the apartment—ah, here. The keys to the ward? Where? On my dresser. No. Damn. Kitchen. *No.* Oh, come on, where did you leave them? Bathroom? No. It's getting late. On the coffee table. No. Check yesterday's jacket. Right where you left them!

It was raining very hard, traffic was slow, crawling, splashing, the convertible top was leaking, every light red, always in the slowest lane. The overpass finally, the budding botanical gardens, the front gate. I parked and ran to the building where I treat Ricky, ten minutes late. Ricky would be beside himself—he could not tolerate my being late. I opened the office door, which was always unlocked, and went in. Ricky, who was usually ahead of me, was not there. The office was empty. I went to the mirror to comb my hair. I was soaked. I looked terrible. I had cut myself shaving in three places and looked gray.

It was a sparse office that the residents shared for treating patients. Outside on the door there was a schedule that we all filled in, each claiming a certain hour on a certain day. I had eight o'clock every day except Wednesday— Ricky's hours. I saw my other patients in the building where my ward was. There were a leather couch and several large leather chairs, a moth-eaten Oriental rug that someone had donated when it became too worn to keep, and a rubber plant with a tiny ceramic footbridge and a pagoda and two small plastic Chinese figures. I would not have minded spending the rest of the day there with them among the blue and silver pebbles.

"Sorry I'm so late," began Ricky, walking through the door. "I came by at eight and you weren't here yet, so I figured that the rain had kept you and I got us some coffee. You take yours black? They only had chocolate doughnuts. Is that okay?"

"Ricky, thank you. I'm starved. I'm sorry I was late."

"It's okay." He seemed to mean it. He didn't look sullen or hurt. He seemed very pleased with himself and so calm and casual that a stranger seeing us together would have thought we worked together. And he had brought me a gift, food.

"You seem relaxed and, well, so calm, Ricky."

"Something's happening to me. Something gradual, something odd."

"What's it like?"

"Well, it started when we began talking about my mother. You know, I thought that you were crazy asking my father and my aunt to bring in pictures of my mother and pictures of me when I was small, but she's become very real to me in the past month. Do you know that today was my mother's birthday? And do you know that for the first time it means something to me? For the first time I feel that I know the person I miss. I really think that I know who my mother was. I began reading her school record and her letters to my father and some of the other things she had."

"Like what?"

"Well, I didn't tell you this yesterday because I wanted some more time to think about things, but last weekend at home I spent almost the entire time in the attic. My father kept running around the house saying, 'Ricky's cracking again. He's hiding.' But I wasn't at all. I found some old trunks and started going through them. I found my baby book that my mother kept of me. A white satin thing, really terribly corny. Did you know I weighed almost nine and a half pounds at birth? I was a fat son of a bitch. You wouldn't believe it to look at me now. I was a regular monster. But my mother made all these little notes in this book—what I ate, who I liked. Did you know that I hated my Uncle Harold even then? My mother said, in the book, that he used to pinch me all the time. I knew he was a cruel bastard."

Ricky lit a cigarette, and his eyes grew glassy and wet.

"She said that I was a beautiful baby and the son that she wanted more than anything else in the world. And she wrote about the games she played with me, and she used to call me 'Sonny' and I remembered that. I remember her calling me Sonny."

He could not stop the tears that were running down his cheeks.

"And she wrote, on my fourth birthday, the January before she died—she knew she was dying—'Happy birthday little Sonny. Poor baby, what will you do without me?' "

Ricky started sobbing.

"Oh, Dr. Stevens, I remember her calling me Sonny."

He got up and sipped his coffee, which was cold, and then put it down. He walked around the room and looked at me.

"You know, you take a lot of shit from me," he sobbed.

"You're not that bad, Ricky."

"Dr. Stevens, are you crying?"

"I guess. Yes."

I stood up and walked over to Ricky and we found ourselves hugging each other and crying together. Then we sat down again. A few minutes passed.

"Ricky, would you like to try working at your old job during the days and staying at the hospital nights?"

"You mean back in the office, in the insurance company?"

"I think you can make it. You've helped out around here a lot and Mrs. Britton, the secretary in the C Building, thinks you can handle yourself."

"She's a patient in C Building, isn't she? Boy, she flies off the handle. Can you imagine depending on her evaluation of me for me to get out of here?"

"I think you can do it. Mrs. Britton may get upset, Ricky, but she knows a good office worker when she sees one."

"My father will be breathing down your neck, saying that you are crazy. I can hear him now: 'You think that a boy who spends all his weekends home from the hospital up in an old attic is ready to go back to work?' My father is a stupid Irish bastard." Ricky looked at me to see if I was serious. I was.

"I'll call for an interview with the personnel manager. He's a good shit. I'll get around him," he said. He was smiling broadly.

"Ricky, you have spent so much of your life running away from your feelings about your mother that in the past you have never been able to deal with what is happening in the present. I see this as a new beginning for you."

"What will happen to our sessions when I go to work? I start at nine o'clock." He was avoiding my comment.

"I'll see you at seven. That's pretty easy to do."

"You know why I didn't mind you coming late this morning? Because for the first time I feel like I have something to fall back on. I'm not anonymous any more. I have a past. I don't have to depend on what is going on in the present to know who I am, or to know whether anyone cares for me. My mother really loved me, you know. She really did, and I remember that, I know that. Your being late doesn't mean that you don't like me—I know you like me. I feel so different."

It was getting late and I had to make rounds on my ward at nine. "Ricky, I'll see you tomorrow."

My coffee was too cold to drink but I grabbed my doughnut. I walked Ricky down the hall and the front stairs, chewing the doughnut on the way to my office. "Good luck, Ricky."

"Thanks, see you."

I was walking on air. Five months of the most intensive work I had ever done had begun to pay off. Ricky was no longer on any medications. He had been on maximum doses of tranquilizers when he first came to the hospital to control his running and wild activity, but he didn't need medicine any more. He had moved out of the locked ward to the dormitory and finally to a single room in the front ward. He worked in the office sorting patients' records and he helped out in occupational therapy. He was extremely clever, and in spite of the fact that he had flunked out of college his first year he had the ability to get through and do well.

Today Ricky had found a missing link in his feelings. It was so rare that this sort of thing happened, so rare that someone understood and felt at the same time. I was whistling and bouncing down the walk, smiling at the patients who had come out after the rain had stopped. An old man was splashing in a puddle, jumping up and down, just like a kid. As I approached him I heard "dum dum dum dum," and recognized him.

"Merrill, how are you?"

"DUM DUM DUM."

Merrill kept jumping away, splashing himself, and I went into my building. The long hall was always filled with patients who had off-ward privileges, which meant exactly that—they could go out on the hospital grounds but had to return for meals and medications. Many of them stayed in the hall waiting for the doctors to ask us questions or just touch us to make sure we were still alive.

"Dr. Stevens, can I go home for Easter?" asked Connie, who had no home to go to. "Please—okay if that is the way you're gonna be. I'll stay here. Do you like my new dress?"

"Yes, blue is my favorite color."

"I got it from the Salvation Army."

"Dr. Stevens." An old Italian woman pushed her way to me. "You gonna find my children? Huh? That's what I wanna know. When you do that? Huh?" The same questions every day, all day.

"They'll visit when they come, but that's not for two months."

"Where are dey? Santa Maria. Don't dey love momma no more?" She started crying and went into the lounge. I opened my office door and walked in.

"Oy vey, are you going to get it," said Mrs. Braverman. Funny, interested, efficient, and fiercely loyal. "You got wolves at your door this morning. Let me lock it so we can talk undisturbed." She got up and bolted the door. Everyone else was at conference. "What did you do last night? Dr. Charpentier, that S.O.B., read your order and just about took a shit, excuse my language. He started raving and yelling. He was going to teach you a thing or two. He said that when he was finished with you that you wouldn't be able to work in a toilet."

"Oh, Jesus." I sat down and put my feet up on my desk.

"You've done it. He and Glickman have been talking since eight, sending out for your record, trying to set up an appointment with Larkin. What did you do? I know, I know. It's Hannah Zimmerman. I can understand your thinking. Oh, they are such bastards. I would have done the same thing. Look, do you want me to call my husband? He's six two and weighs over two hundred. He'll just give them a good clop and that will be that."

"Braverman, sit down. You are making me nervous."

"If your mother knew, she'd have a fit."

"What has my mother got to do with all this?"

"Oy, all men are such bastards. You don't know what your mother had to do with your being here, and you call yourself a doctor?"

I broke up laughing. Mrs. Braverman started laughing too and we went into convulsions, and it wasn't even funny. I was just so afraid that anything seemed funny.

"Look, they are going to want to see you in a conference or something. Now you go in and be real polite, hair combed nice and try to . . ."

"Try to what?"

"I don't know. What did you do wrong? You disagreed with them. That's what you did wrong. You are a chronic disagreer."

My telephone rang. It was Alan. "Bob?"

"Hi, Alan. What's up?"

"It's all around the hospital."

"Are you talking about the fence?" I didn't want to make a joke. I just blurted it out.

"Be serious. Your fight with Charpentier."

"I haven't even seen him today. As a matter of fact, I haven't seen him since last week, and then I just said hello."

"Well, he's been over to my building to get Glickman and they went out together talking about you. Be cool about it and bend a little."

"Thanks for tipping me off, Al."

"Let me know how it turns out."

"As soon as I know anything."

Someone was at the door. Braverman got up and opened it, and there was a messenger with a note for me.

Dear Dr. Stevens,
  Drs. Glickman and Charpentier have requested a meeting with you in my office at 10:30 today. Because of the urgency of the question, your attendance is mandatory.

Yours truly
Harry Larkin, MD

I had met Larkin only twice before. He had seemed pleasant and understanding, and he had seemed fair, but I wasn't sure.

"That's in a half hour. What are you going to do?"

"I'm going to write a short statement. I want three copies." Braverman got her steno pad and took down my note.

"Is that all? It's very short. How shall I address it? Are you sure this is what you want to say?"

"Hurry."

She typed it up, placed the original and the copies in an official-looking hospital envelope, handed it to me, and sat down. We watched the clock in silence until it was twenty-five past. Then I got up and walked through the hall crowded with patients still pushing for the same requests. Residents were coming down from the conference upstairs.

"Hi, Bob." It was Jerry Bieberman.

"Hi."

"You missed a great conference on the use of lithium in manic states."

"You got notes?"

"Yuh, but everything you need to know is in the circular that comes with the samples. Here."

"Thanks, Jerry."

I made my way across the lawn to the administration building. I had timed it exactly. At ten-thirty I was right at Larkin's secretary's desk. She was dour (at least she seemed dour to me) and white-haired, wearing a seersucker summer suit. Older people tend to rush the seasons a little; perhaps they are afraid they will not make it to the next one.

"Dr. Stevens. Go in. They are waiting for you." I started in. "Dr. Stevens, I couldn't help but look at your record when it came across my desk. It's very impressive."

"Thank you." That was very unexpected.

I walked through the heavy door into Larkin's office. Charpentier and Glickman were sitting on a sofa and Larkin was at his desk, being conversational and pleasant.

"Come in, Dr. Stevens. Right on time," he began. "There seem to be a lot of ruffled feathers around here, and you seem to be the culprit. How's that for a direct opening? Would you like a coffee? How do you take it?"

"Black."

He pushed the intercom button. "Mary, bring us four coffees, two black, two regular. Stevens, sit down."

I found a comfortable chair and sank into it. I felt the envelope in my inside jacket pocket. Glickman and Charpentier did not look my way and they did not say anything.

"Well, Dr. Charpentier," said Larkin, "why don't you begin? You wanted this meeting."

"Ahem, hmmm. Hmmm." Charpentier always cleared his throat, even before saying hello. "Dr. Stevens has willfully disregarded an order which has become accepted policy by refusing to place a depressed patient on the drug study. Is that so, Dr. Stevens?"

"Yes," I said.

"Don't try and deny it," shouted Glickman. "We have a copy of the order sheet here."

"Show it to him, Dr. Glickman," said Dr. Charpentier.

"What did you say, Dr. Stevens?" asked Larkin.

"I said yes."

"Yes what?" said Glickman, waving the copy of the sheet in my face.

"Yes, it was true that I refused to place a depressed patient on the study."

"See? See how headstrong and antiauthoritarian he is? I tried to tell him when I was supervising him that his personal problems interfere with his judgment. He won't listen. He's paranoid. That's what he is." Glickman turned red. It was suddenly like a circus, like a game. These people didn't seem real. Larkin was just sitting back taking it all in, looking blank and official.

"You feel that you can disregard authority and policy whenever you feel like it. Is that right, Stevens?" Charpentier was shouting. "You and your impulsive behavior. Taking the short-term answer for problems. If these anti-intellectuals do not allow basic research to flourish then we will never know what it is we are doing. Stevens' attitude is unscientific, wanton, and irresponsible. Dr. Glickman and I have spent a great deal of time trying to talk some sense into him but he just goes and does things the way he wants."

Larkin's secretary came in with coffee and doughnuts and left them on a low table by Larkin's desk.

Glickman stood up and walked toward me, stopping halfway between me and the desk. "Dr. Stevens, I feel, seriously jeopardizes the authority and the morale of this institution. His attitude toward therapy is appalling, and I must be quite candid when I say that he is one of the worst residents I have ever supervised. He is unwilling to heed sound advice, refuses to recognize his own psychoneurotic problems and the way in which they interfere with his work, and he refuses to do anything about correcting them. To top it off, when this suggestion was last made to him he felt so threatened that he had to terminate our relationship. He refused to get the proper permissions before doing this."

Charpentier began, "Ahemm. Mmmm. The depression-drug study is the most important study we have done in this hospital in years."

"What are the conditions which you must meet to keep the grant?" asked Larkin.

"Hmmm. That the patients shall all be diagnosed as depressed, that I follow the protocol established in the original grant, a certain number of patients."

"Was there any date of expiration?"

"Hmmm. Yes."

"When is it?"

"In two months."

"Well, will you make it?"

"It's close, but that should be no problem."

"How many patients do you have so far?"

"Twelve."

"And you need?"

"Twenty."

"I would say that is going to be hard to meet unless you get every newly admitted depressed patient onto that study."

"I knew you would understand."

"It's not hard to understand," said Larkin. "I've done a great deal of drug research myself. It put three kids through college. Tell me, Dr. Glickman, what about Stevens' patients? How are they doing? Do they reflect the way in which you say he is falling short?"

"I believe so, Dr. Larkin. If I had the records here I could show you."

"I had them sent over myself this morning. Very interesting, Stevens. They are right, you know. You certainly have broken with some traditions. Pushing patients, aggravating the staff, having conferences with aides to teach them how to talk with patients when everyone knows that aides shouldn't be aware of the things *you* tell them. They might get out of hand like Stanley Dukakis did and cause a little trouble!"

Charpentier and Glickman broke into smiles that went from one face to the other. Larkin continued. "You pushed people out of the hospital when other people said not to. Most of them came back. You don't go to conferences. Why, Stevens?"

"I came here to learn from the patients."

"You know enough to do that?"

"I don't know. I see a case and go home and read. I find most conferences worthless and I would rather be with a patient."

"It also says in these reports that when you were on the chronic service you sent two patients home. That's where they are now. Dr. Charpentier, you were on that ward for two years when you were a resident years ago. You did not get into trouble. You did not aggravate the staff. You were on a similar ward for a year yourself, Dr. Glickman, and you stayed out of trouble." They both smiled again.

Larkin got up from behind his desk and walked across to an easy chair that his patients used and sat down. "Gentlemen, it's been fifteen years, but do you remember how many patients the two of you sent home in the three years you were on that ward?" The two of them thought and seemed to be counting something in their heads. "Neither of you sent one patient off that ward. Not one patient. But you were cautious."

"Stevens, how many patients did you try to move?"

"All of them, Dr. Larkin."

"You must know that some of these people are hopeless. On that ward especially. What happened there? What is the result to date?"

"Well, John Higgens and Larry Feldman are both out working and live at home with their families. They are very shaky, but they are home. There were six others who went out but were unable to stay, and twelve went to nursing homes because I didn't feel the hospital was the best place for them."

"Too soon," said Glickman mournfully, as if I had ruined whatever I had touched. "You've moved them too soon."

"You don't have our experience, you know," continued Larkin. "We could have told you not to bother. They'll be back. It would be so much easier if they stayed here and you treated them over the long term like Dr. Glickman does."

"But I couldn't just sit and do nothing."

"You see what I mean. This neurotic drive of his." Glickman was having a field day.

"What are the contraindications for including a patient on a study like this?" Larkin asked.

"Besides known allergy to the drugs, I know of none." Charpentier looked pleased and relaxed.

Larkin motioned to me. "What do you have to say?"

I took my statement out and handed a copy to everyone in the room. They read it in silence.

Dr. Larkin walked across his office to the window, and after a moment read my letter aloud:

I have not allowed Miss Hannah Zimmerman to be a subject on the antidepressant drug study because I do not feel it to be in her best interest. First, she responds best to a drug which is not included in the study. Second, she sees research as experimentation, and because she suffered cruelly in the war she would see this as another injury. Finally, her most recent hospitalizations lasted one month at most. To demand that she stay in the hospital for almost three months, merely for the sake of the research grant, would risk her becoming dependent on the hospital and becoming unable to function outside.

Charpentier cleared his throat several times and asked, "Well, Dr. Larkin, are you going to tell him what to do?"

Larkin walked back to his desk and sat down, looking amazingly stern and angry. "First of all, Dr. Stevens, I must tell you that I am the only one in this hospital who sets policy and I do so with a consensus. Second, no resident of mine is ever going to act wantonly or in an antiauthoritarian way flaunt convention for rebelliousness' sake. The first policy of this hospital is that the patient's care is the direct and sole authority of the resident caring for him. No one has any right to interfere with that privilege without prior agreement with the resident.

"I think that your behavior is a little different and even eccentric at times but there is no indication that you have shown poor judgment or acted against the best interests of the patients. Dr. Glickman, I think we can leave Dr. Stevens' mental health out of this. The question seems silly and won't solve any problems.

"Now, regarding this study, Charpentier, it would seem to me that it is Dr. Stevens' privilege to keep his patient off the study if he chooses. We expect that he will be willing to cooperate in research, but it's his final decision. I might add that Miss Zimmerman is not suited for the study."

"Hmmmm."

Dr. Glickman was staring down at his feet. His face was covered with sweat. Charpentier looked very anxious.

"Well, if there is nothing more to discuss I would like to have a word with Dr. Stevens alone." They both nodded in silence and walked out. "Dr. Stevens," Larkin said when the door was closed. "It's Robert?"

"Yes. Robert."

"I spoke to your other supervisor, Dr. Pellegrini, and asked him about you. I think your work with the patients is in keeping with your general record to date. I've seen you at a few seminars myself, so I know you go to the ones you think worthwhile. I wish I could avoid the dull ones myself. Being selective is no crime, but neither is being cooperative. Glickman is especially troublesome. We've been trying to get rid of him and I guess he's trying to get back at us. And Charpentier, well . . . let's not talk about that. I'd like to talk to you about our training program some afternoon."

"I'd like to. I have a lot of ideas."

"I'm sure. Well," he said, holding out his hand, "Robert, keep up the good work. Tell Hannah that I'll drop by to see her sometime tomorrow."

"I don't understand."

"I admitted her to the hospital when I was a resident twenty years ago. We're good friends and I always come by to chat. If you had placed her on the study you would have heard from me."

I started to smile and walked out of the office past Larkin's secretary, who was leaving for lunch. As I was strolling around the grounds slowly, seeing everything in a warm orange light in spite of the overcast sky, I met Dr. Pellegrini, who was coming from the dining room. We walked silently for a few minutes and then I told him what had happened. He was very excited about Ricky and felt that he was really getting better and had made an important step forward in his life. He shrugged his shoulders repeatedly while I told him about the scene in Larkin's office.

Pellegrini sat down on a wet bench and looked dreamily at the breaking clouds. "I am not really sure any more what is sane and what is mad. Sometimes we call things sane just because they seem more logical. That is what's really crazy. Being logical doesn't make something right or more feeling or more humane." Pellegrini put his arm around me.

"Bob, I don't give a shit. If you are not a good person, you can't be a good psychiatrist. You've got to care and you've got to show it. If you don't, no matter how bright you are or how much you know, your patients won't trust you. You can do what some of these clowns do. You can call patients' mistrust by a fancy name and say that it is their fault for not confiding in you. Being a psychiatrist doesn't automatically mean that a person is worth confiding in. Oh, some of the time you'll be right, but most of the time you'll just be covering up for your shortcomings."

I ran to my car, started the motor up, and headed for Connecticut with the accelerator pushed to the floor. I had to tell Anne.

Eleven

The admitting floor was the most jarring, most uncertain, most unpredictable place in the hospital. Ordinarily very little was scheduled there and emergency calls took precedence over everything else. When you were asked to do something it was generally at some hour of the morning when you were least prepared to think things through. There would be an average of three admissions to the hospital each evening, three lost people who would be accepted and taken in.

There were usually nine or ten others who came to the emergency floor. Someone might walk in off the street at midnight, having suddenly decided that something that had bothered him for years had been permitted to go too far, and now he wanted something done about it right away. He would become angry if you said you couldn't help him or if you referred him to the out-patient clinic.

When the weather got colder an entire population of human beings whose existence I had not even imagined would come out of the coal bins of apartment houses and the hallways of steel and glass buildings, from the men's rooms of bus terminals, ring the bell to the emergency ward, and present themselves, shivering and destitute, saying that they were crazy and that they needed help.

Alcoholics were the most frequent emergency visitors. They were very unpopular with the senior members of the staff because they were too difficult to treat and because when the weather cleared up or the ice thawed they would leave the hospital. They made our lives miserable because it was very difficult to refuse shelter to a man when he was dressed in rags and looked beaten and worn out. It was very hard to say, "If you want treatment, come back when you're sober," as you had been instructed to do.

There were others who came in the night, who rang the bell at the foot of the stairs and asked to come in—wives running from their husbands, debilitated old people being thrown out of a nursing home because they were difficult to manage after their room was changed or when they became unreasonable because they had no visitors. I remember a father who brought his retarded son to the hospital after a long, heated fight with his wife over what television program they should watch. She threatened him with the loss of other entertainment and he turned his anger on their son. He teased the boy during the afternoon while she was working and then hid his supper, claiming that the son had already eaten it. The boy threw a tantrum, and the father called him crazy and tried to commit him.

There were prostitutes who had become psychotic and who propositioned me before I had a chance to get their names. There were transfers from medical hospitals who had become disturbed during their stay for a medical disease. Some were sent back to the hospitals, some were sent home, and some we kept.

There were about a dozen rooms on the admitting floor where the new patients stayed and were observed for a few days before they were presented to a disposition conference, and there was also a large examining room and several offices. Very little, it seemed, happened in the daytime. It was always at night when things got busy.

When you had admission duty you were entitled to a free supper, and I always stretched this out as long as I could. It got very lonely in the hospital. The evening would be long and the few colleagues who stayed for supper would soon leave. Unless I felt like playing cards with the aides or making rounds, I would usually sit around and read, waiting for the telephone to ring.

And the telephone did ring! The hospital served a very large area. Whenever someone at another hospital was not sure about what he should do with a patient or could not decide whether the patient was too sick to keep or whether he might get too sick to keep, he sent the patient our way. The police were frequent visitors, and I soon became quite friendly with many of them. They often asked how patients they had brought to the hospital a few weeks before were doing.

There were at least a dozen separate legal forms that would change the civil status of a human being from a citizen of the state to a mental patient, which implied the complete loss of civil rights. But commitment took away an even greater right—the right to be taken seriously and to have your opinions judged on the same basis as those of sane people. People could feel justified when they circled their fingers at their temples. The statement "Well, we all know that he's been in the state hospital" could destroy the strength of any point you could make. Would what was lost by being committed be overshadowed by the potential gains? My power frightened me.

Admission to the hospital created frustrations because even the most innocent of patients' requests would be analyzed by the staff and scrutinized for a deeper meaning, and even when no deeper meaning could be found, patients would feel so unsure of themselves that they became afraid to make a judgment or a move. Almost everything a patient did after he was admitted to the hospital was assigned meaning and would be used to prove something about him or to make a diagnosis. The irony was that after one of the staff had the opportunity to get to know a patient and find out what he was really like, these often meaningless pieces of behavior were usually ignored anyway, and the patient was treated like a person. If he were treated like a person in the first place, and believed in, we probably would not have admitted him. How could we trust a person everyone on the outside said was crazy until we found that out for ourselves? There seemed to be something terribly wrong with this system. It made it easy to commit people unnecessarily and did not offer any help in controlling the very dangerous.

The law that lets psychiatrists commit people has no provision for erasing erroneous statements made and recorded about the patient at the time he is admitted to the hospital. Someday a secretary might refer to the patient's chart when forwarding an important summary, and sometimes the false is easier to remember than the truth, which is often hidden. Sometimes the major source of information in the family at the time of hospitalization is really sicker than the patient himself and the history the relative gives is really a distortion. All in all, people give up a great deal when they became mental patients.

But sometimes they gain a great deal. Frequently I

would find an old friend from the chronic wards sitting in the waiting room when I came down in the middle of the night. To someone discharged after years of institutionalization, the world would sometimes appear too rough, to unfeeling, too demanding to be dealt with all the time. Just being able to come back for a night or two was often all they needed to keep going.

The array of people who filled my life between one and five in the morning: the screaming and the crying, the bizarre, the numb, the inarticulate, the hostile, the unwashed and uncared for, the teenagers having a bad drug experience, the men with delirium tremens, the suicidal and the homicidal. If there was a name to call it, I saw it at its worst.

When people came in the night and asked for help, I tried my best. Sometimes they would not know how to ask, sometimes they would not understand when help was given, and sometimes they would become very angry no matter what I said. Admitting someone to the hospital was something I never enjoyed, and the sounds of violence in the night tearing me from sleep, startled and confused, reminded me of danger in the night when I was young.

Deep night. A horrible sudden blast. What is happening? I am alone in my room, afraid. The fire-signal horn booms across the water. One—two—three—four blasts. One—two blasts, and they stop. Now lights go on and off. I hear fire engines starting up and their sirens screaming through the night air. They drive away. It is still again.

It was a quiet spring night on the admitting ward, hot, sultry, not a breeze anywhere. We tried to open some windows but unlocking and locking them again was more effort than it seemed worth. Midnight, and the ward was still. Since we had admitted only one patient that entire day there was practically nothing for us to do.

"Arnie, why don't you call out to Tony's for a couple of pizzas? No problem. I'll cover till you get back." The nurse put down the phone. Arnie, the attendant on the admitting floor, was always looking for an excuse to get away from the hospital.

"Doctor, would you like a pizza? Tony's makes a great meatball pizza. Come on, it'll clear out your sinuses." Arnie came down and went around the ward to the other attendants, filling out his list, and then left.

The patients had all gone to bed and we were sitting in the lounge watching the television with the sound turned off. It was always hilarious, especially the floor-wax commercials. Then two policemen came in, gently coaxing a stout Negro woman dressed in a very smart bright green suit.

"Here's her commitment papers. They found her lying in the gutter in front of Bonwit Teller's this evening, just as silent and as peaceful as this. Eyes wide open and all. She seemes to know what's going on. Didn't say a word at the station. Not one single word, did she, Jack?"

"Nope, not a sound."

"No handbag, no identification. Nothing, she just sat there for five hours. Didn't even move in the station."

"Not a peep. Not like some we've brought here, huh, doc?"

She stood under a light in the hall, one that was protected by a metal basket but was broken just the same. I asked her to come to my office and she followed very slowly, gliding, sliding, almost as if she were walking in slow motion. She had a flat, dead look, a blank, empty look, and yet she stared directly at me. Directly into my eyes. She refused to sit in the chair and remained at attention and watched me sit down and arrange some papers on the desk.

"I'm the admitting doctor." Even though I knew she

was catatonic and would not talk, I asked, "What's your name?"

Silence.

"Do you have any idea where you are?"

No response.

"Well, it's the state hospital."

Silence.

"Because you were found in the street and couldn't talk and seemed troubled by something and had no identification, you were brought here . . . I can see you don't feel like talking, but I can guess that something has upset you and I'd like to help you clear things up."

Silence . . . a few minutes passed.

"Well, I don't want to put you on the spot and make you feel even more uncomfortable. Perhaps tomorrow you'll feel like talking." I led her back to the sweltering waiting room past the travel posters and the dusty book shelves filled with tattered magazines that were all several months old. She sat down and I began to fill in the admission form.

I guessed at her age. 'A forty-three-year-old, well-dressed, very well-groomed Negro female found in the gutter and brought to the hospital on a Jane Doe warrant, silent but co-operative.' That doesn't make sense, I thought to myself. How can someone be silent and cooperative at the same time?

When I looked up she was gone, but where? I kept writing, thinking that the nurse knew where she was. Then I heard a slow, deliberate, very heavy pacing in the hall outside. It grew louder and more rapid, and I could also hear someone breathing very heavily, growing more intense. I stepped outside.

She was pacing back and forth from one end of the hall to the other, picking up speed. At first she didn't move her arms, and was walking fast, like a giant penguin. Then she flapped her arms wildly and started to run. She ran right up to the wall behind me and crashed into it, picked herself up, and ran again.

A transformation was taking place before my eyes. The placid face was becoming contorted. Wincing and pouting, she smacked her lips. She opened and shut her mouth rapidly with a menacing click. Her arms were now flapping like a wounded bird trying to get up enough speed to take off. She ran up and down the long corridor. People stirred in their beds off the ward and lights were turned on in the patients' rooms one by one.

She stamped her feet and pounded her body, jumping, leaping, bounding. At the end of the hall she turned and suddenly started to run at full speed toward us. Dropping magazines and Coke bottles, the attendants started after her. She was wall-eyed, but still she did not speak. Then she stopped suddenly at the widest part of the hallway in front of a large alcove where we sometimes interviewed patients with their families.

She stopped and looked directly ahead for a moment and then with a sudden motion her whole body quivered, shook—a convulsion. She gritted her teeth and clenched her fists and as she slowly lifted her tightened head and neck upward she shut her eyes.

It seemed as if every muscle in her body was tightening. The veins on her forearms and neck stood out, sweat was dripping from her face. She opened her mouth and her false teeth, first the uppers, then the lowers, glided past her lips as if they floated on her tongue and fell rattling to the floor. And she screamed. A long, high, tortured scream, as if the doors of hell had been opened. The noise filled my head. It stopped me from thinking. The aides were frozen. The nurses gaped. The patients in the hall moved back and some closed their doors and held them shut.

As suddenly as it started the screaming and the movement stopped. We were too stunned to move or say anything or understand what was going on. Then, suddenly, she began to tense all over again. And it came, a flow of speech, a flood of words. A torrent. The dam had broken.

"Jesus Christ our Lord and Savior fill the world with the word. And the blood run from the rocks. And heaven cry unto the wilderness that it was those same God's children who share his plight on Jesus' cross. And heaven bless and keep the harlots of the night and the dark places. Mother Mary come back from behind that rock and wipe his face, you hear me? Wipe the blood off Jesus' face. Wipe Jesus' face. Wipe away my sins and the sins of your children. Slaves and masters, wipe them all away. Hear O Israel, I am the savior of the heathen Malekites, Izzabites, the Tablitites. Save your lord and master, your resurrection, your Mennonite, your damned and your dying."

The hall was filled with confused people rubbing their eyes and trying to figure out what was going on, with angry people shaking their fists because they had been awakened, with hot people crowded too close together, with tired people, with curious people who wanted to get closer to see but stepped back whenever she got louder, with frightened people.

There was a circle around her. No one really wanted to get close. It was a voice like a kettle drum, booming, blasting, hollow and full at the same time. The words spewed out, bounding against the ceiling and drowning us all in leaping vibrations.

"The Hittites, the Ishmaelites, all brethren to serve the Lord. Save the Lord. Serve the Lord. Oh mother Mary, I cry for you. Mary, suck on my breasts. World of blackness everlasting from the depths of destruction and rage rip the poor Tablitites asunder, burn baby away from mother. Bloody nipples crusted over, Mary's forgotten while they kill her chile."

A sixteen-year-old girl with long blond hair who had been admitted to the ward that morning for bizarre behavior sat in the doorway of her room on the ward, giggling and smirking, trying to hold back gales of laughter with her bony fingers.

With a frantic fury, the voice began to scream. Eyes closed, head raised high, a scream.

Some patients headed for their rooms, nervously looking back down the hall as they retreated as if giving a rodeo rider room to ride.

Screaming, her hands slowly started to rise over her head, making rigid and plastic gestures as they did, contorted fingers, pulling and being pulled by imaginary ropes. At once she began to rip off her clothes and throw them into the air, still screaming—her green suit jacket, a silk blouse, her shoes, her bra. Everything seemed to be in the air at once.

An aide, pimpled and anxious, moved to restrain her and grabbed her arm. Two others and a nurse, taking their cue, moved in at once.

Kicking and screaming, down on the floor, arching her back, fighting with demons, rolling and pulling, biting and scratching. Knees in white trousers were pressed against shoulders, ankles, and thighs. Grips were suddenly broken and were applied once again.

Finally, she was dragged, kicking, to a room at the end of the ward and given an injection to quiet her down. In a few minutes it was silent, peaceful, and still.

The nurse walked around reassuring the patients.

"Okay, okay now. Let's everyone go to bed. Come on, Frank, to bed. Frank, to bed."

Frank was very old and very confused, and in the excitement he had dressed himself all inside out. Arnie had just come back with the pizzas and the smell of oregano filled the floor. Frank couldn't understand why he wasn't getting any breakfast. He wasn't the one making trouble.

I was twenty minutes late for the next morning's conference because I had had a very difficult night and had gotten only two hours' sleep. I came straight from the on-call room without breakfast and sat down at the large conference table. The room was filled with people—the admissions supervisor, an English fellow whom I admired, another resident who greeted me by bumming my last cigarette, and the usual collection of aides, nurses, psychologists, and medical students. They were discussing a young man who had been admitted and placed in seclusion during the previous afternoon, before I came on duty.

"Why don't we have a totally objective interview this morning?" the supervisor began. "Stevens, since it seems you have never seen this boy and know nothing about him, I think you are best qualified to give us an opinion about his condition, without history, in the pure state, so to speak." That was not the ideal way to begin a day at the hospital; I would not find anything they didn't already know. They sent for the patient. "His name, by the way, is Gregory Mac-Donald. Scottish perhaps?"

He was about twenty-one or so and was shaking so badly that his chair vibrated against the table.

"I am one of the doctors on the staff here, and I'd like to get to know more about you," I began, angry that I had allowed myself to get into a situation like this.

He sat looking down at his hands.

"Can you tell me what brought you to the hospital?"

He gave no answer and I had not expected him to.

"What's been going on that has made you so upset?"

He suddenly stood up and leapt at me, punched me in the face several times, and scratched me. Two aides ran from the back of the room and grabbed him.

"Gregory, I'm not going to hurt you. If you don't feel like talking, I understand. It's very hard being in this place and I'd like very much to help you get out as soon as possible," I said, rubbing my nose, suddenly realizing that I had probably expressed *my* thoughts as well.

Gregory sat down, or more accurately, was deposited in his chair by the aides.

"Can you tell me how you feel right now?"

He leaped over at me again and this time one of his punches drew blood. The aides pinned him to the floor and then he was taken out unceremoniously.

The conference, which normally lasted only half an hour, was over. The supervisor scribbled a few notes in Gregory's chart. "Tough one, old man," he said, and walked out. It was the only comment made. I wiped the blood off of my face and pressed some napkins against my nose and hunted through a cardboard box and found half a muffin. The coffee pot was empty. There are better ways to start a day.

I called up Miss Owens on the ward to see how things were getting along. On days when I was covering the admissions floor I had to let my usual hospital business go pretty much unattended. It was impossible to keep my therapy hours and when I was doctor on call I canceled them. The only patient of mine who ever dropped by was Ricky. Sometimes therapy patients were upset when I had to work on admitting, but they learned that I was human and was not rejecting them.

"Dr. Stevens, guess what? They're going to give me my old job back." Ricky was delighted. He felt very confident, and would be starting the next Monday. We discussed plans for his discharge and made arrangements for him to continue treatment with me at the out-patient clinic of a large university hospital when I finished my residency in two months. In the past weeks things had moved very quickly for Ricky and he was to be discharged next month. He was beginning to think about school again. He would get better.

It was sad seeing other patients come in who would not be allowed back on their old jobs because it was their misfortune to have less understanding employers or to be older or just not able to begin over again. Every day at the eleven o'clock disposition conference we saw the newly admitted patients who had been completely evaluated and made plans for them. Dr. MacNeil was in charge of these conferences, and they were well attended.

Mrs. Gold's case had just been presented by her ward doctor, whom she despised because he had a purple birthmark behind his right ear. Somehow it wasn't right for a doctor to have a distraction like that where everyone could see it, she thought. She entered the narrow conference room and stopped at the door, turned, and started to walk out again, but there were too many people. An aide blocked her way, so she came into the room, pretending she had changed her mind.

She was dressed in the same yellow dress she had been wearing three nights earlier when she was admitted. She had a haughty, distant air, and in spite of her protests that she did not want to come to the conference and be interviewed, the nurse noticed that she had spent a good deal of time primping in front of the mirror and that she had made a point of doing her nails the night before.

Mrs. Gold felt that she had been taken to the hospital under false pretenses. It had not been the routine physical checkup her daughter had promised, but an abduction, a betrayal, a hurt from one of her own, made out of desperation, and in pain. How clever her daughter had been, packing a suitcase and bring it around to the back and putting it in the trunk. It seemed like the first time she could remember her daughter putting anyone's clothes away. "A routine exam," she had said. "A routine exam."

"This room is jickered and quickened!"

"Won't you come in, Mrs. Gold? I'm Dr. MacNeil. I'd like to ask you a few questions."

"MacNeil is a heel. A pig will squeal a better tune!" She sat down slowly and stared back at the anxious eyes around the table and then locked Dr. MacNeil in a rigid stare.

"How long have you been here?"

"Since the time was mine and mine the time of bed falling feelings. When the morning sun broke the windows of my room and shattered the dark they broke my heart and sent me here. You can't keep a good man down or a good woman. I'm a man who won't be kept down."

"How long ago was that?"

"The days are endless, bendless, senseless, denseless. No density there at all. They're light and bright and last till night. I endure them without fighting. For righting my wrongs, you will have to answer."

"You feel someone has wronged you?"

"What side of the river does the fish swim in? Fishes of silver and gold can often hold garbage and lies in terrible disguise."

"You feel it's hard to trust people?"

"By trusting the busting in custing and lusting in rusting and dusting and gusting like wind!"

"Trust is so much hot air, you feel?"

"We don't have to do these things, you know. We sometimes go to the market and buy apples. There are good pears now. There are pears that sell two for twenty-nine and there are pears that sell two for thirty-nine. The pears that cost two for thirty-nine are better, but they cost more than the ones that sell two for twenty-nine. Then sometimes I buy grapes. I don't like seedless grapes, thank you. I like to spit out the seeds. Then you know you've had a grape. Thank you. Thank you. Thank you very much."

"You sometimes feel like spitting?"

"In the wintertime my mother used to make hot chocolate for me. And I appreciated it. Did your mother make you hot chocolate?"

"Yes."

"Was it good?"

"Yes."

"And did you drink it all up?"

"I think so."

"You're a good boy. Did you appreciate what your mother did for you?"

"Perhaps you'd like someone to appreciate you? What led up to your coming here?"

"Decisions and anger. Misconceptions . . . ideas." She rubbed the back of her neck as if she were in pain. Suddenly she looked her fifty-five years. The make-up grew loud as she became silent. The wrinkles in her face deepened with the pain in her neck. Deep crow's-feet, dark rings around her eyes, the dark roots of her hair leaned forward from her head and seemed to shout her age. A social worker sitting in front of me scribbled a note inviting a nurse to have lunch with her and passed it across the aisle. Mrs. Gold noticed the note and apparently thought it was about her.

"The jickering again. The staring eyes have planned like those who sent me here to kill me and take away what is left of my wretched life."

"How will they do this?"

"The questions that are asked are questions that put the

cart before the horse. Of course I know that the horse is a tale of a different color, a tale not told. I will not again be sold up this river. I will not testify against myself nor will I state any more information than my name, rank, and serial number, which according to the Geneva convention, the Articles of War, the articles of clothing, states that I do not have to wear my own guilt."

"I don't follow you."

"That's what *you* say, but *I* know that *I* have been *followed* here. I know every man who has followed me. He says *he* doesn't follow, yet he wants me to commit myself."

"Mr. Allison, the aide on the floor, told me that you were upset this morning. Can you tell me about that?"

She stood up and turned her hands into fists, pounded the table directly in front of the social worker, and shouted: "Allison the aide, Ballison the bade, Callison the cade, Fallison the fade. Fade! Fade? He's a fag, fagging fade if ever I saw a fag. He accused me of homosexuality. He should die in the back room. Jallison the jade, Mallison the made, Wallison the wade. I want to go back to my room."

"How were you upset?"

"I've answered all the questions I think that the court needs to know. Mr. Allison, my *trusted* attorney, I'm sure can handle matters from this point on. He has handled things *so* well till now. However, with your permission I would like to thank everyone in the room for their nationwide coverage of this famous event. And . . . oh yes . . . you can tell my daughter to stick it up her husband's Irish ass, the homosexual bitch. I rest my case."

She stormed out of the room, followed by Allison.

"Well what do you think, Bob?" asked MacNeill.

"Except for the schizophrenic language patterns, there's very little different here from what is commonly seen in most psychotic depressions of menopausal onset." I said. "I think

the anger at the daughter is really anger that she can't release at her late husband."

"Yes, and especially the way she directs it to the son-in-
law," added MacNeil.

Susan Lundgren put down her note pad and said, "Are
you all aware that she did this when the older daughter got
married three years ago? I saw her on D-7 then. We handled
her by getting her a roommate through the municipal Jewish charities."

"Why is she living with the daughter now?" I asked.

"I'll find out, but I wouldn't be surprised if it's roommate trouble all over again. The daughter is hard to get to
come in. I'll visit at home." Lundgren had made a very
sound point.

Arrangements were made to see Mrs. Gold's daughter to
try to find out what had happened, and Mrs. Gold was taken
off the admissions ward and sent upstairs to one of the wards
on the acute service. She would be with us for a while, it
appeared, and there was much that had to be done.

The afternoon was quiet and I was able to dictate some
charts. There were no admissions and almost no calls. I did
not usually speak with the patients on the admission floor, as
Dr. MacNeil was assigned to the unit and did that. Sometimes, however, when he was out I would speak with his patients and sometimes when he was off for the day I had to
talk with the relatives of a patient who had just been admitted. There was always a lot of confusion and turmoil at that
stage, but I found the admission patients fascinating and
read their charts.

Even when there were no new patients there was always
something to do. Besides covering the admissions floor at
night, I alone was responsible for the care and management
of some thousand patients. Usually the voice on the other

end of the phone belonged to a nurse, sometimes an aide, who wanted to know if it was all right to give someone a particular medication to control him or to ask permission to put a difficult patient into seclusion.

These decisions were very hard at first. Sometimes I wasn't familiar with the particular medication, and usually I did not know the person on the other end of the phone and could not always be sure to trust what they claimed to have observed, and I almost never knew the patient.

At first, I went to whatever building needed me to evaluate each patient, but usually the patients were so upset they were unwilling to talk. Even when they were willing it was often impossible to figure out what the problem was. Sometimes, if the patient happened to be in therapy with someone I knew, I could find out what had been so upsetting. But at night it was usually chaos.

After a while I became more selective and began to trust the judgment of some of the nurses and aides. But it always went against my grain to be reduced to a dispenser of pills, and frankly, that is what the staff had been trained to expect over the years.

One of the most disturbing phone calls a psychiatrist can get in the night is a report that someone has slashed himself badly with a razor or a piece of glass. During my short stay at the hospital I put in more stitches in my twenty-five nights on duty than I had during the entire time I had spent in medical school and as an intern. One particular night would have been fair competition to my past experience all by itself. That spring evening there was a full moon, and I put in over two hundred stitches and referred three cases to the city hospital. I saw anatomical structures I had not seen in so many years that I had forgotten where they were. Even though it has been shown that the phases of the moon have nothing to do with emotional upsets, that night I would have been hard to convince.

Slashing was always a problem in the hospital and would run like an epidemic through a ward, especially one with a lot of young girls. There was a peculiar mystique about having stitches. It separated the new patients with few stitches from the old with many. For some it offered a primitive way of relieving themselves of unwanted feelings. To many young uprooted girls cutting themselves was like inflicting tribal scars of identification and belonging, and they showed off their wounds like a sailor shows off his tattoos and said that now they belonged to something.

While admitting patients could be exciting and challenging, night duty was generally tedious and superficial. It was difficult to find out what happened to the patients you admitted because they were seldom assigned to my ward later, and it was unlikely that the short interview and physical examination I was required to give would effect any change. You were a warden in the night with limited power, checking the doors to make sure that those who belonged would be allowed to come in and that those who must stay would remain.

Twelve

Henry was sitting quietly in the soft shadows of later afternoon, making demands on no one, waiting for something he
did not understand. He had been at a general hospital across
the city most of the day, unable to breathe and threatening
to take his own life. Henry wiped his eyes with a Paisley
handkerchief and said that he had to tell his story or he
would burst. Would I listen, he asked, would I listen without asking any questions? It had been so confusing and no
one had listened to him. We sat in an office on the admitting
floor and he told me his story.

Until today it had been much the same for the three
decades in which Henry and William had grown old and
shared their lonely, quiet lives as one. They had met in the
Army before the war and had been stationed together for

years on some bleak marshland in northern Maine. They had been together then but seemed worlds apart from each other in temperament.

William was older and had joined the service as a way of seeing the world, but had seen only the scant five hundred miles of countryside from New Jersey up to Bar Harbor. He was a large, balding man with a full mustache. He had a sharp head for business and a keen eye for antique glass.

They had spent the war years in Maine searching through every barn and attic they could get into, gathering glass. Henry, younger and rounder, was shy and retiring and had a sensitive, sad way of collecting. They planned to open an antique shop together as soon as the war was over. In his mind, Henry would spend entire afternoons arranging the cartons of glass on the shelves.

If, when rummaging through some farmer's house, Henry found a piece that was perfect except for a little chip that was hardly noticeable, his face would darken as he appealed to William, handing him the glass to see if he felt it was salvageable. After holding it to the light in the endless dusty attics, William would gently hand the glass back and put his arm around Henry's shoulder. "We'll find another, just as nice, but perfect. We don't have that large a collection yet that we can afford to take anything that isn't perfect."

Henry would stare at his feet on the way home in the car. "It really wasn't such a big flaw. I know someone would have bought it."

They invested their pay together for years. William insisted on taking only perfect pieces and Henry remembered every cracked or chipped one that was refused. Though he saw the soundness of William's thinking, he felt hurt with every rejection. And when a new purchase reminded him of one that William had put aside months before, he would say triumphantly, "Now *that* would have gone perfectly next to the yellow pitcher you wouldn't let me buy in Boothbay Harbor." William, endlessly patient, would smile and give the top of Henry's head a ruffle and a little push.

They collected more than sixty cases of glass, and Henry was so anxious on the day they moved that he covered his eyes when the movers came to put the cartons in the truck. William gave Henry an errand to keep him out of the movers' way and from getting too upset, but Henry was so anxious he couldn't remember what he was supposed to do and had to come back for new directions twice. And he lingered, holding his breath and gasping as he anticipated the movers' stumbling.

They moved to a small farm on Cape Cod when the war was over. Henry ran into the kitchen and held his breath. It wasn't as modern as he had remembered when the broker showed the house, and that sink was impossible. He made shopping lists and began the process of cleaning up the house. It had a large barn that needed work, and William remodeled and painted it alone. He put large windows in at one end and laid an oak floor. In one short summer it became a shop. Henry painted the name "The Loft" in gilt letters on a red wooden slab and William set it out in front. Henry also made a smaller sign in simple black letters, "Antique Glass, 300 Yards," and set it down the road.

For years they lived together in the frame house. Henry cooked and did the shopping and William chose the wines and drove the car. William had tried to teach Henry to drive, but Henry couldn't concentrate on the road. He would look across a field and say, "I bet that house has an attic just full of stuff," and William would have to grab the wheel to avoid a collision. It was simpler for William to do the driving.

In winter they went to antique shows and bought glass

and sometimes sold to other dealers. Occasionally they went to auctions, and it was understood that William would do the bidding. They still went through barns and attics, but Henry said it was not like it had been before—"even all those chipped things would sell now."

They were respected by other antique dealers for their good taste and honesty and forthrightness, and many customers were sent to "The Loft." They had local dealers over for tea and played their record collection for them.

Every Tuesday Henry played bridge with three ladies who owned an antique store in Dennisport. Mostly they talked antiques, but it was usually about furniture, in which Henry had only a casual interest. "I like furniture, don't misunderstand me, but to live with, not to buy and sell." Henry traded recipes (he was an excellent cook) and stories about other dealers, and he played bridge.

The years passed and the community stayed about the same as it had always been. The summer was the busy season, with browsers coming in and asking for specific but sometimes hard-to-find pieces of glass or wanting directions to the summer playhouse. Traveling and bargaining was William's job, as was the crating and lugging. William aged and Henry worried because he worked so hard.

One fall William received a letter from his mother's sister in Toledo announcing that she was going to move in with them. She did not ask. She was simply arriving. When Henry heard the news, his asthma began to act up for the first time since he was a boy. An eighty-year-old woman living with them! And there was no return address. William said that they couldn't refuse his mother's sister, his only family.

She arrived in late September. William was digging chrysanthemums and Henry thought she was a customer and couldn't understand what she wanted. Then William came and took her bags from the taxi as she slowly walked across the gravel walk. "What a filthy place, a disgrace," she said before she had been inside for a minute.

"I'm allergic to dust, and William usually dusts tomorrow," Henry said, as if apologizing. The aunt was determined to be an asset and show them that they needed her to keep house.

"How many years has it been," she asked, "since you had a good meal, William?" Henry ran outside to the barn with tears streaming down his face, waiting for William to come and promise him that she would not stay. But she stayed.

Two in the same kitchen was almost unbearable for Henry. "She cooks the good out of everything and doesn't know the first thing about herbs," Henry complained. William made suggestions and tried to keep the peace, but it was impossible. There were fights and tears.

"She's just trying to be helpful and earn her keep," William would explain.

"She's welcome, if you really want her. Just keep her out of my kitchen."

After a while they seemed to get along a little better, but there was always an undercurrent, always some kind of friction. Henry's bridge friends tried to help.

"When my mother-in-law came to our house, I put my foot down. Henry, you should stand up for your rights!"

Henry resolved to force a change, but the old lady had a stroke that same day, almost as if he had wished it upon her. He felt sick at his own anger and tried to help her get around. She was forgetful and frequently lost her balance, and often fell down while they were out shopping together. Beet-red with embarrassment and wheezing from the strain, Henry would put his arms around her and pull her up from the sidewalk, but he usually needed help from a passerby.

William picked them up at the market and they would drive home in silence. When the old woman was placed safely in a chair and they were out of hearing, Henry would complain, "You don't know what a perfect fool I felt like, her falling all over me. And trying to help her up. I really can't stand much more of this."

William listened, but that was all. He was not feeling well himself, and seemed to age suddenly. He had lost more weight than he could blame on the friction at home. Business was slow and he was not so busy, but he still felt weak. He stopped taking his long walks on the beach and that winter he stayed in the house even though it was one of the mildest in years. "The Loft" exhibited at only two antique shows that winter. Because William felt so weak he could not take care of the old woman, and she went to one show alone with Henry.

The aunt had been failing and Henry was not used to making decisions. He couldn't keep his mind on the glass at the antique show and watch out for the shaking old lady touching things that she might break. He could not guess what William would have paid for things or at what price he would let a piece go. Henry could stand it for only a few hours and they took a taxi home from Providence.

William was surprised to see them return so soon, but he was glad because he had been in a great deal of pain and was too weak to use the phone. He asked Henry to call the doctor. Henry disliked doing that sort of thing—somehow it was too real. He disliked pain and preferred to think that it would go away on its own, and he could not remember William ever having any pain. It was all so sudden, what was happening. William had never complained before.

The doctor came and examined William on the blue velvet sofa in the living room. After he finished he took Henry and the aunt aside in the same kitchen they had contested over for so long. "I'm afraid it looks like cancer. We'll have to bring him into the hospital for tests."

William slept in the living room and Henry stayed up, sitting and sobbing into the afghan that a bridge friend had made and that he had placed over William. He watched the sun come up through the small paned windows in the front of the house and through the several dozen pieces of glass on the long windowsill that William and he had felt were too fine to sell and had decided to keep for themselves. In the driveway the last few mounds of dirty snow were awakening from their reprieve in the cold spring night and were beginning to thaw again and lose their struggle to the sun.

The next day they went to the hospital and the diagnosis was confirmed. Henry choked on the sterile hospital fumes and began to wheeze when they told him that William had little time left to live. For hours he sat in the patients' lounge. He refused a ride home and walked the five miles back to the house. The aunt did not seem to understand and asked only when William would return.

The spring passed quickly and business was poor. Henry became irritated at the fat women in sundresses who were looking for bargains or who asked, "Is all you carry glass?" And many customers who in other days would have bought something were sent across the gravel walk lined with red wooden boxes (which were empty of flowers for the first time in years) to search for discoveries and bargains elsewhere.

William became weaker and finally, when the truth of his condition became obvious even to him, he called Henry in and told him that he knew he was dying. There was the matter of the mortgage, the accounts, and the unpaid bills that he had tried to manage in the hospital, but he was too weak and Henry would have to take over, and also take care of the aunt.

He died during the first week in August. The heat was

stifling and depressing. Henry made the funeral arrangements and spent too much money on the casket. One of the
ladies who had been his friend finally stepped in and took
care of the details when Henry became overwhelmed. Henry
was like a man sleeping, hoping to wake up from a dream.

The day of the funeral it was different. Henry was
alone. He sat in the front row of the white colonial church
with the aunt sitting next to him muttering and asking
where William was. The soft, hot wind blew open a side
door. Looking into the brilliant sun of noon, Henry could
see the ocean in the distance. There was a small sailboat
with a bright red spinnaker. The straw grass was very bright
and the light hurt Henry's eyes. He thought: I really don't
know the business. I don't know how to buy or sell. I'm just
a lost and empty little thing with no one to care for me.
What am I going to do? And this woman. What about her?

The old woman kept tugging at Henry and asking where
William was and why they had to be there and couldn't
Henry get her a sandwich.

It seemed so sudden. The minister had known them
both for years. In his eulogy he called them "close friends."
When the service was over Henry walked with the old
woman and tried to help her along, but she fell several times
and a friend stepped into line to help Henry with his burden. Henry walked by the open casket and through the door
to the limousine that was waiting to drive them to the cemetery. And his wheezing started again and he could not
breathe.

His asthma grew worse through the fall and by the end
of winter he could hardly breathe and had to be hospitalized. Nothing seemed to help. Late in the spring he remembered the events of the year before and thought of killing
himself.

Henry was crying. It was the first time since William's

death that he had been able to. He wanted to stay for a few days, just to get his bearings, he said. I suggested that the social worker might be able to get the old woman into a home while he was at the hospital and that I would be pleased to come by. Things went well and his wheezing lessened as he learned to cry. He only stayed one week before returning to the Cape and a painful struggle in an empty house that he would have to learn to call home again.

Thirteen

Most patients I saw at the state hospital were prisoners of their own disease, but those I saw at another hospital—a prison for the criminally insane—had broken the law. They were confined in other walls and so were doubly kept. Twice each week I drove from Boston to an ancient, dilapidated prison on the Cape where I was the only resident doctor. No one else would take the job. I took the position to make some extra money because my wife was pregnant again. The professional staff was primarily medical and none of the doctors had had formal psychiatric training. They were trying to do the best they could with limited resources and some times limited expertise.

I was in charge of a rehabilitation ward where I treated patients in an attempt to get them ready to go to trial. At the administrative level the prison staff was generally kind and interested, but among the lower ranks the level of interest deteriorated. There were exceptions—there always are exceptions—but for most of the correctional officers it was just a job. I saw these forgotten patients and tried to help, but I found that the institution itself and the other forces that operated on the patients from the outside were as difficult to overcome as the forces that controlled them from within.

My supervisor was Dr. Kamin, a psychiatrist trained in legal medicine. He was so concerned with the legal processes involving the patients that often he was as slow to act and carry out my requests as the courts themselves. In part this was because there was a great deal of unfavorable publicity about the deplorable physical state of the prison, and the correctional staff was overly sensitive to change and suggestions. Although Kamin called his inertia caution, he seemed afraid to endanger his reputation by making a move even when the path was relatively clear.

We would sit for hours and discuss how patients on the ward were doing. He would make suggestions and I would ask for help in getting a particular patient placed on a court docket so that, after being kept at the prison for ten or twenty years without a trial for a crime for which the maximum penalty was one or two years, the patient would be able to be tried and possibly released. Such patients were usually transferred to another hospital, because after being kept so long in such horrible conditions they were often unable to return to the community or to work, or even to find what was left of their family. Then, after spending half their lives in the damp darkness, if the men were finally found to be innocent, as many of them were, they would be able to get the psychiatric help that they had needed years ago. But usually, after so long, time had worked its paralyzing effects and there was little anyone could do. It was frustrating beyond belief.

I learned that no man is so unjustly held as the insane criminal. When an ordinary criminal is sent away and his world restricted, he can look with hope to a day throughout the years when his confinement will end. The criminals I saw were sent to this hospital prison because they were also sick. They were doomed to languish and live with endless time and receive neither the rehabilitation of the prison nor the care of the hospital. They spent their lives between the walls and waited, only waited.

The hospital was a forbidding place rising unexpectedly out of a cornfield; approaching it, one was surprised by its massiveness, as a visitor to Chartres is taken by the sudden dominance of the cathedral rising out of the land. Electronically operated iron gates, steel bars, grates, locks, doors were the way of that place. The most powerful precautions guarded the most fragile minds.

On the wall of the prison yard these words were scratched in stone:

"VOID AND EMPTY ARE MY DAYS,

NO HOPE FOR ME TILL DEATH"

The older prisoners, uniformed and broken, dead yet living, ignorant of the ways of their past like the distant descendants of a civilization long decayed, passed their years in front of this monument which has survived, unable to read the silent voices in stone, showing the way out.

In that great yard the years of a man's life were surrounded by a wall, covered by sky and a relentless sun, and sealed in at the floor with a carpet of imperfect grass. Many of the men were forgotten. Many had forgotten why they were there.

Many of them had been taken from their homes and led away in chains, the rattling of their leg irons the only protest they would ever make.

Even those whose crimes had been small had been

thought to be too sick to go free and were locked away and forgotten for years, while their children grew up without them or any memory of them, their wives found other solutions to the problems of their absence, their visitors dwindled and, if they had any, their friends and family died.

Many were there indefinitely, as the law had prescribed, and received little help or care. They became hardened in their ways. And each morning when they shaved, with a razor shared among a dozen men, they watched their youth gray at the temples in the mirror.

The feared and hated drives that long ago had led them astray aged, too, lost the greater part of their sting, and were no longer the force by which harm could be inflicted on others. Time had disarmed these men.

The doors and bolts and steel and bars built to hold the raging bulls were now too heavy even when unlocked for the men to open by themselves. The officers whose role it was to protect the world from their prisoners found themselves protecting the prisoners against the ravages which age is heir to.

One night there was a fire in one of the cell blocks and the sorry old men had to be carried to safety in the arms of their captors, so great was their infirmity. The officer in charge, laughing at the folly of it all, ordered that the doors to their rooms be left unlocked at night.

The men are now all alone and have grown fond of their keepers, who are their only family. They have no attachments among themselves and do not seem to grieve another's passing.

In the hot summer days they can be seen motionless in the heat, moving only to catch the mantle of shade from the wall as it moves across the yard, hiding them from the sun until they are called inside.

The old coal cellars were painted and used as day halls. Here wife murderers and felons play pool and follow the cue ball's course from side to side with heavy steps. The staccato of a ping pong ball punctuates the silence. Others sit in a corner, staring at test patterns on an old TV.

In the sharp shadows of a single bulb's haze they fill their time mindlessly, waiting for their turn to play and to die.

If what went on in most wards was terrible, what happend daily as a matter of routine on the maximum-security cell block could only be described in terms of darkness and empty horror. Here the patients stayed in their cells and came out only to be sprayed with a hose or given occasional exercise. To them the others in the hospital seemed to be free.

Above the cavernous black brick room there was a fan and one lonely light bulb unequal to the task of lighting all the cells. Each cell had a door of solid steel and a gloomy grate that served as a window and whose bars were crusted with the dry remains of food that had been spilled as it was hurridly passed through the narrow space.

Inside twelve cells, twelve patients stood, some laughing to themselves, some pounding on the door, not understanding that they should be tired. Some were beating their heads against the floor, and all in nakedness.

For those who had been there too long the boundaries between reality and their minds, already shattered by crimes too terrible to tell, grew more indistinct each day. They watched the shadows from the churning blade of the fan moving over the walls of their cells and saw in the passing shapes their lives played out in mimicry, a shadow play, a dumb show given in the umbrage of their own desperation.

When it was time for medication or time to eat, the brilliant lights in the cells were turned on overhead. The moaning and laughing stopped as mechanical men moved toward the unlatched grates, which fell with a rattling clatter as they were opened by the officers moving in a great circle around the ward.

The prisoners appeared in grotesque silhouette against the sudden brightness of the rooms behind them. Their eyes searched through the grates as they directed—in morbid community, in anguished disarray—their collective despair to the world outside their cells.

Their shadows, cast by the bright lights behind them, mingled on the rotting wooden floor outside, their only contact with each other. This communication ended with the click of the light switch, and again they were covered in darkness, each left to conjure up again his own world from memories of another time.

Everyone in the hospital wanted to leave. On my ward the promise and the hope seemed only to add to the pain. False hope is worse than death.

Mr. Hardy bid us all farewell and went around the prison yard shaking hands, saying goodbye to everyone he knew, saying that the life in him was ebbing, that he could feel it go, and that we would not be seeing him again. He said his sickness had consumed him, that it had sapped his tired brain, withered his weakened limbs, broken him.

He settled his account at the prison coffee shop. It was three months overdue. Because he worked, he was considered a good risk and no one was after him to pay.

"Where are you going all of a sudden?" asked the prisoner who ran the concession.

"I am going to die."

"What's wrong with you?"

"I said, I'm dying."

"Look, why don't you speak to your doctor?"

"There is nothing he can do. How much do I owe you?"

"I'm sure he can do something. Talk to him."

"How much do I owe?"

"Look . . ."

"How much?"

And in the carpentry shop where he had worked for years, he put his tools away and straightened out his unfinished work. He scribbled directions to the others to complete the pieces he had been working on.

Mr. Hardy shook our hands at night before he got ready for bed and told us he would miss us and hoped that he would be on the right side of things in the next life. He shaved his graying beard with tears in his eyes, showered and washed his hair as if he had an important engagement and was preparing to go into the world the next day.

We stayed up all night to watch him. He lay on his back in bed, barely breathing, his eyes closed, asleep. And we wondered what it was all about.

In the morning, he did not get up. He could not be aroused. We shook him and pinched him. He was alive, but his pulse was slow and his breathing was very shallow. We could get no response at all.

He was fed by tube for nearly a week and did not even gag as it went down. After ten days he became restless and began to move in bed, and finally awoke to a different day and time. We ran to see him as he opened his eyes. He asked who we were and what we wanted and said that he had been reborn and that the world was a different place.

He had built a wall around the past and had killed all memories so that he might live. He was much quieter and seemed more content on the surface. He even appeared happy at times. But without the past, there can be no future, and he would have to wait years for another death before he would leave the hospital again.

It was not hard to understand Mr. Hardy. I remember

falling asleep as a child and knew how the world could seem
new in the morning.

Eddie White has the fastest speedboat on the bay. After
supper when I am put to bed I prop my pillow up against
the wall and look out over the water and watch him get in
the last few runs before it gets dark. The water is very still
in the warm sunset, and a golden shimmering reflects on my
ceiling.

The motor has stopped. I lie back, looking at the ceiling
and the buildings below drenched in deepening orange and
gold. It is very still. I can hear the voices of older children
playing in the distance grow dimmer in the afterglow. All
around it is growing dark and my ceiling is turning gray.
Lights come on and streak across the water whenever an automobile turns this way. Doors close, someone laughs. The
sheet feels heavy upon me.

One patient, Charley, actually did leave the hospital
prison while I was there.

The baby they say Charley killed (it was his sister's
baby) was only two months old. He had just returned home,
a collection of fragments of the boy who had left to fight the
Germans in the Second World War.

In his best days at home Charley was timid and withdrawn. He was rushed through basic training and sent over-
seas to fight. He was asked, with his comrades, to challenge
the Germans on a front Hitler swore would never be allowed
to fall and which he had bolstered with Rommel's best
troops.

Charley's company was ambushed in hilly terrain and
he was pinned under the bodies of his own men, a trickling
shield dying over him. For three days he dared not move.

When he finally did, it was in darkness; he ran, stumbling over the fallen and the rotting, screaming, with his own screams echoing in his ears. He was found wild-eyed, incoherent, weeping and laughing, saying something about having killed everyone.

They peeled his crusty fatigues from him. The medic found a bloody handprint on his back and said that it must have been rough. He was shipped back to the States in irons, locked up for his own security in the brig of the ship. When he was quieter he told a nurse that he was glad they had put him away, because he was a murderer.

After a year in an Army hospital he was better, quiet, controlled—he had a nervous smile for visitors. His mother had died the year he was away and when he got out he went to live with his sister, her husband, and the new baby. He was not ready to look for work, and his brother-in-law resented him for sitting around the house and insisted that he make himself useful. He did odd chores and carried the bundles when his sister went shopping.

One summer evening his sister asked Charley to give the baby a bottle while they visited some friends. He sat in the rocking chair and slowly gave the baby a few ounces. He burped the baby and put her back in the crib to sleep and then returned to his chair in the corner, his newspaper, and his war.

After a while he noticed that the baby was very still. She did not seem to be breathing. She had spit up and had suffocated. When he picked her up she fell limply all over him. He carried the dead baby to the phone and in a panic he told his sister that he had killed her baby. When they came home they found him crying, trying to burp the baby.

At Charley's arraignment the baby's father pressed for the maximum penalty, but the judge read his past record and sent him away to a hospital for the criminally insane. Month after month his stay was extended. He quieted down and was assimilated into the walls, the walks, and the cells of the place. His case never came to trial and for twenty years he sat in the back reaches of the prison.

It was difficult for the staff to convince him that a lawyer had been assigned to him to present his case and bring him to court. He had already served the maximum sentence, and even if he were found guilty the judge would set him free. But in spite of all the arrangements each time, nothing seemed to come of it.

One court-appointed lawyer came, one went. Each time the case was reviewed anew and each time the letters to the district attorney proved barren or unanswered.

There was one highlight during his stay, one moment when it could have been said, this was a good day. Once during his twenty-third year of confinement, when he was working on the farm attached to the prison, he bought an egg for two dollars which he had managed to borrow from a friend. He loved a fried egg more than anything—nothing fancy, just fried and a little crisp around the edges. There was no grill in the hospital and the only eggs served there were boiled or scrambled. But this fine day, this happy day, he lit a fire beneath a small, flat rock and when his wet finger sizzled touching it, he cracked open the egg and fried it.

Very little happened the next year.

Charley's luck started to change when a new ward with its own psychiatrist was formed and he was picked to be a patient on it. Now he could see a doctor more often and a new effort was made to get him to trial. Dr. Kamin saw him at first. Charley accepted this with the same anxious smile that he had worn for years, which served as his greeting and as his farewell.

A dozen letters were written. The first ones by Dr. Kamin, the more recent ones by me. It took a month to get replies. It was finally shown that he was being illegally held, and he would have a hearing and the charges would be dropped. He could go to a veterans' hospital, perhaps even out onto the street.

When I told Charley the news, he smiled. He would go to court before the summer recess. He walked to his bench just beside the bocce court and stopped and walked back to me again. He smiled broadly and took my hand.

It was all set. A writ of habeas corpus was sent and he was to return to court. When the sheriff from his district came, the writ could not be found. It had been misplaced on someone's desk. Everything was searched and finally the search was abandoned. The sheriff returned to court alone. Charley stood silently in the first suit of clothes he had worn in twenty years. They took off the handcuffs and took back the suit.

It was too late to send another writ and Charley would have to wait for the fall session. I thought that I would have to console him, but the new suit was proof enough that he was on his way. "I can wait one more month" was all that he said.

It was a very wet summer and much of the time the men were forced to stay inside. At the end of August the second writ came. (The first had been found being used as a bookmark.) The second writ would not be lost. On Monday he was to return to court. Freedom was assured.

Charley spent the weekend saying farewell to the officers and men he had shared his life with, and on Sunday he walked slowly around the yard, surveying the stones that had measured his world. He finally settled on his bench and sat smiling, watching a game of bocce.

Charley did not make a sound. His right hand went up

to clutch his chest as he fell forward to the ground, silent, dead.

There was nothing anyone could do, and it was impossible to convince the other patients on the ward that they would leave, that they would ever leave.

Fourteen

The geriatric service gathered its patients from the rest of the state hospital as well as from the outside world. What the healers could not cure over the long years of a hopeless hospital stay was left for time to set straight.

Many patients stayed in bed, too frail to encounter what was left of their shrinking world, but many others could not stay in their beds at all. At midnight, figures floated across the halls to find mops and brooms, and haunted the ward with the sound of their pails and brushes, clawing away at the darkness.

There was a quiet resignation on that ward, in that building. None of the staff expected much and no one was disappointed—except sometimes the patients. Although the staff no longer seemed to care or notice that the patients were there, the patients sometimes still had hope, even there. What on the other wards of the hospital seemed the meanest residue of life or form appeared in that place only as its fading shadow.

The memories of my childhood that had been coming back to me during the year became more and more real as I worked with older patients. Their building looked familiar and had a familiar smell . . . a smell of age, of old people, of death, that is always the same . . . always.

The snow had come in the night, blowing drifts, sealing the doors shut. Ice was frozen on the kitchen windows and the wind cooed at the pigeons scratching on our wooden back porch. A great rumbling shakes the house and I run to see the plow push by, boxing cars and driveways in, creating fortresses of frozen white.

I am never dressed in winter, I am bundled up. I think of myself as an arctic explorer or an Eskimo lost in some snow canyon. Icicles are forming on the gutters; clotheslines and railings catch the morning sun. They make wonderful targets for snowballs and broom handles. It is beautiful, white, and cold with snow covering the gray-brown wood two- and three-family houses and the trees in front of them.

I cut through a back yard to reach the street behind. The snow is very deep and dry, and the wind blows it swirling into my ears and nose and clothing. Down the hill I go, tripping and sliding, exploring the drifts.

At the bottom is a car with the door open, and the snow has almost filled it. The headlights are still glowing faintly. With the sureness of a trapper having cornered his prey at last, I spring forward to investigate. The snow is waist high and blowing everywhere. At the back of the car there will be protection from the wind.

A man in a black coat lies flat and still on the ground.

Snow had covered his hat. His face is gray. His ears are pur-
ple. He does not move. I can feel myself grow tight.

"Mister, are you okay?" He does not answer. I think I
knew that he wouldn't. His eyes are open and covered with
snow. I stare fixedly at him, terrified at what I have found,
and even more frightened by the possibility that he might
start to move and come after me.

Seeing someone dead does not fit into my world. Death
is a stranger. How could he lie there in the cold? He must be
freezing. Why doesn't he move? I am chilled and he does not
even shudder. No one is home at the house. It is empty.

I climb up the hill to the street and stop a stranger and
tell him that someone is sick and has fallen.

I start back. I am a hunter who has gone out in search
of the unknown and have found something beyond my reck-
oning, and I run home, fearing that some day it will come to
hunt me.

The patients appear tired and did not seem to move
very much, and when they do it is in slow motion.

Her papier-mâché face, fixed in anger by time, leans
out over the rotted green wood of the crumbling ward porch
like a gargoyle over the parapets of Notre Dame.

Held in her hands, it stares out and down, watching in
endless angry sadness the merchants' trucks making their
scheduled stops on the circular drive below.

She studies the husky delivery men from a healthier,
younger world, joking with each other as they unload their
burden.

They are unaware that they offend her and do not know
that they are being watched, but they are remembered and
they are judged.

From the shaky heights of the third-floor porch she
chronicles her world and time in the wrinkles on her face.

"The thing that stands out most in my mind in my fifty-three years here? Hmm. Let's see. Can't say. Well, now, wait. Two things. Uh yuh. Back in fifty-one—no, it was the spring of fifty-two. Yuh, that's it. I was coming back from the G Building, minding my business. I found thirty-five cents, a dime and a quarter.

"Well, I hadn't had any money since I came here so it was kind of a windfall. I picked it up and thought about it for a few days. Then I decided to buy one of those candy bars, a Milky Way. It was very good, so I saved half, very good. I had the quarter broken into small change. It made it seem like more. I bought one of those large Tootsie Rolls the next month, but I didn't know you couldn't eat it with no teeth. So that was kind of wasted, but I kept it anyway. I finished the other half of the Milky Way instead. And somehow, I lost the rest.

"Then, the other thing. There used to be this large old beech tree on the south field where they built the A Building. Well, during the hurricane in thirty-nine it blew down. I used to spend my summers under that tree. Cool and shady. There were a bunch of us who used to lie there. Small, tasty little nuts in the fall, too. After it came down, the old group just broke up. I didn't do very much the next two summers, as I recall."

Two splendid cherry trees in my grandfather's back yard. I could have all I wanted. "Don't swallow the seeds. Spit them out, Bobby."

One worn slippered foot, bent and pointed, motionless and halting. She appears at the landing, her withered skin glaring pale beneath the hall's harsh shadows, which are her only raiment.

I, Theresa, empress and queen, properly heralded by

Mahler's Second, floating from a radio in a chamber above, begin my daily entrance.

A white mustache and stubbled wart crown her pointed chin. At her next birthday she will be seventy-eight. Last year there was a small party. Her daughter baked cookies, but had to leave early to relieve the baby sitter. The ladies of the ward passed the box around and emptied it before she got even a crumb. She banished her daughter to the palace dungeon where, the year before, in a fit of anger, she had had Goethe hanged.

No matter. Today . . . today there is brilliant sunshine falling on the steps just as she had commanded. A fitting entrance, she thinks, as she takes the first step. Mahler's music was beginning one of those very long, sweeping, swelling cadences.

For breakfast I do not think I shall have pheasant eggs again. My private physician says that they upset my constitution. Look at them stare at me even now. My greatness and femininity are eternal. God, how they adore me. See, they smile. I delight. In my majesty, I delight. How grateful they are for the sun. We shall have it shine until evening for them.

But she, the one in white, she does not show proper breeding. She turned her back. She will have to scrub our private sewer again.

I have found a way to keep them apart, not like the days before when they were allowed to come close. Even the exhalted grow weary of closeness. They may look at me, but I forbid them to speak. They dare not.

We still enjoy ruling them, but we shall not receive them.

Another arthritic step, another swaying naked hip, she descends.

"Robby, help Pa down the stairs, dear. Help him."

Every morning for a decade she has packed her cardboard suitcase to go home and carried it down the two flights of stairs to the empty wooden porch in front.

She stands looking down the drive to the gate on the boulevard until dinnertime. Then she struggles upstairs, unpacks her bag, and mutters to herself on the way to eat.

A suitcase! A suitcase from the upstairs hall. With the stickers from my aunt's trip to Europe. Yes, one of them was a sticker of Venice . . . Venice.

Fat in his faded pajamas, he stands with his nose pressed against the mirror over the washbasin, a hand resting on each hip. He stares into the eyes that are staring back at him.

Which side of the mirror am I on? Which side is real? How can I be sure? Everything on this side is on that. If I pinch the person on this side, ow! See, the person on that side winces too. Which person am I, this or that?

He puts his short, fat hands into the bowl and washes them and throws the bubbles up onto his face. He pulls the plug and watches the soapy water go down the drain in lazy eddies.

Suddenly, as if remembering, he looks at the other side to see if the water there is going down too.

My grandfather, in his striped pajamas, standing confused somewhere. Pa!

Old, a crow with black matted hair, he stands in the newly raked pile of yellow and red autumn leaves that reaches as high as his flabby arms.

Motionless, listening for the wind to stop, he suddenly bends down and scoops a giant armful to his chest and throws it into the air as high as he can.

As the leaves fall all around him, he makes a long blowing sound, places his hands by his sides, and waits till the leaves are still.

Then quickly and suddenly, he begins again.

Burning leaves in the back yard. "Stay away from the fire, Bobby. Don't get too close. Here, you take the rake. That's a good boy."

When I touch my finger to this stone and speak my name backward three full times, the villages of Greece will crumble in the snow, the Amazon will overflow its banks with ice.

By the power placed by Gabriel in this stone, commanded by the Lord God full of love, at my discretion I am here to choose the time of tide and speed of wind and bird, to say which ship shall leave upon the flood, which vessel swallowed by the swirling deep, when furtive love be in joy requited, when treaties broken and promises kept.

When I touch my finger to this stone and speak my name backward only twice, I will have the doctors send me home and turn this hell to paradise.

They are little black boxes, phylacteries, which rustle softly when I shake them. They are held together with worn-smooth leathers and I cannot find a place to fit my screwdriver to pry their secrets apart. My grandfather used to wear them when he was a boy. He showed me how he wrapped the leather around his arm and tied one box fast; a piece was torn from the other box and he could not bind it to his head so he held it there with his middle finger and said, *"Like this, I wore them like this."* I never saw him pray in the morning and I guessed it had been a long time since he had put them on.

The only time he was religious was at Passover, and then he would read the Hebrew of the Passover story so rapidly that my sister and I would turn red holding back our laughter. Then he would become very slow and dignified and it would be my turn to ask the Four Questions, which I had learned from memory and really didn't understand. When, finally, I was old enough to know what I was saying, I was no longer the youngest and a cousin took my place asking the questions.

In time my grandfather himself grew vague and difficult to care for. He was admitted to this hospital and . . . Oh, God, I remember . . . he died . . . on this same ward.

When we grow dim at the end of our years and sit nodding in our chairs, we place the world a little distant and wear that glad indifference as protection against the losses the future brings. How much more distance could these people add? How do you separate from a world you have never allowed to get close?

Fifteen

Epilogue

Closing my office door for the last time; the month has turned, the season has changed, it is summer again, and I must go.

I had the last night duty and the hospital showed its sadness. The old doctors were leaving. Even on the back wards, where sunlight did not filter in and where we felt least known, the patients put on their saddest faces and turned their backs to me, angry at me for leaving, sorry to see me go.

The whole year they had been silent, and now that it is almost too late they showed me that they liked me. And I had the strange feeling as I turned the key in the lock that in some abstract, crazy way it might have made a difference that I was there to see this.

I had followed them into the darkness in the belief that

somewhere there was light. Perhaps it was insane to try, but I had believed in trying and had wanted very much to win. In spite of all the failures, even the patients who refused to be moved would know that I had tried to move them and they could believe in that.

I left with mountains of work unfinished; some patients didn't notice and some didn't care and some cared too much. I had mixed feelings as I walked across the grass and said goodbye to a hundred plaster faces, accepting their good wishes spoken in the same voice with which they asked for a second cup of coffee.

I had felt that I did not know how to enter their world and I had despaired of trying, but on leaving I found that somewhere along the way I had become part of it.

I had come to the hospital frightened, as much by the risk of failing in a personal sense as by the apparent hopelessness of the patients themselves. I had cared about them; I had been criticized for caring too much. Sometimes, in my greenness, I had been overwhelmed as much by the obstacles fate had placed in the way of my patients as by their and my own inability to combat them.

I had lamented hospital conditions, the pipes that leaked into the cafeteria food and onto the patients' beds at night, the hollow wards with fifty beds in one room where time was measured from the turn of a key in the evening to its echo the next day, freeing men from their sleep but not from their dreams; but for all my efforts I had not changed things very much.

I had grown furious at husbands and wives for deceiving, for bringing in upsetting news to fill the empty hours, for eating the chocolates they had brought during the long silences as they sat visiting, and because they had resolved their loneliness in other ways and were afraid of a homecoming.

I had been angry at children and parents for abandoning each other, for exaggerating the sacrifices they made. I had been angry at the visitors for making the patients feel like a burden to be visited, when really the visitors were thankful for the peace and quiet they had with the patients out of the home at last.

I had been angry at society for malforming children and at teachers for beating them because they could not learn or even try because of their daydreams, the only place they had to hide. I had been angry at the law for throwing confused boys into cells when their only crime had been to run away from a cruel father, when their mothers, perhaps only the year before, had committed the same crime and had gone unpunished.

I had been angry at nurses for being naïve, for letting their medicines come before the patients, for being unrealistic, and for sometimes not caring. I had been angry at aides for their brutality, for confronting frightened menacing patients by rushing at them, for leaving the patient no choice but to fight and be beaten.

I had been angry at my predecessors for their stupidity, their missed diagnoses, and their poor judgment, which hindsight allowed me to see. I could easily find their defeats and hunted for their gains, only to find that they had vanished with time.

I had been angry at my patients for resisting my efforts, for not trusting me, for testing me with lies, and for being preposterous. They had wasted my time with pranks, delaying actions, and talk about the weather. Mostly, I had been angry at them for not getting better, for not wanting to get better.

I had been angry at myself for not being any different from the rest. I had silently encouraged patients who irritated me to go into treatment with someone else. I had sometimes made the admission procedure so difficult for an especially obstinate patient that he finally left in disgust. I had sometimes seen my patients' failings as faults of my own and, because I feared to admit them, I had failed to take them into account.

And then I had mellowed and learned to tolerate despair and to see it as part of life in the place. I grew, and saw myself as able to give. I felt, gingerly at first, but I learned to share my feelings when sometimes I thought I had none left. I reached out and my hand was often slapped away. I was attacked in the parking lot, in the dimly lit hall outside my office, on the lawn. I was garrotted, spit upon, and punched. I was showered with urine and spattered with feces, kicked in the groin and laughed at as I caught my breath in pain, while other patients stood in silence, faceless, and, in watching me being beaten, beat me in their own silent way.

My hand was softly taken by old ladies who vaguely remembered my name and by other children who didn't know my name at all, and I had shared silence in the touch of a hand. My eyes had filled with tears in learning to deal with grief and I had learned I was grieving on my own for my own. I was adored, despised, scorned and berated, exalted and exaggerated. I was both kind and cruel. In helping people discover themselves, I had discovered more of me and, in the bargain, I became more human.